If you've read a few of my books you know I tend to write mainly in British English. With this one I thought that's just too easy, why not make it harder for myself and a whole lot more confusing for my editor. Switch it up a bit, you know. So I went and did that.

All I can say is that you can find a mix of British and American English in this one, depending on who's recounting the events. It just felt like the right way to go. Sorry, not sorry.

Book playlist

Red Cheeks

I rushed into the foyer at my best friend's mansion block, slipping through the front door as an older lady walked out. She stopped outside under the little roof barely covering the two steps leading to the door and admired the downpour. Me? I escaped the rain about five minutes too late.

Dripping my way over to the lift, I stabbed at the call button with more force than was necessary. It was plenty cold in my thin T-shirt, tucked into a short skirt that clung to my thighs like a second skin. The cotton bra I wore was clearly the wrong choice for the occasion, since it did absolutely nothing to hide my hardened nipples. Good thing I was almost there and nobody was around to see me in my obvious state of distress.

I squeezed at the edge of my skirt while I waited for my ride to arrive, and a stream of water trickled to the grey tiles of the hallway.

Glen better have spare clothes to borrow.

I wouldn't say no to a hot shower in her bathroom either. The idea sounded absolutely amazing, in fact. Yup, her shower had my name on it. Her reasons for calling me over 'right now! It's an emergency!' could wait another ten minutes, or thirty, while I made sure I wasn't going to go home with a sore throat or, God forbid, cystitis.

The ding of the lift was music to my soul, and I hopped on with a wet squelch, repeatedly pushing on the twelfth

ELEVATE

with me

Ellie,

Trust yourself to know
what is best for you.
No one else can know
it better than you do.

Victoria Liiv

LEVELS OF YOU BOOK ONE

This book is dedicated to @blanreginbooks and here's why

blanreginbooks 09/24/2024   ...

My life could not be more embarrassing!
I LITERALLY closed the elevator doors and trapped a guy with them. I was MORTIFIED!!! (Still am)
And that's my life 😅

♥   ◯ 7   ↻   ▽

Replies   View activity >

vicwritesbooks 09/25/2024   ...
That would make an awesome opening scene in a romance book!

♡ 2   ◯ 1   ↻   ▽

blanreginbooks 09/25/2024   ...
Well, it's where my bestie lives so maybe I'll see him again 😵‍💫 😅 (Although I probably would ask the earth to eat me so I don't have to remember the embarrassment)

♥   ◯ 1   ↻   ▽

vicwritesbooks 09/25/2024   ...
😈 but ut would be so much fun!!

♡ 1   ◯ 1   ↻   ▽

blanreginbooks 09/25/2024   ...
Agree 😅 😅 😅

♡   ◯   ↻   ▽

floor button as if that would make the doors close quicker. I hadn't even noticed I wasn't the only one trying to get on, and while the doors didn't particularly slide close fast, the man stepping in behind me wasn't quite as nimble as I had been. Oh, no, he took his time getting on, unaware of my rush and the doors closing in on him as he fumbled with the strap of his umbrella.

His surprised *oomph* made me finally drop my hand from the buttons. His eyes shot up from the impossible project in his hands and landed on me, one eyebrow quirking up. The umbrella slid halfway open once more, but he'd given up on it anyway.

"Sorry," I mumbled, hoping to God he wasn't going to do one of those full body checkups men tend to do, but of course I was out of luck. His gaze slid over my face, taking in the chestnut-brown hair curling up more than usual, courtesy of the rain. Then travelled down my chest, stopping for an unnerving amount of time, then finally checked out my thighs, his lips forming a rather sexy smirk.

"Sure you are." His deep and clearly American drawl brought goosebumps to my skin. No, that was the cool breeze called upon by his strong push against the metal doors sandwiching him to give him enough space to squeeze through.

I was so dumbstruck I stood frozen in my spot as he stalked a step closer and leaned over me to get access to the floor selection buttons. A whiff of manly cologne swept over me in his unwelcome nearness, and I told myself I didn't like the scent of it. Yeah, that's why I was gulping it in, as if trying to memorise every aspect of its distinct smell before it dispersed. Sandalwood and something spicy. It was out of my vicinity too soon. Or not soon enough. Definitely not soon enough.

Mr. Umbrella leaned against the opposite wall from my position after he'd selected his destination, lazily staring at me with half-lidded eyes. I pinned my own stare at the faded floorboards that held stains from heaven only knows what sort of atrocities. My heartbeat strummed in my neck, and any attempt I made to swallow it down only caused the lump in my throat to tighten.

Oh god, oh god, oh god...

Counting floors in my head to get my body under control was of no use when he hummed quietly from his position. My eyes flicked to him before I could stop myself, and he grinned victoriously.

He was comfortably dry, having been protected by the umbrella. Bright green eyes studied me with interest as his short-cropped hair did nothing to hide his gaze. Scruff on his jaw indicated he should shave soon. Or not. Maybe not, it looked rather hot. He held himself with the confidence a man surviving a downpour with dry buttocks should, but his smirk unnerved me nonetheless. As if from an unspoken joke, he chuckled to himself, and I hated the deep, raspy sound of it. Shit! I hated it, right?

Heat surged through my body, and I was surprised water didn't evaporate from my clothes in one sizzling second. It would have been possible to fry an egg on my cheeks alone. I wasn't only wet from the rain, but also sweating, and starting to smell significantly less pleasant than my lift mate, who had decided I was the main attraction for the duration of our short ride together.

I apologised, what more did he want? To chit-chat, apparently.

"Nice weather, am I right?" Mr Umbrella mused.

Fucking lovely.

I shrugged, uncertain if he was trying to make a joke or if he truly enjoyed rainy days. Perhaps he'd moved to England just to enjoy our many sunless weeks. Those people existed, I was sure, but I did not belong to that group.

My foot began tapping away impatiently as the lift made its slow ascent. Too slow. I pursed my lips and stared at the floor again until the saving ding almost made me jump out of my skin. I pushed toward the opening doors as if there were many more people in the lift than just the two of us, and I was the only one leaving on this floor. I probably took it a notch too far, elbowing invisible people out of the way because he chuckled behind me.

"I'm pretty sure this is my floor."

My eyes flew to the floor selection buttons in time to see number ten flicker and stop shining, while twelve was still bright as a beacon. I hadn't even checked which floor he was going to. Of course, it was lower than mine, this building only had fourteen floors and the chances of him living on the last two were slimmer than the odds of him leaving on, lets say, the tenth floor.

Shiiiiiiiiit.

Hot. I was so hot. My head swam and my stomach did somersaults as I gingerly stepped away from the doorway giving him space to exit. Once he was off, I let out a long breath only to find him looking back at me with a smug smile.

"Nice meeting you, Red Cheeks," he called through the now closing doors.

Oh my freaking God. That did not just happen!

Proposition

I looked left and right as I exited the lift on the twelfth floor not to be taken off guard again, but the hallway was clear. Still, I squelch-ran my way to Glen's door, thumping on the metal impatiently with my fist when I stopped behind it.

Halfway through my next series of knocks, it swung open, leaving my hand hanging mid-air. My mouth opened to recount the mortifying events of the last five minutes, but one look at Glen told me my story would have to wait. Her eyes were red and puffy from crying, dimming the freckles usually so vibrant on her cheeks.

"Glen, what's wrong?" I rushed into her entrance hall, shutting the door behind me as she stood back and followed my movements with a drawn expression. "Your cheeks are nearly as wet as my clothes, and I'm only saying 'nearly' because my clothes are outright drenched."

"It's raining?" she asked, her voice flat and devoid of emotion. "Sorry."

"It's always raining, that's no news," I muttered, dragging my wet shoes off to hide my frozen toes in a pair of slippers. "What's wrong?" I asked again.

"I'll tell you while you get changed." Without looking back, Glen turned on her heel, her ponytail swishing from side to side, and shuffled deeper into the flat, expecting me to follow.

Torn between urging her to speak now and needing to get out of my wet clothes, I begrudgingly stomped after her.

The living room was crowded with antiques Glen had acquired from her grandmother along with the flat itself. Dark wooden shelves in different shapes and sizes, with intricate grooves and detailing, took up most of the wall space without appearing cluttered. A vitrine cabinet, a bookshelf, and a vanity exhibited bits 'n bobs from a different century that begged for attention as we passed them by, but the Victorian-style parlour chair was the actual star of the space. That and the matching lounge suite, which right now was hidden under blankets and covers to keep the actual blue satin seat safe from wear and stains.

We passed all of that into a much more modern looking bedroom, where Glen took a pair of cosy pyjamas out of the closet and threw them at me. I caught them gingerly and admired the pattern on them.

"Cats?" I asked as I traced one of the black figures with a finger and was met with soft, inviting fabric.

"I got those for you for our next sleepover. It was supposed to be a surprise, but we'll probably never have a sleepover ever again. At least not at my place," Glen murmured, stomping one of her feet on the fluffy white carpet that covered the space from the foot of her bed to the closet.

Peeling my wet T-shirt off my body and removing the wet bra next, I only managed to give Glen a questioning "mph?' and a quick glance. Then the pyjama top was over my head, restricting my view and ability to speak as it slid down to hide mischievous nipples and the few folds on my belly that even the dancing I had been doing almost daily hadn't managed to smooth over. The dry warmth wrapped me in its welcoming embrace, and I sighed before I remembered the topic at hand.

"Don't be silly, we'll have plenty of sleepovers." I tugged at the skirt, the only wet thing I was still wearing while staring at my best friend with a furrowed brow. "And I'll be wearing these. They feel absolutely amazing."

"No," Glen sniffed. "I'm going to have to sell the flat."

The skirt slid through my fingers and down my thighs until it fell with a heavy squirt as I stared at her. "What do you mean, sell the flat? You can't sell it, it's like a family heirloom. Your own grandkids will be inheriting it once you're gone."

Glen's shoulders slumped. I quickly pulled the pyjama bottoms on, taking no time to admire the kittens traipsing around on them, but still managing to appreciate the softness of the fabric against my thighs. All wrapped up in dry clothes, I could focus all my attention on Glen, who was rolling her lower lip around unhappily.

"Remember when I told you A&R's wasn't doing so well business wise? Well, they've decided to cut me loose. Very likely the entire company is going down, at least that's what they said while withholding my last pay cheque. I can't afford this flat without any income."

A&R's stood for Antiques & Restoration and was like a second home to Glen who had grown up admiring her grandmother's pretty furniture pieces before she even learned how to walk. If the company was going down it was to no fault of hers because she'd do anything in her power to see it thrive. Paying her last cheque was the least they could do!

"What?" I squeaked. "No, they can't do that!"

"It's already done, Hallie," Glen sniffed again. "Today was my last day. They said that the contract ends immediately."

"No, no, Glen, they can't withhold your pay," I argued.

She was an immaculate worker, I knew she was. With her knowledge in antiques and history passed down by her family, she was the best any antique shop could want. At her age any company would try to underpay her regardless of her qualifications, but they couldn't have had anyone better for the job.

"There's nothing I can do about it." She looked so miserable with her slumped shoulders and red cheeks—no, not *red cheeks*, definitely not that one—swollen eyes, I doubted she even realised just how much she could do about it.

"You know my mum is a solicitor, don't you?" I said in case she'd forgotten. Of course she knew; we'd grown up together. She was just shutting down and not thinking clearly. "You can sue them, I'm sure my mum would help. I'll be scrubbing dishes for the rest of my life for her services, but she'll help. You would at least get your last pay, they can't keep it from you."

"That doesn't change the fact that I'm now jobless."

"For now," I insisted. "You are jobless for now. You are so incredible. I have faith that you'll find a new job in no time."

Glen rubbed her toes on the fluffy carpet, swiping at her eyes. "I've looked. Don't you think I've looked? I knew being let go was always an option. There is nothing else, Hallie. I'm going to lose my grandmother's flat."

Shaking my head, I refused to accept it, but with the mood Glen was in, it was impossible to reason with her, so I offered the next best thing. "I bet you have ice cream in that bottomless freezer of yours."

Grabbing her hand, I pulled her out of the bedroom, across the antique living room and into a kitchen that fell somewhere between the moderness of her bedroom and antiqueness of the living space. It could possibly be called a country kitchen, only we were nowhere near the country, so it felt wrong to call it that; perhaps country chic or modern farmhouse. Whatever it was, it held the fridge and the ice cream I was certain I'd find inside.

Rummaging in her fridge left me empty handed, however. I turned an accusing gaze at Glen, whose despairing composure hadn't changed since.

"I was here yesterday," I claimed, flicking my gaze between the clearly ice-creamless freezer still hanging open from my search. "I could swear I brought in an entire carton of ice cream and we only ate half."

Glen's shoulders raised in a pathetic shrug. "You were in class when I messaged, then took another thirty minutes to arrive," is all she replied.

Of course, she ate it. Silly of me to assume it was still here. I nudged the fridge closed and crossed my hands over my chest.

"So you've gotten your sugar rush already, huh?" I narrowed my eyes when all she did was tap her foot to the tiled kitchen floor. I clearly sucked at this cheering up thing. "You want more sugar? I mean, I suppose I could make hot chocolate, instead."

No answer. Right, I was talking to myself now. With that in mind, I resumed shuffling around in Glen's kitchen, opting to prepare the most sugarsome treat I could with the limited ingredients available. The proof of the ice cream's early demise lay in an almost overflowing bin, which I opened to throw away a wrapper that once belonged to a chocolate bar I'd hidden away in her dry-goods cupboard a week ago. I knew she wouldn't find it there. And right I was, at least in this small matter.

Heating up milk took longer than I thought, and I contemplated telling Glen about my lift encounter while the liquid took its sweet time to get warm. One look at her, though, and I knew that no matter how awkward my retelling would be—and it would surely be more awkward than the encounter itself, which was godawful—it would not cheer her up in her current dejected-mood. Probably nothing I would say would, so I opted to just stay quiet and prepare hot cocoa Nutella sandwiches—with the chocolate bar hidden between the slices of bread. After careful consideration, I revealed another one of my snacks-hiding places in her kitchen and pulled out some chocolate covered raisins from under a teacup solely meant for me. I added that to our definitely-best-supper-choice pile. Glen didn't even blink an eye at the revelation.

By the time the hot chocolate was steaming, I was certain my growing belly had nothing to do with how much I exercised, and everything to do with what I was going to stuff my face with. Today was not a day to cut down on sweets, though, so I attempted to put that thought aside, along with the smug face of Mr Umbrella that kept rising to the forefront of my mind.

We consumed our calories on Glen's Victorian sofa, wrapped up in blankets, and opted to watch the 'Sisterhood of the Travelling Pants'—yes, *pants*!—on the flatscreen TV perched on a vintage cupboard when Glen suddenly blurted, "Why don't you move in with me?"

Cat pattern jim jams are the new fashion trend

"Move in with you?" My mouth fell open as I considered her words, with my impulsiveness urging me to not think too hard.

We'd been best friends for almost twenty years now, having met in preschool at the age of five. Inseparable ever since, we did everything together, including ravaging havoc on Glen's grandmother's flat when we were ten and hiding from my parents in a shabby shed in my back garden when we were thirteen. Growing up together in each other's living rooms and basically sharing families, it had never crossed my mind to actually live together.

Her kitchen was like my own already. Her bed was as comfortable as mine as I'd fallen asleep in it gossiping more times than I could count. I knew each and every valuable piece of furniture in this living room, as well as the history they carried, and could appreciate the slightly mismatched look of them together better than anyone else could. Besides, I was here at least every other day anyway.

The fact that I hadn't thought about it first was not lost on me, but if there was one thing Glen was good at, it was coming up with brilliant—or sometimes not so brilliant— ideas.

"What?" Glen straightened from where she lounged against me to give me a judgemental stare. Her arms folded over across her chest, and she huffed out a sharp breath. "You've been looking at flats for months now and not finding anything suitable. I have a spare room."

I had been looking for a flat, ready to move out from under my parents' roof with an unmatched eagerness for almost half a year without much success. Ever since I graduated with a business degree that I'll likely never put to use and started giving dance lessons full-time next to my waitressing shifts in Turtle Bay.

I had enough income to not deal with the recurring clashes with Mum. She always meant well, but I was a grown-up now and didn't need her advice every time I walked out of my bedroom. Dad just shrugged and smiled, but that didn't make it better. So yes, I wanted out, but I'd also been picky with my choices, and never once had I considered Glen's free room.

"It was your—" I said carefully.

" —my grandmother's. Yes, I know," Glen finished for me.

It was a sore topic for both of us since we had both loved her dearly. Glen hadn't likely opened the door to that room since her parents tidied it up four years ago. I know, I hadn't. The thought of invading Mama Jones' space gave me the creeps and made me the one worrying at my lower lip.

"It's either that or I'll lose the flat," Glen pouted.

I was sure the situation wasn't that dire yet. Nobody was going to take the flat away from her. She might lose warm water, WiFi, electricity, sure, but the flat itself was hers. Paid for and all.

I hesitated. "Glen, I..."

Her pouting turned into a scowl, and she slouched back into the seat, no longer leaning against me. Arms remained locked across her chest, and whatever little shine the movie had sparked in her eyes dimmed out. For some reason I thought of Mr Umbrella again and his intruding gaze. I would likely run into him more often if I were to live here. Not sure if I appreciated the idea or if the kerfuffle in my stomach was from discomfort alone.

I bit the inside of my cheek. "I mean, I could stay for a while?"

"Yesss!" Glen squealed and suffocated me in a squeezing hug.

I gulped for breath as she attempted to coerce the Nutella sandwich I'd consumed back out. When she was done celebrating, we shared a meaningful look.

"Your grandmother's room," I murmured.

"Yeah," Glen whispered.

Then we resumed watching the rest of the movie in contemplative silence, digesting our heavy meal and the idea Glen had come up with.

Once the movie had run its course, there was nothing left to distract us from the elephant in the room.

"Have you...?" I swallowed the lump that had risen in my throat, unable to complete that sentence.

Glen knew, though. She always knew what I was thinking. Her only response was a slight shake of her head.

After a moment, where the silence sizzled and vibrated in my ears, I braved another question. "Do you want to...?"

"I think we should," Glen said quietly.

As if rehearsed, we both stood at the same time and tiptoed to the door we'd been avoiding for the past four years and stood staring at it, while gathering our courage to pull it open. Glen wriggled her clasped hands in front of her chest, clearly not going to be the one to open the door, so I took a deep breath and wrapped my palm around the knob not giving myself the time to chicken out.

The hinges whined a sad song from not being used for so long. Goosebumps raised on my arms. A shiver ran down my spine. For a moment, a sense of eeriness lingered around us as a dust cloud puffed up from the motion, obscuring my vision. I coughed, but once it settled, we both stared motionlessly at the room beyond.

"It's empty," Glen finally breathed. "Completely empty."

And so it was. Bare wooden floorboards covered in dust were the only spectacle in this room. Darker rectangular spots indicated where the furniture used to stand, but there wasn't even a tabouret in sight.

"Did your parents empty it out?" I wondered out loud as Glen pushed past me, leaving shuffling footprints on the grey film covering the floor.

"She used to have a canopy bed over here," Glenn said, staring at the big open space in the middle of the room. "I always found it funny that she'd need extra curtains around the bed when the windows already had black-outs."

She spun around to face the opposite wall. "And there was a chestnut Renaissance wall cabinet," she continued. "Easily worth more than a couple thousand pounds if sold properly. The detailing on it was done by—"

"I remember," I said, joining her in the middle of the room. "She had an old rocking chair in that corner."

"Not just any old rocking chair," Glenn huffed. "It was Hitchcock's rocking chair."

"Right," I agreed.

"They took it all?" Glenn despaired. "How could they take it all?"

"How could they not tell you they took it all?" I echoed.

Parents were simply the worst sometimes, I decided. The emptiness of the room did make it easier to come to terms with the idea of moving in, however. Mama Jones' ghost was long gone, the only scent left in this room was from stuffiness and mildew; after only a few minutes of standing in the middle of it, I itched to scratch my nose. We'd need to give it a good scrub, that's for sure.

"So, how much do you pay for the utility bills?" I wondered, squeezing my eyes shut in anticipation of the number. I didn't know why, because she'd clearly been able to afford it on her antique shop assistant salary so far.

"You would only need to cover it until I find something new," Glen wriggled, avoiding the answer. "Then we'd split it."

"How much is it?" I asked again.

"About six hundred per month," she mumbled.

Holy shit! She'd been paying almost all of her salary to the energy bills alone to keep this flat. I'd been looking to rent for about the same price, but already owning a place and still paying this much every month? That sounded like thievery.

"We might need to look into that," I decided.

There ought to be cheaper providers, but that wasn't the priority just now. We talked about the move and planned everything out as much as we could until the sun began to set.

"Okay, since I'm not really officially living here yet," I said, standing up from her sofa to stretch, "I need to get going before my parents come knocking, or decide to call the police about a missing twenty-five year old."

Glen snorted. She was in a much better mood than when I'd first arrived. "They wouldn't! Your mum would lose her credibility with the authorities if she went crying wolf every time you stayed out past midnight."

I laughed. "You know her as well as I do. Nothing would stop her from giving me a house arrest despite the fact I'm not a child anymore."

"To her you'll always be a child."

The short trip to Glen's bedroom revealed that neither of us had thought to pick up my wet clothes from where I'd left them. Crumpled up as they were, they hadn't only remained wet but also acquired a strong stench.

Wrinkling my nose, I picked them up and threw them in the washing machine in the kitchen along with a few random things piling up in Glen's laundry basket.

"I don't suppose you have anything more... presentable to borrow?" I wondered, giving Glen a hopeful look while batting my eyes.

"You saw the laundry," she replied. "I'll be happy to find a clean pair of knickers for myself in the morning."

"You will not be working tomorrow, though."

Glen flinched. This topic was still raw. I got it, losing a job sucked, but I wasn't going to pick my wet clothes back out of the washing machine, and I wasn't going to traipse through the city in pyjamas either.

I was wrong. Glen had said there'd be hardly anyone out this late, which had persuaded me to leave her flat, gripping my phone in one hand and keys in the other, still wearing a cat pattern all over my body. I'd trusted her like I would an older and wiser sister had I had one, so it came to me as a total surprise when only two floors down from her place the lift yanked to a stop.

The ding of the doors opening carried an ominous air. There were three other flats on this floor, and for a second I held onto the hope that the person on the other side of the opening doors was anyone else but *him*. That hope died with the first crack in the metal enclosure as a familiar figure standing on the other side came into view.

I held my breath as Mr Umbrella slid his gaze over my outfit with a spark of amusement lighting up his eyes.

"I'm not sure this is an improvement on your previous outfit," he said, stepping into the tight space and pushing all the oxygen out into the hallway in the process. "Your boyfriend didn't have any of his clothes to spare? A knee-length T with those heels could convince a casual passerby you were headed to a bar or a club, but this?" He shook his head, grinning. "This'll not convince anybody."

I was not going to correct him on the facts he'd gotten wrong any more than I was going to give his handsomely smug face the attention he clearly craved. So, I huffed out a breath and faced the dials on the side wall, following the trail of the numbers lighting up and dimming as we descended.

"Right. Not in the mood to talk. I get it," Mr Umbrella said, and it took every ounce of me to remain nonchalant. I would not look at him. The reminder of his smile already seemed to be tattooed on my brain, and a refreshment would only make it fade slower. "It's cute, you know, the PJs. It's the heels that ruin the look."

"I didn't ask you for fashion advice," I blurted. "What would you know about it anyway? Maybe cat-patterned jim-jams are a new fashion trend and wearing high-heels is part of the protocol? Ever stopped to think about that? Besides, don't people in America wear stranger things outside than this?"

He laughed, and my eyes jumped to him in time to see his head fall back and his Adam's apple bobble. He wore a sleek button-up clearly meant to impress, the hem of it tucked into the waistband of his dark jeans. He also still carried the umbrella, and my heart lurched at the idea that it might still be raining.

"That obvious, huh? You don't need to get defensive, I have indeed witnessed stranger things. I also said it was cute, didn't I?"

I retorted, "For your information, girls don't like to be called cute."

"Hmm, is that so? What do they like being called?" he challenged.

"Stunning. Beautiful. Gorgeous. I don't know, anything other than cute. Cute is reserved for Hello Kitty, and you know, things that are actually adorable." The answer left my lips before I could stop to think about the implications. Having him call me stunning? Really, Haylee, really? You couldn't just swallow it down?

Mr Umbrella gave me another once over but didn't compliment me. Of course, he didn't.

"Girls wearing kitten PJs should expect to be called cute at least once," he insisted instead.

I narrowed my eyes at him, but he only chuckled in return. He wasn't wrong, I supposed. Hello Kitty and my pyjamas were almost the same thing. I refused to back down, however, and glared at him until he gave in.

"Okay, fine. I won't call you cute, you have your boyfriend for that."

I didn't see as much as felt the sting of his studious gaze on my face, while I tried to maintain a neutral expression. He didn't deserve to pry into my personal life after our two most mortifying lift rides together. Lift rides that lasted way too long if you'd ask me.

Mr Umbrella hummed as if my face had told him whatever he'd been looking for, despite my strongest efforts to keep it from him. He didn't say anything else for the rest of the way down, and I kept my own mouth welded shut, too. It would have been easy to forget he was there at all if it wasn't for the faint scent of masculinity slowly filling the space from his cologne and the tickling of my neck.

He stayed back, letting me exit first when we got to the ground floor. I got a distinct impression that he was checking out my bum, but if he was he didn't let on as he walked with me to the front door.

Even before I was close enough to see through the glass rectangle in the middle of the door, it became evident that it was indeed still raining. The soft tapping that had been muffled by the buzz of the lift grew louder as we reached the door.

I cursed in a very unladylike, very uncute way as I stopped under the little roof just outside the hallway. Mr Umbrella stopped right next to me, breathing in the scent of rain.

"I assume you don't have a raincoat hidden up your sleeve?" he asked, taking in my falling face.

I wasn't even going to joke as I sucked on my lower lip and shook my head. God, I fiercely hated the rain. Getting continuously soaked through was the worst of the worst one could ever experience. And yes, I could have also carried an umbrella like Mr Smartpants over there, but somehow, despite my hate, I kept forgetting to take one with me.

"Can I give you a ride somewhere?" he asked, genuine concern making his voice rougher.

I shook my head again. "No, thanks."

His arm reached out, breaching the space between us. "Here, let me at least give you my umbrella. We wouldn't want these clothes to turn transparent, too, now would we?"

I turned beet-red at the reminder, barely comprehending the umbrella changing hands, but I was clearly gripping the handle of it now. It was warm under my palm, and I could almost imagine his hand wrapped around it under my own.

"Ah, there it is," he said smugly, clearly referring to the blush colouring my cheeks. "I'll be waiting for you to return the umbrella when you're done with it, Red Cheeks."

I didn't have the chance to reject the umbrella when a car pulled up in front of the mansion block and Mr Umbrella, now umbrella-less, stepped into the rain and jogged to the passenger side. I was still standing on the front steps when the car drove off into the night.

Innocent and naive

The kitchen felt too full when I went to grab breakfast the next morning. It was early and Dad was drinking his coffee with a newspaper spread out in front of him, while mom clinged and clanged with about anything in—and out of—her reach. Henry, already energised like a Duracell bunny, ran circles around the island, chasing Drixie for whatever naughty plan he had for the cat this time. I wished he'd leave her alone, and I bet she thought the same when she bolted past me and slipped through my ajar bedroom door.

"There you are, Haylee," Mum said, not looking up from scraping sandwiches together, while Dad gave me a sweet smile. I cringed from the expectation of where this would go. "We made plans with Beckleys this weekend so I'll need you to babysit on Saturday. You weren't here last night so I decided it for you."

I stopped in my tracks, flipping my gaze to my brother, who now stood just outside my bedroom, trying to coax the cat out. Giving up, he prepared himself to tiptoe into my room, thinking I wouldn't see it.

"Henry!" I shouted. "You know the rules. Get your filthy feet out of my room!"

He flinched, yet did what I told him to. Once he dragged his feet back into the kitchen, I turned my attention to Mum. She was looking at me with a furrowed brow that said, 'be nice to your brother,' without her lips needing to move.

"I can't." I set my jaw and opted to stay firm in my decision.

Mum's eyebrows furrowed even further as she took in my rebellious stance. "What do you mean, you can't? As long as you're living under this roof you are expected to contribute. We've talked about this."

"Are you not familiar with the term? It's when something isn't possible for the person saying it."

"Don't get cross with me, young lady."

I sighed and my shoulders drooped slightly. "I have plans, I am moving out this weekend."

Glen and I hadn't really decided whether it would be this weekend or the next, but I could arrange it in two days if it meant getting out of here sooner.

"Moving out?" My mum asked, incredulous. "That's a bit short notice, don't you think?"

"Just like your request to babysit," I retorted. I only said 'request' because I didn't like the thought of her ordering me around. "Did you ever stop to consider that I, too, have plans?"

"Not very often, you don't," my dad chirped in helpfully, and I gave him a side-eye. "At least not something that can't be rearranged."

"You go rearranging your plans this time," I huffed.

Mum didn't even pay attention to the side conversation and continued as if Dad hadn't said anything at all. "Yes, but moving out? Shouldn't that come with a longer notice than two days?"

I crossed my arms over my chest. "You know I've been looking around for flats."

"So nice of you to find something so quickly," Dad said, "but can't you postpone it until next weekend? What's the rush?"

Nah, nope, not gonna happen. What's the rush, he asked? It was born from the suffocating feeling growing in my lungs the longer this conversation kept going. The way they treated me as if I was still a child because, at twenty-five, I was still stuck under their roof, unable to escape their judgement. It was the fact that I had offered to contribute to the household with my hard earned money, but the only currency they took was the hours wasted looking after Henry, or cleaning after Henry, or worse yet, listening to how it somehow still wasn't good enough.

Having to arrange my life around their expectations of me and not my own wants and needs wasn't how I planned on spending my entire adulthood. Especially since I'd already failed to become an attorney like my mother always wanted for me. Instead, I'd fallen in love with dancing and broken her heart. Now she tried to get me under her command in every other way possible.

She'd stopped packing sandwiches all together to give me a hawk-eyed stare. "When did you get the confirmation? Is it closer to the studio?"

"Yesterday," I said because it was true, "and it is not really closer, but it is easier to get to."

To get to the dance studio from here, I had to take a bus, change twice, and worry about the arrival times. From Glen's, I could take the Tube, even if it was a twenty-minute trip and a five-minute walk thereafter. The peace of mind it would come with surely was worth it, wasn't it?

Mum's mouth fell open before she screeched, "Yesterday? Honey, no respectable broker makes transactions that quickly. Are you sure this isn't a scam? Did you pay already? Let me have a look at the contract."

"If it's not closer, hon, maybe you should stay here longer and find something better suited," Dad chirped Having discarded his newspaper, he was now sipping his coffee.

"So you could enlist me into babysitting whenever you feel like?" I was getting mad, and I realised I was acting childishly, but their trust in my abilities to actually take care of myself were clearly nonexistent. Not once did Mum ask me to clarify where exactly I would be moving and how I'd found the place. Oh, no, she had assumed I was naive and had managed to get myself into trouble.

"Of course not, Haylee, so that you would be safe," Mum replied. If she'd left it at that I'd have considered spoon-feeding her the information I'd withheld, but she had to go and ruin it. "You and I both know how reckless you can be. Now let me see that contract."

I squinted at her as the ball of fury in my stomach grew and sizzled with vengeance. "There is no written contract," I offered stubbornly.

"What? Haylee you did not lease a flat on verbal confirmation only! You know better than that. Give me their contact information and I will sort this out for you right now. This will not be happening."

"I did," I said, gritting my teeth. "And no, I will not give you the contact. I am moving this weekend whether you like it or not. What you can help me with is borrowing Dad's van for the job, but that is the only thing I need from you."

I turned around, forgetting breakfast, and marched right back into my bedroom to grab my phone and my keys. I couldn't stay a minute longer or I would explode right into my mother's disapproving face.

"Haylee, come back here right this second!" she called after me, but I ignored her.

Once safely behind my closed door, I took deep breaths to calm my raging thoughts and thumping heart. I'd just stuffed a pair of joggers and a shirt into a backpack when the door slammed open behind me and my mum's scowling face disrupted my escape.

"Don't walk away when I'm still talking to you," she said while Dad tried to restrain her with a, "et her go, she needs to learn from her own mistakes," that didn't help soothe either of us.

I took a deep breath and tried to swallow down the bile rising in my throat. "If I don't leave now, we'll both regret it." Very adult of me to say—very reasonable—and with that I hauled the bag over my shoulder and stormed out.

I couldn't believe I had been on the fence about moving in with Glen when she first suggested it. Anything would be better than staying with my parents another day longer than I had to. Even taking over Mama Jones' old bedroom and living with her ghost. Not that I believed in ghosts. And dating would become so much easier, too, if I didn't have to tell men I was still living with my parents. Nobody had asked, of course; I'd made sure not to give anyone reason to get close. That could change once I moved. I could not only put my mother's judgement behind me, but also the past *recklessness* she so often liked to bring up.

Rushing to cross the street as a double decker turned a corner and made its way toward the bus stop, I tried to get that thought process out of my head, but it was stuck in there with a Super Glue.

I cringed imagining how that would play out with Mr Umbrella: *Oh, you know, today my nipples are safe since I decided to wear a padded bra, but I'm still living with my parents, so there's always that...*

Yeah, not happening. I wouldn't bring up my nipples in the first place, that was too close to thinking about the past I was to leave behind. Besides, Mr Umbrella would be one of those men not really inquiring about my situation, so this would never come up.

Either way, moving in with Glen would be for the best.

Freedom

The students in my dance class were in for a workout since my morning hadn't quite turned out the way I expected it to, and I needed an outlet. I didn't even bother to take them through the new choreography I'd planned to teach and had them all on their backs doing sit-ups. My own muscles screamed at me to stop since I'd been at this tempo for a third class in a row, but I might have been punishing myself, too.

With the chocolate horror of yesterday's supper fresh in my mind, I counted down from twenty, then went lax on the mat. Several sighs sounded across the studio.

"Stretch," I said, reaching my arms over my head as far as they could go, feeling my abs strain in the process. A minute later I had us on our stomach lifting the upper body off the floor until my back burned.

Up, one-two, down. *No more chocolate suppers*, I told myself with each excruciating lift-up. Up, one-two, down. *No more fights with Mum.* Now that one was much harder to accomplish, but distance ought to work. Up. *No more walks across town in pyjamas.*

Fun as it sounded, it had been a total nightmare, and I was not eager for a repeat just like I wasn't eager to return Mr Umbrella's umbrella. The thought of seeing him again made my stomach churn.

Could it have been any more embarrassing? Not only once but twice had he found me in a compromising attire. I had made a complete fool of myself, I'm sure, although my memory was a tad bit foggy from all that aforementioned embarrassment. I couldn't quite remember what we'd talked about. His smug face, however, was clear as day in my mind's eye. That four o'clock shadow framing his lips so perfectly you couldn't help but land your gaze there. And that glint in his eyes? He'd clearly had fun on my account and wasn't going to forget our encounters for a completely different reason that perturbed my thoughts.

I had the class stretch again, deciding I'd had enough torture and that it wasn't distracting enough. "We'll spend the last twenty minutes going over the choreography from the previous class."

Cheers erupted in the studio as I switched the soundtrack and mats were returned to their place in the corner of the room. I stared at my reflection in the floor-to-ceiling wall of mirrors, while the class settled behind me into their positions. Strands of hair fell out of my ponytail, framing buffed red cheeks Mr Umbrella would surely call attention to. The shirt hugged at my curves, highlighting each and every one of them, most importantly the belly that refused to flatten out. The fabric didn't show, but it was slick with sweat and clung to me almost uncomfortably. The joggers hung low on my hips and pooled around my ankles, being a bit too long for my short frame. I liked the bagginess of them, though, so I wore them anyway.

I was used to being seen in class this way since my students were all in various states of disarray as well, but I wouldn't walk out of the studio without at least changing my shirt and redoing my ponytail. Why, then, did the thought of me standing in that damned lift with Mr Umbrella in this state of dishevelment cross my mind? Ah, maybe because I was starting to become slightly obsessed. No, that couldn't be. Just to prove myself how much I was wrong, I took the class through the steps in slow motion only once before rushing us to dance them to the music.

All else faded as the rhythm took over. The lingering embarrassment and shame, the anger at my mother, the anxiety over actually moving out. It became irrelevant as my body moved to the music.

Gracefully beautiful. When I was dancing, that was the only time I really felt like that. As if I'd left my physical body behind, and the light of my soul could finally be seen. That's what brought me back to the studio time and time again, until I chose to volunteer to give a class at the age of seventeen, and they officially hired me a year later. It was also why following my mother's footsteps into the stuffy suffocating courtroom had never been a real option. Studying law would have been the complete opposite of the freedom dancing gave me.

And the waitressing on the side? Well, a girl's gotta do what a girl's gotta do. While I hadn't really needed the extra money living under my parents' roof, it had gathered me a decent savings pot for the flat hunt and would come in handy moving in with Glen.

I let myself get excited about the idea and smiled through the heavy breathing. We completed the set of moves we'd rehearsed, came to a standstill, and rewound the song to start from the beginning once more before our time was up. Yes, this was what I'd needed in the first place. To dance my heart out.

When you are looking forward to something, it takes much longer to arrive. I used to look forward to summer when I was a kid, and the rest of the year would always take an eternity to trickle by. Or to my birthday, or Christmas.

Getting obsessed with counting hours or days only slowed down the passing of time. It wasn't a surprise that the two days until the move went by at snail's pace, despite the decision being rushed and 'oh-so short notice' as my mother liked to keep reminding me.

"Are you absolutely certain?" she would ask, passing by my room and seeing me packing up my bookshelf. "You know you don't have to take all of that with you." Or an hour later during supper, "Haylee, honey, have you come to your senses yet? Shouldn't you take more time to think about it? Tell her, Arlo."

Her jabs had the opposite effect of what was desired, as every time she opened her mouth, my conviction to leave only grew and my resolve to not tell her anything about my arrangement grew. I was almost certain Mum had talked Dad out of lending me the van for the move, and was ready to drag a suitcase full of clothes over to Glen's to figure out the rest there. So when he stood at my bedroom door with the keys dangling from his fingers on Saturday morning, I did a little celebratory dance.

"Do you want me to drive you and check out the place for you, Haybear?" he asked, trying to tread carefully around the minefield Mum had built around the entire topic.

"That won't be necessary, Dad. I'll be staying with Glen." There, I said it. It was easier to admit it to Dad, and it just slipped out of my mouth without me even thinking about it.

The gears in his brain were visibly turning when he put the entire story together. Crinkles appeared next to his eyes, and his lips turned upward in an involuntary smile. "When did you plan on telling your mum this?"

"When she asked." I shrugged, pressing my lips into a stubborn pout. "She never even asked."

"When do you want me to tell her?" Dad pondered.

"When she asks?" I laughed and he shook his head.

"How about I give it a few days and let her know then. You know she's as stubborn as you are, she won't ask."

"Serves her right," I blurted.

"Haylee, you don't mean it!"

I dropped my gaze to my feet and sucked in my bottom lip. I thought I meant it, which is why I said it in the first place. I did mean it, didn't I?

It's common for people to try to put words in your mouth that you didn't even think of saying at first. And perhaps speaking in anger wasn't the best way to go, but taking one's words back because someone didn't like the sound of them couldn't possibly be the right way, either. How would we learn each other's true thoughts if we tiptoed around one another all the time?

No, of course, I didn't mean to be rude. I wasn't brought up like that. I was brought up to eat my own words and pretend I didn't feel the things I felt, to put my own desires aside and be thankful for every judgemental guideline that turned me into the girl who couldn't even own up to standing dripping wet in an elevator with a stranger. While my nipples were showing through my T-shirt. Jesus Christ, worse things had happened to people, and they weren't constantly getting edgy at the thought.

How did I end up thinking about Mr Umbrella again? *Shit.*

"I'm sorry," I muttered begrudgingly. "That was out of bounds."

Dad smiled sweetly, swiping the topic away with a motion of the hand. "Do you need a hand with any of this?"

I did a one-eighty circle in my room, taking in the boxes stacked up on top of each other, and chewed at my bottom lip. This move was about independence. Doing things on my own, in my way. Taking life by its horns and finally being in charge. But then again, wrestling the bed frame and the bookshelf into the van on my own would be a challenge and a half.

"That'd be nice," I agreed.

Two hours later. I'd parked the van in front of Glen's mansion block and tapped my fingers on the steering wheel, not quite ready to depart yet. Moving out was the right thing to do. I knew it. And it wasn't like my parents were all that far away if I had a change of heart, like my mum kept wishing. I spent plenty of time at Glen's to be totally at home there. Despite all of that, I had to take deep breaths and urge myself to let her know I'd arrived.

Dad wanted to help me bring my belongings up to the flat, but Mum whisked him away to the plans they had made. Henry was sent off to our aunt, with a frown and a 'such an unnecessary hassle' pointed towards me.

Deep breath. Freedom was right there outside this van.

I texted Glen. There, simple as that.

Mathematist—mathician...

"*You expect us to* get all of that up to the twelfth floor on our own?" Glen stared at the assortment of items stuffed into the van in wide-eyed horror. The bed and the shelving unit being first to go into the van were neatly tucked furthest from the doors, while boxes of every size crowded the rest of the space.

I'd run a red light, being too late to stop, and swerved away from an eager driver crossing the same junction. As a result, most of my stacked piles had fallen over, making the task at hand look more challenging than it actually was. I should know; I dragged them all out of my bedroom just fine.

"We'll just use the lift. We'll be done in no time. Two hours, max." I dragged one of the boxes out, feeling my arms protest a little.

I was already two hours in, and I'd been pushing myself harder at the studio these past days. Just two more hours. Piece of cake.

"Tell me again, why couldn't your dad help us with this?" Glen huffed.

I gave Glen a raised eyebrow and nudged my jaw towards the boxes, urging her to pick one for herself. "He and Mum had plans. Socialising and such. Don't ask, I'm just glad not to be babysitting."

She scoffed and grabbed a box of shoes. "They sure do a lot of socialising."

ELEVATE WITH ME

We made a little tower next to the lift before we called it down to pile it all in. I was already breathless and sweaty. The little rest I had, standing still in the lift, was well needed, but my body remained on high alert, and my heartbeat picked up as we rode higher.

Seventh floor. Eighth floor. Ninth floor. Tenth… and we passed it without a hitch. My nerves remained on the edge nonetheless, as we unloaded the lift, then dragged everything to Glen's grandmother's room—or, I supposed, my room now.

It had been dusted since our last visit and rays of sun brightened up the space, bathing it in a warmer light. The beige patterned wallpaper was old-fashioned and had faded with time. It was due for replacement, but it wasn't a priority, and removing it felt like overstepping. It added character and a reminder of who this room used to belong to.

We were quite done with carrying things already when we reached the challenging items. The lift was getting tired of us, and I was more than tired of the lift. Especially since every ride up and down made my stomach tie in knots when we passed the tenth floor. Not once did we make an extra stop there. We did leave behind a family of four on the seventh floor once while going up, though. They couldn't have fit in with our stacks of boxes even if they'd tried.

The bed was taken apart into smaller manageable pieces, but the bookshelf was still in one piece and the mattress? It had been hell to get that into the van even with my dad's help. Glen and I eyed it together with reasonable trepidation.

"Tell me again why…" Glen started, and I just shook my head at her.

"We can do it," I encouraged but didn't move an inch to pull the mattress out.

God, we couldn't really do it. My arms felt like noodles at this point, and the memory of how heavy the mattress had been was still fresh in my mind.

Glen turned to look at me. "Oh yeah, we sure can. Maybe if we drag it across the ground? Good thing you've wrapped it in plastic."

"Dad's idea," I muttered. I wouldn't have bothered, but if we were indeed going to have to slide it the plastic would come in handy.

"Good one," Glen said.

Neither of us moved for another minute, until I cursed myself. "Okay, last spurt. Let's go, let's go." I clapped my hands and bounced on my heels, getting ready for said last spurt, while Glen snorted, and then folded over in laughter.

"Let's go, let's go," she repeated through giggles.

"Shut up and help me with it." I dragged the mattress to the edge of the van bed, waiting for the second set of hands to latch onto it.

"Give me a moment," Glen said and I peeked at her from behind the mattress with a raised eyebrow.

She had her phone camera directed at me and a wide grin on her face. "You are tuning in with Hallie and Glen in the middle of a moving mayhem. Hallie here thinks we can most definitely, with all our sanity attached, get this mattress to the twelfth floor. Thoughts?"

I rolled my eyes. "Do you have to?"

"Yes, I most certainly do." She nodded emphatically, the phone wobbling in her hands slightly along with the movement, and I cringed at the thought of my image on it already looking less than stellar without the added effect.

"Okay, if you really have to know, we'll certainly not make it if you don't put down that phone and help me with it."

Glen's lips formed an adorable pout. "Ouch, someone's getting cranky. I just thought it could be fun to document this milestone."

I rubbed my face, groaned, then pushed at the mattress I still held onto, so that it wouldn't hang too much over the edge of the van and drop onto the ground before I let go and faced the camera.

"You're right. Exhilarating," I mumbled. "It's just that I've been at this moving business since this morning and you've been at it for the past hour and half, so you have no idea how cranky it can make you when your best friend pulls out a camera when you're looking like a horror show."

"You look fine," Glen said. "Let's talk about how happy it makes you to move in with me instead."

I snorted. "Only if you turn that camera around and show it your own glorious sweaty self."

Glen clicked her tongue and puffed. "Okay, fine."

She turned the phone around in her hand, smiling at the invisible audience. "There, happy?"

I grinned. "Thrilled!"

"So, we have this mattress to somehow get out of this truck," Glen went on as if the previous debate hadn't even happened. "Where are them big strong men when we need them? Hm? It is a distress call!"

"Don't forget the bookshelf behind it," I reminded Glen who had turned the camera toward the van to showcase the magnitude of the mattress. She swung it right over at me again, however, and I took it like a champ. "But other than that and the bed frame, we're basically done. And you know what? It hasn't even been raining today, which actually makes this entire process more enjoyable. Now, would you put that phone down and help me? I'd like to get this done before my body gives out on me, and I think that's just about soon."

Glen giggled again. "Yes, Mum."

We had the mattress up on one side for the least ground contact after we hauled it all the way out of the van. Glen was pulling, I was pushing, and the plastic was covered in scraped against the asphalt as we manoeuvred across the car park. Somehow it had grown in size and weight since I'd dragged it into the van with Dad.

"Are you even pulling it?" I huffed, putting all my weight against it and feeling like I was trying to dislodge the entire mansion block.

"Wait! Wait! The steps!" Glen screeched in response, and I almost dropped my half of the mattress. Although, it was barely even off the ground at this point, maybe hovering by about a millimetre.

Oh gosh, the steps! I hadn't even considered the steps. There were but two, but if we weren't able to lift this thing off the ground on equal flooring, the steps were an obstacle we might not be able to surmount.

"You've got to come on this side!" Glen decided after another second of stumbling, so I left my side of the mattress leaning on the ground and joined Glen on her side.

We flipped the mattress over so it now laid flat on the ground, and I felt like dropping on it and sleeping under the sky right in the middle of the pavement. The only thing stopping me from doing just that was the idea of Mr Umbrella finding me like that. Yeaaah, no, that was not happening, so I squeezed my fingers under the mattress next to Glenn, and we both pulled it halfway up the steps. Halfway because there was no way the entire length of it would fit. And to get it through the front door, we had to turn it to its side again.

I was sweating worse than after my most excessive workouts. If Glen had said I looked fine when she made her little hilarious memento, by the time we got the mattress to the corridor, I was an absolute mess. I know because she herself had looked fine before, and now... Well, let's just say we both needed a shower – badly!

Wiping at my forehead was no use when my palms were just as wet. I could track droplets travelling down my back beneath my soaked shirt. No cotton bra this time, thank god. I was properly secured in a sports bra, but that didn't ease my mortification when the lift dinged, and none other than Mr Umbrella walked out, almost colliding with my mattress.

That's one way to get the man into bed. Just trip him with a mattress, that would certainly do it. No need for further conversation or permission at that. Consent was fickle anyway, I would know... No, nope, not going there.

"Careful where you put your—" His eyes travelled from the mattress parked way too close to the lift doors to me, and his furrowed eyebrows smoothed out, a grin blooming on his lips. Even his tone changed from annoyance to bemusement. "Oh, hey there, Red Cheeks. Didn't expect to see you again this soon. Wet again, I see."

I flushed the instant I felt his eyes on me, try as I might to hide from his gaze. Oh no, I was intensely fascinated by the pattern on my mattress. Had it always had thin light blue parallelograms on it? I can't quite remember seeing them before. Fascinating.

"Red Cheeks?" Glen retorted, pinning me with a questioning stare that made my cheeks burn hotter. "You know each other or something. Wet again? What kind of wet are we talking about?"

Oh my sweet lord, take me now and spare me from this embarrassment.

"Rain, Glen, we are talking about rain. And sweat, apparently. And no, we don't know each other 'or something,'" I rushed to say, wishing the ground would swallow me whole.

"No?" Mr Umbrella mock-scoffed. His amusement was growing by the minute. On my account, really. He was making fun of me the way boys often did. "I thought we went way back to the time you trapped me between the elevator doors."

Glen gasped. "Hallie, you did *not*! How have I not heard about this?"

"That was three days ago," I mumbled. "I was hoping it had only been in my imagination."

Glen immediately realised why she hadn't heard about it. Three days ago was when she had her little meltdown, after all.

"Oh." That one word was enough.

"Definitely not in your imagination," Mr Umbrella replied, though there was a look in his eyes that made me wonder whether he wanted to spend time in my imagination.

I noticed he didn't carry an umbrella this time, though admittedly, he'd given it to me. It was somewhere upstairs in one of the boxes. I had been wondering whether to pretend forgetting to give it back and keep it on display in my room to—I don't know—torture myself with the memory of him. Or just simply go ahead and give it back, as was proper.

I made a mental note to return it as soon as possible. Oh yes, that would be better for my sanity. Maybe I could make him wait here while I went and grabbed it right away? Who knew, he might need it to keep his chinos dry. Never mind that the sky was a brilliant blue.

"So, *Hallie*," he said my name as if testing it on his tongue. "What are you doing with that mattress?"

I did not bite my lower lip so much as chewed it raw. "Taking it upstairs, naturally."

"Naturally," Mr Umbrella echoed after me, his amusement growing by the minute, and I didn't know what in the world he found so hilarious. Unless it was my dishevelled appearance yet again. He should be used to seeing me looking less than stellar at this point. I doubt it could get any worse than our two previous meetings, anyway.

I waved with my hand in a shooing motion to get him to step aside from the *elevator* doors, as he called them, so we could continue our quest. "Do you mind?"

"Oh, you were going to use the elevator? I'm afraid that's not going to fit." He stepped aside anyway and even pressed the button so that the doors reopened for us.

My flushed face stared back at me from the mirror on the back wall and my stomach recoiled. "What do you mean it won't fit?"

"I meant the mattress, of course." His gaze flicked to the lift and then to the offensive object between me and Glen, a grin spreading on his face.

Of course, he'd meant the mattress, what else could he have—ohh… No, Haylee, he had meant the mattress all along, I was the one thinking about other things. There were no flirty suggestions thrown around in this corridor. Only in my head.

"You're welcome to try, but I'd say it's bigger than the six by six space. "

"Six by six what?" I stammered, looking to Glen for help, who shrugged and studied the lift.

"Feet," Mr Umbrella said.

I dropped my eyes to his feet clad in brown leather dress shoes. He was talking about feet and inches, not his actual feet, though. I realised that a second later. And yes it looked like a tight fit, but we had to get it up somehow so I was willing to shove it in, press the button, and then run up the stairs if I couldn't squeeze in with it. Who was he to say my seer will wasn't enough to make it fit?

"What are you, a mathematist—mathician—Christ." My brain was short-circuiting. Must have been all those non-existent flirty suggestions it was conjuring up that halted my usually bright enough thought process.

Glen picked this moment to be helpful in the most unhelpful way possible. "Mathematician," she whispered.

"Nope, just a realist, although I do like the last guess."

"What? Mathematician?"

"No, Christ. I imagine worship could be fun when done right."

It was in my head. Only in my head, right? Staring at his smirk, though, it was clear he had actually said it out loud. Oh my goodness. I shook my head trying to encourage blood circulation, then rolled my eyes. I was not imagining that along with him. Of course, I wasn't! Okay, fine, my brain was very eager to go there. Way too eager. Over-eager. I really needed to stop thinking about it. Like right now would be great.

"I can help you carry it upstairs," Mr Umbrella suggested casually, flicking a button open on his blue jacket without waiting for a response. He continued to loosen buttons in a lazy manner while studying my reaction. I was flushed already, so there wasn't really anything more he could get out of me with his playful undressing. Perhaps he expected me to decline the help.

Of course, it would have been stupid to refuse the offer since we already experienced the two small steps in front of the building. An actual staircase with just me and Glen was not going to be in our power to overcome. Also, I was too stunned to outright deny him.

"To the twelfth floor?" I gaped at his neat button-up shirt under the jacket he hung on a railing, while he resumed to unbutton the cuffs and fold them up, revealing strong forearms in the process. My mouth was not going dry.

He smirked. "I remember the floor you live on, Red Cheeks."

Was he for real? Was he actually for real?

"I could always call my dad for help." I should have done that to begin with. Should have begged him to come with me and make sure I'd be fine. But no, my pride had to get the better of me. Some things I really couldn't do on my own.

"Or that boyfriend of yours?" He cocked an eyebrow, daring me to spill it.

I'd stayed silent last time he mentioned the nonexistent boyfriend and planned to do so this time, too. Glen, however, reminded me I was not staring at Mr Umbrella's bare forearms all by my lonesome. Oh no, Glen was also gaping, and she was invested in our conversation.

"Boyfriend? Hallie doesn't have a boyfriend."

I swear he grinned. I wasn't looking, but I swear he did. "I will not ask about your midnight walk of shame if you'll allow me to help you."

"I told you, cat patterned pyjamas are in fashion," I huffed.

"Mhmmm, I'm sure they are. Now tiptoe over to the other side of this bad boy and help your friend lift it, we've got stairs to climb."

Nicknames are for forever

Even with Glew aud and me putting all our efforts into pulling the mattress up the stairs and an umbrella-less Mr Umbrella supporting the bottom side with unmistakable prowess, it took us a long sweaty while to get that damned thing up to the twelfth floor. The entire weight of my king-sized bed fell on his shoulders, and he still somehow managed to keep staring at me. That more than anything made me stumble on the steps countless times.

"So, Hallie," Mr Umbrella said when we were on the fifth floor, taking a breather. His voice didn't carry even a note of wheeze, while Glenn was hunched over with her palms on her knees, and my own lungs burnt like something had caught fire on them. "How come you're moving furniture?"

"It's not just furniture I'm moving." Okay, I was breathless as hell, and it came out more like 'itshhh not jhhhust fuhhhrniture 'm mohving.'

Mr Umbrella was fluent in wheeze, because he didn't even blink an eye at my response. I mean, it shouldn't have come as a surprise really; he left plenty of women breathless, no doubt.

"No? What else will be moving?" he asked with a quirked eyebrow.

"Me and my cat."

"Drixie?" Glen gasped through her own breathlessness. "We didn't talk about Drixie moving in with you."

I turned all my attention to Glen. "Of course, she is, I can't leave her behind."

"What about the antiques? I don't want claw marks all over them."

"She doesn't do that sort of thing, and you know it." I crossed my arms over my chest and narrowed my eyes.

"She might! She's never been around antiques!"

I scoffed, shaking my head. "No, Glen, but she's a cat, and I don't think it matters how old anything is for her to leave it well alone. What are you really worried about?"

Glen's shoulders deflated. "Drixie doesn't like me. I don't think we'll get along."

"Nonsense," I scoffed. "The only person Drixie doesn't like is Henry. I'm not leaving her with him."

Mr Umbrella cleared his throat, and we both turned in his direction. His eyebrow raised in question. "The nonexistent boyfriend?"

"Brother," I muttered, while Glen went "Eww" at his question.

He nodded understandingly. "Fascinating. Go on."

I shared a glance with Glen, and we unanimously decided it was a topic to discuss when it was just the two of us. No audience needed, thank you. Also, holy camoly! Time for a distraction.

"Don't you have anywhere to be?" I asked at the same time Glen said, "How about we 'go on' carrying this hellish thing?"

Mr Umbrella glanced at the watch on his wrist, clicking his tongue, then looked from me to Glen and back again. "Okay, ladies, I see what you're doing, but you are both right. I do have somewhere to be, and we need to get this mattress out of the hallway."

Somehow he managed to keep talking while we continued our climb up the stairs. "So what kind of cat do you have, Red Cheeks?"

I was red all over at this point, so I couldn't really fault him for the nickname. I buffed out air, trying to answer as we reached the next landing. "Just a normal black cat."

"Ah, and why doesn't she like your brother? Henry was it?" Mr Umbrella asked.

"He's twelve," I huffed as if that was an answer enough. I really didn't have any breath left in me to explain the torture Drixie went through on daily basis under his uncareful hands. No more!

"Right," Mr Umbrella nodded as if that made perfect sense. "Gotcha." He was getting breathless himself, which was a pretty good indication of his immaculate stamina, since we'd reached the eighth floor at this point and had to take another break.

I shook my hands, trying to get blood flowing and the tenseness out. Glen sat on the stairs again gasping and wiping at her brows. Mr Umbrella was staring at me again, so I stood up straighter despite wanting to vomit my insides out.

"You know my place is closer," he joked. I hope to God he joked, because that was bad as far as pick-up lines went.

"No. Nope. Nah. You signed up for this all by your muscly self, you don't get to back out now."

"Oh, I'm not backing out," he grinned. "Far from it."

It was at least fifteen minutes later when we dropped the mattress in Glen's spare bedroom—my bedroom. At last! I was most definitely dripping with sweat. Glen was all sweaty, too, and I knew we'd be fighting for the bathroom. Even Mr Umbrella's shirt was sticking to him but in a delightful way. Nothing like the two of us. I think I'd prefer to show up in pyjamas again to this drenched-in-sweat look, but there was no going back now.

Mr Umbrella gave the antiques in the living room an appreciative look as I guided him out.

He wiped his palms on his trousers. "I'd help you with the rest of your stuff, but I've really got to run now. I'm actually quite late."

"Thank you for your help. I don't think we could have done it without you."

"Sure you could have, you seem like a resourceful girl." He winked. "It was a pleasure."

"Oh, it was far from pleasant," I retorted, stopping at the doorway and leaning against the frame trying my best not to think about the bed and bookshelf still in the van downstairs.

"Hmm... If you say so." He backed away toward the lift, looking smug while at it. "I hope to see you around, Red Cheeks."

I hoped to be looking decent for once when I'd be seeing him around, but I didn't say anything when the lift doors opened on our floor and he stepped in. I did give a little girlish wave as the doors closed, taking him away. Then I shook my head, dropped my hand and reprimanded myself. Because really? What the bloody hell was that?

Way to make a good impression, Haylee. Oh, it was disastrous.

Glen came to stand next to me, peeking into the empty corridor. "So, Hallie, who was the hottie?"

I cringed. "Hottie? Didn't we grow out of that word after highschool? It sounds... I don't know, lame. And I don't really know his name, I've been calling him Mr Umbrella."

Glen snorted. Honestly, it sounded absurd when I said it out loud.

"He lent me his umbrella." I shrugged defensively. "It made sense when I came up with it."

"Well, this Mr Umbrella fancies you," Glen announced with a wide grin, pulling me into the flat and closing the door behind us.

I was too exhausted to complain about stopping our moving activities, but I had enough energy to deny her suggestion. "He does not!"

Glen threw a look my way. You know the one that says, 'Girl, you're blind or joking or just better believe me on this; you have no idea what you're saying.' I did know, though. Nobody in their right mind would fancy me after the three embarrassing encounters we'd had.

"He carried your mattress up twelve flights of stairs," Glen insisted. "He is into you."

Right, I didn't know how to explain that away, but I wasn't ready to give in just yet. "I bet that's just a regular Saturday for him."

Glen shook her head. "He gave you a nickname."

I rolled my eyes. That damned nickname. "He probably walks around naming girls left and right. He seems like the type."

"What type?"

"The type to nickname everyone," I groaned. "The type to flirt and sleep around."

Okay, I sounded bitter about it. Jealous at the mere thought of it. It was unlike me to make conclusions out of first impressions, but his confidence had to have come from somewhere. More often than not experience was involved in that. He'd had a fair share of girls falling for that devilish smirk and burning stare. I was certain of it. It would be smart of me to stay away, because I was not looking for a player even if they played a perfect gentleman.

"Red cheeks sounds cute, though." Glen had stopped by the bathroom door, ready to tear her clothes off. We were clearly done carrying things upstairs.

"God, don't mention it."

"He is quite good-looking, too."

I snorted. "He is outright gorgeous is what you mean."

Glen screeched in delight. "So you do like him!"

I pushed her into the bathroom. "Go take a shower, so I can go take a shower after you. I feel nasty."

"Not before you admit it, Hallie!"

"I do not like him," I crumbled.

Glen crossed her arms on her chest. "Hallie!"

"I do not!!"

She did not agree with my answer. Well, so be it. I nudged past her into the bathroom. If she wasn't going to use it, I would. We could discuss Mr Umbrella after I felt like a person again. Or not discuss him. I think I'd much prefer the second option. Thank you very much.

Good reasons

After we were both clean and all but forgotten about the rest of the furniture, Glen reminded me why I was getting fat. I was done rummaging through boxes for a clean comfortable pair of jeans and a baggy T-shirt, and Glen had finished blow drying her hair when we rendezvoused in the living room.

"We deserve a treat," she said convincingly. "Let's go grab some cake from the cafe across the street."

I wrinkled my nose, even as my mouth began to water. "I shouldn't…"

"Oh, come on, why not? Is it because of that mathematician guy? The Mr Umbrella."

I scoffed. "Of course not."

"It is, isn't it!" Glenn squealed. "Haylee's got a crush. Haylee's got a crush!"

"Oh, come on, I do not have a crush!"

My cheeks were blazing just at the thought of him. The embarrassment! Would it ever let me breathe freely again?

Naturally, Glen did not take my word for it. "Yes you do. It's written all over your face. When were you going to tell me about him?"

I groaned. "I was hoping to forget about him, actually."

"Well, forget about him with a piece of cake and a coffee, while you tell me all about the way you two met."

I dropped my head back, staring at the ceiling panels. I knew she wouldn't let it go so I sighed and agreed. "Today you win. But only today."

Glen laughed and pulled me out of the door. "We shall see, Red Cheeks. We shall see."

Oh, hell no! She would not take over that horrible nickname. I would not let her.

The coffee shop was literally across the street from Glen's—our—mansion block if you exited from the street side of the building and not to the car park behind it, where my van waited impatiently to be relieved of its burden; plenty of time for that later.

The welcoming aroma of coffee beans and biscuits mixed together in the air and convinced me I needed the sugar rush. Pastel-coloured chairs warmed up the mostly wooden interior of the small place. The chairs, and the heater alike.

There was a chill in the air that managed to get under my skin during the short walk over, and the warmth wrapping me in its embrace as we stepped into the cafe was much appreciated. Especially since, unlike Glen, I let my hair air-dry, and it was still slightly damp from my shower and curling up rather wildly.

No, I was not expecting another 'wet again' joke from Mr Cocky since I knew he'd left in a hurry after his heroics. No, I was not still thinking about him. Heaven help me, I was still thinking about him!

"Cappuccino," I told the barista as I eyed the cake selection.

"And the chocolate brownie for her," Glen chirped in from behind me.

The barista looked from her to me, raising an eyebrow. I wished I could raise just one eyebrow the way she did, it looked cool. I bet Mr Umbrella could raise an eyebrow. On him, it would look hot as hell. Yeah, not thinking about him at all.

Glen nudged me, and I sighed. "What the hell, why not. One for me and one for her, too. Anything else you want, Glen? My treat."

"Oh, if it's your treat," Glen grinned, "I'll have a big caramel macchiato. Thanks."

I nodded a confirmation to the barista, paid and let her prepare our coffees as we chose a window seat to settle in.

A candle in a cute little clay tray flickered on the table, and my fingers itched to press into the liquid wax in a childish reflex. Ah, to hell with it, I gave in and painted my fingertips in candle wax like it was a totally normal thing to do.

"So, Hallie," Glen began. Her eyes poured into mine as I tapped at the table with my 'reinforced' fingers. "Tell me everything."

"There isn't much to say, really." Tap. Tap. Tap. And a bite of my lower lip.

"That's hard to believe, since his eyes were literally glued to you the entire time. Don't think I didn't notice."

"That's his problem, not mine."

"Problem? Hallie, he is hot, and he was basically undressing you with his eyes. I don't see any other problem here other than you being too timid to do anything about it."

"He needn't bother. The day I got rained upon gave a good enough impression of what's under my clothes," I muttered.

"Oh my God, Hallie! Your shirt was basically see-through."

"I know, I was there." If embarrassment was a living, breathing entity, it was sitting on my chest at that moment. "It was horrific."

"I see why you would keep it from me. He seemed like a perfect gentleman today, though."

"Maybe he was trying to make up for the unpleasantness of our first meeting. Not that me trapping him between the lift doors really helped my case that day. Nor the fact we ran into each other again when I was leaving IN MY PYJAMAS!"

Glen burst out laughing and didn't stop even as the coffee and cake arrived. I tolerated it with a piece of melting brownie on my tongue and thoughts of sweet revenge in my mind. She had her own explaining to do, and I would be on at her as soon as she stopped giggling.

"About Drixie," I said after too long of a moment. "She'll be moving in with us."

Glen's face fell, and she fidgeted in her seat. "I told you, she doesn't like me."

I crossed my arms on my chest, momentarily letting go of my coffee mug. Eyes narrowed, I stared at Glen as she twirled her own mug round, and round, and round between her fingers. I let her fret for a moment, finishing my brownie while she took her time trying to explain her reasoning.

"Remember when I picked you up for Jay's birthday? You took your time getting ready, and I waited in the living room. Drixie, she hissed at me and left when I sat next to her on the sofa. I didn't invade her space or anything, I know cats at least that much. I sat two places from where she was laying, but still she complained. That's not even the first time, but it's the time I decided she hated me."

I furrowed my eyebrows. "Jay's birthday? You mean the one two years ago? The one where I was made a total fool out of and we never spoke to him nor his friends again?

That one? That's a long time to hold a grudge against Drixie without telling me about it."

I'd taken my time getting ready that day because, despite despising crowded social gatherings, I wanted to look pretty for Jay. We'd not really been dating, but I'd thought he'd wanted to. I wasn't an expert in that department, that's for sure, because all he did want was to play around with me, then have his friends walk in on us to catch my humiliation on camera. I bet Glen would have owned up to her tits hanging out of her shirt and skirt improperly pulled up. Me? Scarred for life!

I'd just stood there in shock letting them catch it all in a video that ended up on social media. That was the last time I hung out with any of the influencer folk Glen had connected with through her channel. Not only was I mortified, but explaining it to my mother had been a total nightmare. She lectured me for hours before she had one of her contacts take the videos down. By then, it had been seen by fifty thousand people all over the world. I think it was around that time that I started having regular clashes with Mum. What a coincidence...

"There were other more substantial matters to discuss back then," Glen said. "Like what an utter prick Jay was!"

I snorted. "Such a prick."

We sat in silence for a while, sipping coffee and listening to the chill tunes trickling through the speakers.

"I'll let you in on a secret," I said at last. "Drixie owns the sofa, and she's not sharing. She'll act all disappointed no matter who sits on it. I get hissed at on a regular basis. It's not you."

Another secret I'd been keeping close to my heart? I didn't trust men, even if they looked like knights in shining armour. Mr Umbrella was an intruding thought—wishful thinking, perhaps—but the way we met hit a bit too close to my most humiliating day ever. I would never be able to look past that.

Stainless shirts are no good

I drove the van back to my parents' house after Glen and I managed to unload the rest of my things. She was still on the fence about Drixie, but that didn't stop me from urging the cat into a carrier bag. She resisted, of course, and attempted to hide from me, but even the trepidation of the carrier and what it stood for couldn't keep her hiding for long when I opened a can of tuna.

Her soft paws tattered right over and into the carrier when the scent of fish got too tempting to resist. I locked her in with the treat. By the time she realised her misfortune, all she could do was give me a betrayed yowl. She stomped around the small space, rubbing against the net in the hope I'd feel pity for her. She'd learn quick enough that that wasn't going to happen.

Before I left my childhood home behind, I wrote a note on the fridge: "All settled in. Thanks for the van. -H." I dropped the keys on a hallway cupboard where they were impossible to miss, slipped on my shoes, and grabbed Drixie's carrier bag. She protested one more time before she settled down in defeat. What she didn't want to admit was how much she actually enjoyed seeing the world behind the window. Since I'd given away the car keys we'd need to take the bus, and Drixie could observe more of the city... through the windows of various public transportation vehicles. I was quite done by the time I reached the mansion block I should start calling home.

Want to guess who else was done with wherever he'd rushed to after the last time I saw him? Mr Umbrella, of course.

The bus stopped just behind the mansion block, giving me a view of the almost full car park. It was impossible to miss the man stepping out of a Toyota, possibly the very same car that'd picked him up when it was raining, and pat the roof of it the way only men do. He laughed, with his head dropping back, then shook his head, replying something to the driver before he swung the door shut and the car took off.

It'd be fine, I told myself. If I walked slowly he'd be in the lift before I reached the front door, right? Wrong. Since I had a clear view of him through the parked cars, he also had a clear view of me. As if feeling my stare, his gaze landed on me, and I swear I could see his eyes sparkle even from this distance.

His hand came up to cup around his lips as he shouted, "Hey, Red Cheeks!" His other hand waved me over with a wide, almost theatrical arch.

There was no avoiding him after this. Even several passersby stopped to observe my stumbling walk toward the man who was content to wait in the middle of the car park.

Grinning from ear to ear, he crouched to peer through the netting of the carrier bag. "Look at who's with you. Hello, Drixie," he cooed, tapping at the bag softly and pulling away just as she gave him an annoyed frown. Straightening, Mr Umbrella asked, "So you got it sorted, hmm?"

I bit the inside of my cheek as one of my feet did awkward circles on the asphalt. His eyes burned right through me, the intensity leaving my mind blank, and my heart racing. It was just a look. Just a look, nothing more. And an innocent question, really. *Snap out of it, Haylee.*

I nodded, then shrugged, forcing my feet to still and not start a tap-dance at the tension building within my body. "Sort of? You could say that. I mean, yeah."

Mr Umbrella laughed. "Sounds like a no to me."

I studied him with interest. Men I'd gone out with rarely knew what 'no' meant even when said outright. My stuttering just now would have been misinterpreted for sure. Somehow, Mr Umbrella had learned to speak the universal language of women, and while I didn't mean to be impressed by this one simple comment he'd made, I couldn't stop wondering what else he knew.

The moment he caught me looking, I dropped my gaze to our feet and started fidgeting again. Devil's nuts, his attentiveness was nerve-wracking.

"Hmm…" Mr Umbrella hummed, and his dress shoes took a step closer to my trainers. "We've learned that I'm not a mathematician, and neither are you. It's my turn to guess, are you an artist?"

My heart hammered in my chest as I slowly raised my gaze from his quirked lips to his sparkling green eyes.

"What?" I gasped.

He stood close enough now to reach out his hand and tap at my shirt, just below the collar, in the same fashion he'd tapped at Drixie's carrier. I followed his finger to where it was still touching me. All air flooded out of my lungs, leaving me breathless.

"Artistic," he murmured as I incredulously took in the brown splotch marring the otherwise gray fabric.

It hadn't been there this morning so it must've happened during my coffee break with Glen. I had no recollection of spilling anything, but I must have since there it was, in all its glory, proving once again that I could not look decent in the presence of Mr Umbrella. Not even once. Not at all.

I closed my eyes, hoping the offending stain would disappear, and groaned. "No. Not an artist. Just clumsy, apparently."

I did not expect that Mr Umbrella would take this opportunity to raise his offending finger and boop my nose. What the actual fuck? My eyes sprung open as my mouth fell to the ground. Heat was a living, breathing thing within my body while air was nonexistent. I was growing lightheaded just standing there and wished for the ground to swallow me whole.

Mr Umbrella laughed good-naturedly, backing away from me now that he'd made his case. It did make it easier to breathe, but my nerves remained on edge, and my heart refused to settle.

"Aren't you going to tell me it's in fashion, Red Cheeks?"

"Coffee stains? In fashion? Even I'm not going to pull that lie off," I muttered.

"I bet you could," Mr Umbrella insisted. "Come on, give it a try. I promise not to argue."

I took a deep breath and stomped past him to the mansion block. He followed me to the front door. "Oh," I said theatrically, "didn't you know stainless shirts were out of fashion? You've got to have at least one strategically placed splotch to stay trendy."

His throaty chuckles carried all the way to the lift where we stopped side by side, and I braved a glance at him. His half-lidded eyes lazily roamed over my face before meeting mine. "I believe you. You've sold it, really. Makes me want to get all dirty. Since you're the expert here, I might need some assistance on that account. Think you can help me stay trendy, too?"

Holy camoly, he did not! He…did.

Speechless and unable to calm my racing heart that was now beating in my ears and muffled out the ding of the lift, I stared at him for way too long. He was smug about his suggestion, too. Or quite possibly about my reaction to his suggestion. Or both.

"Well," he waved his hand to the open doors. "Fashionistas first."

I broke our staring contest and stumbled into the lift. If standing in the corridor had been suffocating, the tight lift was worse. So much worse. My only salvation was Drixie's carrier bag that established a barrier of sorts between me and the boundaryless Mr Umbrella.

He pushed both tenth and twelfth floor buttons and let the doors close at their leisure. The silence was only breached by the constant hum of the lift slowly raising upwards. Did I already mention how slowly it rode? Probably slowly enough to take Mr Smug up on his offer to get dirty right there and then in our cramped enclosure. He was thinking about it, for sure. I was *not* thinking about it in the slightest.

The silence was so loud between us it left my ears ringing. And yet, I had no clue how to breach it after clearly rejecting his advance. He was perfectly content to stay silent, wiggling his fingers in front of the netting to Drixie's carrier, getting the cat inside to follow the movements predatorily and paw at the confinement when his hand reached out playfully.

"I think she likes me," Mr Umbrella said eventually, his eyes finding mine. Still sparkling, still green, still full of mischievous intent.

"She only dislikes my brother," I murmured.

"I remember," he replied. "And your roommate."

"That was a misunderstanding."

"I'm sure you're right."

"I am right."

Mr Umbrella nodded solemnly. "Good to know, Red Cheeks." Then the lift dinged to a stop, and he left me standing there alone, flustered and confused.

What's a heart for?

Cooking always helped to clear my mind, and after meeting Hallie, I sure needed the distraction. Just to keep my hands busy and my mind blank, I decided to make calzones.

Only my mind did not stay blank. Not when I was mixing the dough. Not when I was rolling it out and certainly not when I was folding it closed over the salami, ricotta and mozzarella filling. Those red cheeks stayed right there in my mind's eye despite me trying to forget them.

I overstepped this time. It was clear by her reaction in the hallway. *No sexual jokes from now on, gotcha.* Just chill. Or better yet, forget about it. Yeah, just forget about it. Because that's been going super well since the first time I saw her. Haha, no. The joke was on me.

Too many little pizza pockets ended up on my oven plate, and I hadn't even calmed down after the tray went in the oven. Three hundred and five degrees Fahrenheit; the oven was showing one hundred and ninety, however. Getting used to the temperature being measured in Celsius wasn't the biggest change moving to England had brought with it, but it was sure easy to stay focussed on it every time the weather forecast announced it would be fourteen degrees and raining. Always raining, just like the day I'd met Hallie.

There you go, my one-track mind took me back to her. And in circles it went no matter what else I attempted to think about. In the middle of the next lap around my scrambled thoughts, my phone rang. After wiping my hands in the towel that hung off my shoulder, I accepted the call.

"*Ciao, Papá*," I said. "It's not Sunday yet."

"I know, I know, *fagiolo*," my father said on the other side of the line. "I just wanted to call and see how you're doing. *Nonna* had this distinct feeling you might want to talk. A womanly intuition, she called it."

Every Sunday, whether I was in the UK or back home, we would cook and have dinner together. Currently, that had resorted to video calls only. We would prepare the same meal, just on different sides of the world. And while it would be in fact an early dinner for me, it was around lunchtime for him and *Nonni*.

"I'm fine," I said. "In fact I just put calzones in the oven and was about to watch the news."

"You only make calzones when—" Dad was interrupted by a muffled female voice on the other side. Of course, *Nonna* would be listening, too, if her womanly intuition was involved. Sometimes that intuition was damn strange, but this time it was nothing to call about.

"I just had a lot on my mind, that's all," I said, to which the phone changed hands, and my grandmother's voice was loud and clear in my ear.

"Don't be brushing it off, Luca. You were making calzones, *fagiolo*. Calzones! Last time you baked calzones there was heartbreak involved. Listen to your *nonna*, no girl is worth your beautiful heart breaking. You pick those pieces right back together and tell me what she done so I can kick her *culo*."

I laughed. "No asskicking necessary, *Nonna*. I swear. I am not heartbroken."

"But there is a girl?" Dad's muffled voice was just loud enough to make out.

"I did not say that—"

"Of course, there's a girl," my grandmother interrupted me. "There always is, and none of them know how to treat our *fagiolo* right."

I closed my eyes, listening to the friendly bickering between my father and my grandmother, until they both quieted down on the other side of the line, and I could try to give an explanation that would ease their worries.

"It's not like that, *Nonna*. She doesn't even like me." I imagined Hallie's adorable red face that I took a bit of pride in, and the image jumped to my mind with surprising ease. Man, I was getting a wee bit invested. A smidge smitten. *And a whole lot British*. "I think I make her uncomfortable, but every time I see her I can't help but tease her. It's making it worse."

"It's not you, *fagiolo*. It's the girls you choose," my grandmother said matter of factly as if she'd been there in the elevator with us and witnessed the entire confrontation. "God only knows how it is possible that, when it comes to finding a good woman, all the Ombrello men are so useless."

I sighed and my father groaned. It was a known topic, and Granny never failed to express her feelings about it. And every time, she would turn to her husband, pat him on the shoulder, and smile sweetly. "I'm not talking about you," she would say. "You did good."

I didn't have to be in the same room to know how the scene played out. My father would grumble about her never approving of my mother, no matter how they started out, and then finally his dejected, "She was right at the time," that ended the conversation, for him at least.

Me? I had nothing to say to that accusation. I'd pretty much given up on the idea of a 'good woman' before I was

ELEVATE WITH ME

quite literally trapped by one. Was Hallie good? No idea. She was amusing, however. She was almost impossible to look away from.

Pretty, very pretty, despite always being disheveled. I couldn't wait to see her all put together, ready to take my breath away. Or completely nake—not going there! Certainly not going there. Not now, not before I knew for sure I stood a chance against all the proper skirt-chasing Englishmen. The little unplanned tease when I first saw her all wet was engraved to my mind, of course. But I didn't plan on doing anything about it. Until I saw her again and lost the functioning part of my brain...

My oven dinged, providing an escape from the prying questions about my dating life that were about to come. "That'd be the calzones," I said. "I've got to go, but I'll talk to you soon, okay? I really am fine, and there is absolutely nothing going on with Red Cheeks."

"Red Cheeks," Dad mused before I had a chance to end the call. "Sure doesn't sound like nothing, Luca."

"It is nothing. One hundred percent. You know you'd be the first to know if it was otherwise."

"Just take care of your heart, Son. That's all I'm asking."

I wouldn't weasel myself out of it during tomorrow's dinner, but for now, they would have to settle for the knowledge I was fine and not in love.

I pulled on the oven mitts, and then dragged the tray out and onto the cooking plate as the stuffed pizza pockets sizzled in their heated happiness. Too many of them for only one person to eat. Way too many.

Before I even registered moving I'd grabbed an aluminum foil and started stacking calzones on top of it with every intention of taking them two floors up to my unforgettable neighbour.

Wrapping them up in another layer of aluminum as if the short trip up would cool them down instantaneously, I took deep calming breaths as my heartbeat picked up.

Just say, 'Hi.' Just say, 'Sorry for earlier.' Give her the calzones, smile, and leave. Easy. Only, it wasn't really this easy, was it? Not when my brain was fixated on doing much more than just saying, 'Hi.' And my body was preparing for a battle with the amount of endorphins coursing through my veins. I shouldn't go at all. Just take the baked goods to the office on Monday, or eat them for the rest of the week myself.

No, I shouldn't go. I definitely shouldn't. What would that say about me? Obsessed. Obtrusive. Stalkerish. Couldn't read the room.

Several deep breaths later, I stood by my door, keys in hand and the damn calzones basically pressed to my chest in the hopes they would stop my heart from making a run for it. I really was obsessed, goddamnit. But not in love. Nope, not that.

Too fidgety to wait for the elevator, I took the stairs two at the time until I stood on the twelfth-floor landing. Called the elevator up before I stopped behind the girl's door. No reason I shouldn't have a quick escape plan.

Get on with it, Luca. Just do it.

I knocked. Fisting my palm helped to redirect the nerves, and I welcomed the cool metal bounding against my knuckles. Then I waited as only silence met my inquiry. The thing is, I knew she was there. She'd ridden the elevator up with me just an hour ago. The elevator that now announced its first and only boarding call while opening its doors.

I heard footsteps behind the door, then Bickering. Right, that was my cue to leave. It was a bad idea to begin with. I dropped the warm package on their welcome mat, which depicted four cute paws and hadn't been there when I'd helped Hallie with her mattress. Then I backed away, hands raised like a criminal caught in act in case they were still looking through the peephole. I was just in time to slip into the elevator when the door opened and two blushing girls peeked out.

I did not say 'Hi.' I did not say, 'Sorry for earlier.' I grinned, waved, and pressed the 'Close Doors' button as Glen shrieked, "Oh my goodness, this is hot." Then I chuckled to myself as the nerves fled, and my heart was still safely in my chest. If nothing else, I just found a new entertainment.

Sweet unreachable dreams

My morning schedule didn't appear to align with Hallie's. For the next week she managed to evade me so thoroughly I began to assume she was avoiding me on purpose. Obsessed, obtrusive and stalkerish as I was, I would have probably avoided me, too, if I wasn't so stuck with myself.

Doing my best to forget about the girl upstairs and her red cheeks, I went about my days just as I would have otherwise with only one little side effect: she was constantly on my mind. Always awkward. Always blushing. And almost always dishevelled in one way or another. Most often as a result of my hands on places they shouldn't be.

My imagination got me waking up with a cold shower on Wednesday morning, and her name on my lips on Thursday as I couldn't convince myself to take another. By Friday, I was too far gone, and I wasn't sure I could face the video call on Sunday with my family without knowing where she stood, and whether I needed to jerk her off of my system more vigorously than I'd already tried to. *Nonni* would ask about her. I knew she would.

After another unwarranted, wet dream I was certain this obsession was getting out of hand. I stood in the hallway, waiting for the elevator that morning, hoping to finally catch Hallie leaving at the same time, so I could try to talk to her in a way that wouldn't scare her away. Or sound unhinged. Insane. But she was driving me crazy even when we weren't stuck in an elevator together—elevating together, elevating my blood pressure among other things —so there might have not been a lot of hope for that. I should have instead hoped that my insane matched hers. Was there even a chance?

The elevator doors opened with a ding and the first thing I noticed was a pair of furry slippers. I was already grinning before I raised my eyes from those feet to meet the eyes of... Glen, the best friend.

Shaking my head, I kept the grin on a moment longer, though it now felt a little stretched, and stepped into the elevator.

"If it isn't Mr Umbrella in the flesh. I thought the lift rides with you were reserved for Haylee only." She smirked at my raised eyebrow at my apparent nickname. Or had she said Ombrello? If so, how did they know?

I also took note she'd called Red Cheeks Haylee and not Hallie this time. I liked Haylee more. Or Hals? Another thing to ask her about.

"Actually, I haven't seen her the entire week." I shrugged as if it didn't affect me as much as it really did. "What did you call me?"

"Mr Umbrella?" She pointed at the one I was holding in my hands.

I had to get a new one since it seemed Haylee had no intention to return the one I loaned her. This one was bright red. Red like her cheeks. Red like desire.

I chuckled. "So close it's funny."

"It's Haylee's nickname for you," Glen explained, not understanding my meaning. "She said it's how you met."

"So she does talk about me?" I pried, my heartbeat picking up without any real reason for it other than I wanted Haylee to be talking about me.

"I am not allowed to discuss such matters. Best friend's privilege." Glen made one of those childish movements where she took an invisible key and locked her lips with it.

"Ah." I nodded knowingly. A true smile formed on my lips. "I understand perfectly. What else has she said?"

"No, no, Mr Umbrella, you do not understand." Glen shook her head and swiped her finger left and right as if scolding a child. "When I say I won't disclose any details about it, I mean it."

"It's Ombrello, actually," I said, taking in Glen's wrinkled eyebrows.

"What?" she asked.

"Mr Ombrello, not Umbrella. Although, that's cute," I explained, twirling my red rain protector around between my palms.

"You're not serious." She had her arms crossed over her chest with a funny look on her face.

I shrugged. "I'll allow it this once, since I did fail to introduce myself."

"You'll allow it?" Glen gasped theatrically, then shook her head, her red pony tail swishing left and right. "Just like we'll allow Red Cheeks, just because it makes Haylee squirm."

"Ah, does it now? I'll keep that in mind."

We were both quiet for a while, or relatively quiet as Glen muttered 'Ombrello' under her breath a few times in a row, thinking I wouldn't hear.

While Haylee tended to drop her gaze to her feet more often than look at me, Glen had no reservations against staring. It was a strange change that I did not totally appreciate, but couldn't point out either. I had an inkling that my own tendency to stare at Haylee was similar, so I made a note to try and amend my behavior around her the next time I saw her. I could force myself to look at her shoes, too, right? Right.

"So, Mr Gorgeous," Glen said slyly. "What are your intentions with my best friend?"

"Another one of Haylee's nicknames?" I wondered out loud.

Glen laughed. "Oh, this one is entirely mine, though she did not oppose."

"My intentions?" I hummed and tapped my fingers against the handle of my umbrella. "Let's see... Stalking. Kidnapping. Maybe tying her to my bed. Nothing too crazy."

Glen laughed harder. "I hope you won't suggest those things to her, she'll run the other way. I, on the other hand, appreciate the humour."

"I thought you might." My lips twitched. "Also, thanks for the heads up. Maybe you could also advise me on how to approach the subject of asking her out? You know, in a way that doesn't make her run the other way. Or should I forget about it?"

The question just slipped out. I pretended to play it cool while she laughed at me some more, and the elevator dinged, announcing we'd reached the first floor, or ground floor, or whatever.

Glen stepped out, her slippers dragging on the tiles a little, then turned to point her finger at my chest. "I like you, so that's a good start."

That's all she said before shuffling her way to the main entrance and leaving me wondering what that meant. Overall, I didn't learn anything new whatsoever from this interaction, while she walked away with some juicy gossip material and possibly a red flag to shove in Haylee's face in warning. Stalking? Kidnapping? Oh boy, that went worse than expected.

I was still standing in the hallway when Glen marched back through the door and pointed another finger at me. I was anticipating the worst when she blurted, "You didn't happen to bake those pizza things yourself did you?"

"Actually, I did." That's all I said. *Just keep it short.*

"Okay, I like you a lot," she said, then marched out again.

Well... okay then. One teeny tiny problem right there, she wasn't Haylee.

I walked into the conference room in the Lewis & Walker Law Group ten minutes late, which was better than the last time. We shall not mention the last time, that was when Haylee needed her mattress carried up twelve flights of stairs. Let's just say, I've made better impressions.

Lewis was a man in his sixties. His hair had turned almost as gray as his eyes, and his face held more wrinkles than anyone else in the room. He turned his eyes on me and smiled wryly before the rest of the room turned their attention from Walker, who'd been showing the first slide to my presentation to the group and saying something informative, I'm sure.

While Lewis held humor in his eyes, Walker's gaze was strict and judging. She tapped her wrist with an index finger as her mouth formed a thin, unpleased line. Perfectly controlled curls framed that hardened face, failing to add a softer touch to her very lawyery appearance.

"You're late, Mr Ombrello," Walker barked, before she moved away from the spotlight to sit on the empty chair next to Lewis. "I hope this is not becoming a habit."

"Give the boy a break," Lewis chuckled. "At least he ain't sweating like a sausage on a heated pan this time around. That's an improvement, don't you think?"

I ignored both the friendly jab and the narrowing eyes of Walker, who didn't seem to think a joke was called for. Some of the people in the room could not hide their smiles, and Walker's eyes narrowed even further as I took the place she'd occupied before. Nice and centered, with everyone's eyes fixed on me.

"What's an improvement," I said, "is the new system we are implementing, and I can say that for a fact."

Even Walker had to agree with that, since she'd gotten a close look at the product I'd been working on for them the past six months.

"We are already beta testing the functions, and what I've heard is that everything runs smoothly, which is why we are gathered here today. It is time to switch fully over to Rembre systems, and I'm going to explain how it is going to work." I met the eyes of the closest department heads, before I switched to the next slide on my presentation and resumed describing the process step by step. Once at the end of my presentation, I said, "Remember, I'll be here for another month to make sure everything runs smoothly. If you have any questions, do not hesitate to reach out. After that, the system updates and occurring issues will be taken care of remotely."

While everyone piled out of the conference room, those last words kept rolling through my mind over, and over again. Especially the part about me being here for another month. Just a month longer. That came as a stab out of nowhere, since even though I was expecting to go back to Colorado soon, I had not thought I'd find something worth staying for. The thing is, I had no clue where my attraction to Haylee was going, but having only one month to find out got my stomach twisting uncomfortably.

I hadn't realized me and the two partners were the only ones left in the conference room, when Walker turned her scowling attention toward me. "What is it about 'sweating like a sausage' Lewis was talking about?"

I closed my eyes, sighing. "It was an emergency meeting on a Saturday. I was helping a friend with something heavy. It won't happen again."

Walker's narrowed eyes did not stray from me. "Make sure that it won't. This is a respectable workplace. Image is important, and I will not tolerate undisciplined behaviour during your employment."

"Of course, I understand."

The thin line of Mrs Walker's lips didn't even twitch. I imagined that stare scaring the shit out of any witness and having them blurt out all the hidden evidence that'd save the case. It didn't work on me since I had nothing to hide, and my grandmother had given me plenty of disciplinary glares during my teenage years. She'd also squinted at all the girls I'd considered dating and the one I managed to convince to actually tolerate dating me for a time.

"Don't listen to her, Luke," Lewis chuckled. "Discipline isn't everything. You're doing splendid with the program."

I was glad when I finally escaped the office. Lawyers kept ungodly hours at most times, it was more so when they had set a goal to finish something before heading home. Today the entire office had been convinced they needed to learn the new program inside and out and had me running from one computer to the next, explaining the same functions over and over again, until I grew sick of hearing my own voice. Apparently they too thought a month would pass by in the blink of an eye.

When I reached the apartment building, I slowed down my walk, searching the parking lot for a familiar shape, but of course, she wasn't there. I practically dragged my feet to the front door, craning my neck to see behind me and almost stopping when a bus turned a corner. She wasn't on it.

Just one month, I repeated to myself. A week had passed in a hurry, and I hadn't caught a sight of Haylee. A month wouldn't be all that much slower. *Forget it.*

I reached the elevator and stared at the closed doors. I couldn't forget it, though. Fuck, I couldn't forget it. Was she up there in her apartment already? Was she on her way home? What should I do? Surely, there were guidelines for this type of situation.

Minutes ticked by, and I hadn't pushed the call button. An elderly woman entered and gave me a strange look as I kept on standing in the hallway after the elevator opened its doors for her. The hum of it riding up accompanied my uncertainty. I groaned, walking to the mailboxes and fumbling around in front of mine longer than necessary, all the while keeping my eyes on the door.

Several more tenants rode up and down and up again, before I decided I couldn't wait any longer. This was getting ridiculous. I was ridiculous. I called the elevator down again, resigned to trying to forget about it. I was pacing the length of the hallway when the front door opened, and Haylee walked in.

I froze in my steps, staring at her. Her brown hair was pulled up in a bun that must've been neat at one point. Stray hairs fell out of the confinement framing her face in wild curls or stuck to every which way on top of her head. Her eyes widened, and her mouth fell slightly open when she saw me. My first thought was of kissing those plump lips, which was the very thing I was supposed to forget about. How was I to do that when my blood was suddenly pumping twice as fast, and my brain was fixated on her smooth round cheeks.

I told myself to play it cool, but my brain had other ideas when "Hello, Gorgeous" left my lips. There was that flush. She stumbled in her steps, and her eyes dropped to the ground. There, I went and made her uncomfortable again. Shit!

Complimentary mockery

I didn't run into Mr Umbrella for an entire week. An entire week! How that was possible, I have no clue, since it had previously seemed like he was there every time I took a step outside. Waiting in the lift. Driving up and down in it for a chance to see me. Absurd.

But no. He wasn't doing any of that, and I didn't know if I was disappointed or relieved that he hadn't had a chance to comment on my appearance. Possibly disappointed, since I'd been meticulously making sure I looked my best whenever I left the flat. This is why Friday evening—after four back-to-back dance lessons—was the worst time for another encounter with the man.

I was exhausted to the core and skipped the shower routine this one time to get back home quicker. While the sweaty joggers and T-shirt dried quite decently on the Tube, my hair remained in a messy bun, and my body's aches showcased themselves in my slumped posture. I just wanted to get back home, shower, and spend the rest of the evening on the sofa with a complaining Drixie and a moping Glen. What I didn't want to do was walk into the mansion block to see Mr Umbrella pacing the corridor waiting for the lift to arrive.

He halted the moment he saw me. My own steps slowed as my eyes darted between the lift and the stairs, searching for a quick escape.

"Hello, Gorgeous," he said, just as the lift dinged its arrival. He averted his gaze, cleared his throat, and waved at the opening doors. "Ladies first."

I walked past him, hoping he couldn't smell me, but that fleeting hope dwindled when he stepped into the tight space after me. There was no way he wouldn't smell me. No way at all.

I stayed silent, counting the floors in my head. To my surprise, Mr Umbrella stayed quiet, too, and focussed his attention on his feet as his fingers danced against his thigh.

That was new.

As if his quieter demeanour invited me to study him the same way he had done the previous times we'd stood in this lift together, my eyes drifted over to him with greater ease.

He wore his fancy shoes again, although this time simple dark jeans replaced the khaki trousers. Hands in his pockets pulled the waistline lower. I involuntarily licked my lips, then raised my eyes higher where the button-up shirt pressed against his abdomen. The jacket was the same as last time I'd seen him.

If there was one of us who could call themselves stylish it was him. Yet, I would fight with every fibre in my body should he call me out on my sporty outfit. In fact, I was surprised when he didn't say a word.

When I studied his face, I was happy to note he was content keeping his four o'clock shadow and hadn't done a full shave. Mr Umbrella's eyes flicked to me and back to the ground as if he felt me staring and didn't want me to stop. His lips twitched. I sucked my lower one into my mouth on reflex.

"I expected you to talk more," I finally blurted. "Especially after the mocking greeting."

"Mocking? Red Cheeks, I wouldn't even dream of mocking you." Unable to keep his eyes pinned to the ground, he met my narrowing ones.

I should have possibly stayed quiet, because his gaze was intense and made me fumble with the hem of my shirt. I couldn't even come up with anything coherent to say after this. Luck was not on my side when it came to the interactions with this man. I got it. Not meant to happen. Better off this way anyway.

"Hasn't anyone ever called you gorgeous before? I find that hard to believe."

We'd reversed our roles again with him staring at me, and me staring at the battered floor and chewing on my cheek.

"Not when there are clearly no reasons to use that word," I replied.

"And why wouldn't I have a reason to use that word, Haylee?"

My eyes flicked to him and met his green ones. There wasn't a trace of mocking on his face, more like an intense curiosity.

"Well," I started raising a finger to count all the reasons, "the first time you saw me I was dripping wet, the second time I wore cat-patterned pyjamas. Third? Wet again. Do you want me to go on? Because there was also the time I splattered coffee all over my shirt. Surely, everything you've seen of me so far has been the exact opposite of gorgeous, so excuse me for calling you out on the lie."

"You are neither wet nor wearing cat-patterned PJs today. Unless you'd like to tell me something." He drawled, and my mouth fell all the way to the ground.

Oh my actual God, no. He did not just... But he did. Yup he had said that, and there was no taking it back. Just like there was no cooling off my heated cheeks.

"Um, no, but I am clearly not dressed up either."

"And yet you manage to look gorgeous, Red Cheeks."

Silence.

God, that silence was thick and suffocating. I couldn't form words, he'd closed his eyes, and his head fell back.

Deep breaths didn't really help with the rhythmic beat of my heart. I could dance to it if my limbs were still working. Is there a proper way to respond to that? Certainly not after a forever lasting silence.

"I'm sorry," he whispered to the ceiling and swallowed hard. "I didn't intend to make you uncomfortable. I just can't seem to figure out how to act around you."

Stupefied, I glared at him until he righted his head and smiled sheepishly at me.

"Maybe we started off on the wrong foot. I haven't even introduced myself." He reached out his hand tentatively, searching my face for who knows what. "Hi, I'm Luke."

Biting my lip, I met his hand halfway, and his engulfed mine in a cocoon of warmth. Luke's thumb slid over the back of my hand, eliciting shivers across my entire arm.

"Haylee," I squeezed through my tight throat. "But you know that already."

"It's a pleasure to meet you, Haylee." He still held my hand hostage, and I tried to hold it perfectly still as if not to draw any attention to our clasped hands as his thumb kept on caressing the back of mine.

Ding. Tenth floor. Ding-a-doo! And the doors opened.

Mr Umbrella—Luke—looked from me to the corridor beyond those doors, to our clasped hands, and up to me again, rubbing the back of mine one last time before sliding his hand out of my hold. I immediately missed the warmth. What a silly thing to say, but at that moment it was true.

He swallowed again and rolled his tongue in his mouth as if convincing himself to say something. Anything.

"That was my cue," he said eventually. "I do hope to see you again—" Luke stepped out of the elevator and looked me straight in the eyes as the doors began closing again —"gorgeous."

"So, I saw your Mr Umbrella today," Glen said after I'd showered, changed, and said hello to Drixie who now laid on my feet.

We were in the kitchen, and I was trying my hand at something excotic that was supposedly healthy and hopefully tasty, while Glen sat on a wooden dining chair with her elbows propped up on the square table opposite the countertops. We didn't eat here often, just like we didn't eat healthy often.

"Not mine," I huffed. "And his name is Luke."

"Luke Ombrello?" Glen mused. "That sounds strange doesn't it?"

"His last name isn't actually Umbrella, you do realise that, right?" I turned away from the vegetable to throw a concerned look at Glen.

"Not Umbrella, *Ombrello*. That's what he said, anyway. Maybe I'm pronouncing it wrong. It doesn't sound American. Did he say he's American?"

I shrugged. "No. He only said his name is Luke. After he called me gorgeous."

"Oh my god, Haylee! What are you going to do about it? You know he asked about you today."

I focussed on chopping my vegetables, pretending it didn't mean a thing. "What did you say?"

"What do you think I said?" Glen challenged me with a laugh. She loved to keep me on the edge. Me? I hated when she did that. Barely tolerated it.

"Knowing you, Glen, it could have been just about anything. Something scandalous?"

"I would never!" Glen basically shouted. Drixie stretched on my feet, gave her an annoyed look, then trotted out of the kitchen.

When I turned around, Glen had her palm against her heart as if I'd given her the utmost insult. "I said nothing. I figured if he was truly interested, he'd better work for it. There ain't no shortcuts in love."

"Well, he was uncharacteristically quiet after he said I'm gorgeous, until I called him out on it. You saw how I looked, his claim was ludicrous. And then he introduced himself. That was all."

"You're always gorgeous, Hallie. You are your own worst critic."

I cringed. "No, that's my mum."

"Don't let her ruin this for you. I feel like Luke could do you some good. Are you sure he said his name is Luke? Because he really did say his last name is Ombrello. He seemed amused about you calling him Mr Umbrella. Like very amused."

"I'm ninety percent certain he said Luke."

The vegetables were frying away on the pan, and I followed the recipe with my finger, smearing oil on the printout page as I did so. Add white wine? Ugh. Oh... I suppose we can skip this step. What's next?

"Luke Ombrello," Glen mumbled, typing it into her phone and going through the search results. "If that's his name he's a ghost."

"At least he's not an influencer. I don't think I can go through that again." I flinched the moment those words left my lips. Maybe I wasn't ready for anything. With anybody. Thinking about love was one thing, but actually putting myself out there?

I wanted to, but the walls had to come down for that. Walls I'd worked so hard to build. The ones that kept my heart safe, kept me from doing something stupid. You know, those walls. Without them, I was exposed and vulnerable. Would Mr Umbrella be worth the risk? I just didn't know.

Desire, shame and pure fury

I was sitting behind the PC in my living room, connected to the servers of Lewis & Walker Law Group as I created backups for each and every case that had come through the agency, then buried them behind several firewalls. That was better than cursing myself for the way my latest run in with Red Cheeks had gone. I hadn't even dared to ask her out after I blurted out the greeting. What a fool!

It would be for the best if I forgot about the little flame that sparked within me every time I saw her. I was leaving in a month. I shouldn't put myself—and Haylee—in a position where heartbreak became an actual possibility. I was getting to her, though. I was certainly getting to her. She'd been checking me out, and I'd let her, because it had excited me. And then I went and made her uncomfortable and adorably flustered. What was I going to do about that? Nothing at all? *Dio mi aiuti.*

I focussed on the screen sorting through file after file, hoping to distract the yearning settling deep in my chest. It was all nonsense to me. Random names, dates and locations, sometimes accompanied by the accused crime or claim, sometimes not. A few search words helped me organize the endless information under different topics, or crimes levels if you please. My program also separated all files according to other filled-in information that I'd rather not get into. Just know that in the end, Lewis & Walker

Law Group would be better off for it and I'd be back in Colorado where I belonged.

In the blur of the program doing its thing, a name caught my eye as it was sorted under cyber bullying. I pressed pause on reflex, and the folder in question stopped dead on my screen, baiting me to open it. I shouldn't go snooping around other people's case files, let alone ones that were classified and hidden behind passwords by none other than Lisa Walker herself, but my curiosity got the better of me. The file in question was named 'Haylee.' No other specification, just that one name. A name that already rolled around in my head relentlessly without the added help from my PC.

I don't know what I expected to find, but a folder full of emails and video files was not it. The icon tiles loaded into preview pictures painfully slowly, while my heart sped up, searching each and every one of them for a familiar face. Most of them showed a guy in his twenties. Wild blond hair, grey eyes and a cocky smirk creating an image of the bad boy he undoubtedly was. The last video, however... had a pair of perfect tits, barely covered by wavy curls on the preview picture. Curls that were awfully distinct. Haylee's curls.

I blinked at the screen, dumbfounded, before my finger involuntarily double clicked on the image, and it popped open in VLC player. My heart thumped loudly in my ears, but my eyes locked on the mobile film clip following Haylee—my Haylee— through a packed party into an empty bedroom.

"Is this necessary?" she waved at the camera shyly before biting her lower lip the way she often did.

A guy chuckled behind the screen before it blacked out, then showed a wooden panel of a door accompanied with more laughter. Shit, I did not like where this was headed, but I was now along for the ride whether I wanted to see it unfold or not. Transfixed on the screen, I swallowed painfully as a rough hand pushed the door open to catch that blond asshole pulling Haylee's shirt off.

Desire, shame, and pure fury fought for control in me, the last one winning when Haylee shrieked and raised her hands up protectively. The look on her face was the worst thing I'd ever seen, right before the jackass pulled her arms away from her chest and ripped her bra clean off. On cue, the boob shot just before the device went flying out of the filmmaker's hands, and a very pissed off Glen shouted at the men before the video cut off.

I shouldn't have seen that. I had no right to have witnessed that, but now the scene was fried to my brain as my knuckles itched to punch something. Preferably the blond man's jaw.

I rubbed my fist as my gut recoiled. *Leave it.* I should have just left it, but after a long silent moment I clicked on the next video, then the one after that, and one after that. Fuck, I watched all of them.

They weren't all as incriminating as the first. In fact, most of them were of the blond man talking. Jay... of Jay talking. The topic always being Haylee, although her name wasn't uttered in any of them, pictures of her flashed on the screen several times, some of which should've stayed private, as he made whatever jokes he thought would amuse his crowd. By the time I'd gone through everything, I wanted to do more than just punch the guy. I wanted to suffocate him, make him drink his own piss, and cut off his dick. He did not deserve to walk around with one.

I was so worked up, I needed a better distraction. Distraction that always seemed to work. So I started baking calzones again.

Two hours later with a third patch of pizza pockets in the oven, I took a deep breath and leaned against the kitchen counter. I'd poured out my anger and frustration into the dough. Now my chest held an empty void that ached when I exhaled, but it was better than swirling heat. I'd take the void any day over rage.

The fact that one woman got me so worked up in the first place was a testament to my waning self-control. There was just something about her—*don't go there!*

Yeah, just leave it. For now.

The oven hummed a comforting tune, while the calzones inside sizzled happily. A scratching accompanied the soft melody playing in my speakers, all to encourage calm vibes. I urged to call my grandmother, but we'd talk soon enough on our Sunday cooking time, so I just fidgeted with my hands. God, I could still feel the softness of Haylee's skin under my thumb—*Stop!*

The scratching sounded again, and I perked my ears, searching for the source. Not the speakers. Definitely not the oven and the calzones. I pushed off the counter and took a step toward the living room. My work desk in the corner was in disarray, but I'd turned off the computer, not trusting myself to leave the files I found in peace. My TV was off. The sound came again, this time accompanied by a sad *meow*.

I raised an eyebrow as I walked to my front door and opened it. Without hesitation, the black cat that had been begging for entry slipped through and padded into the kitchen.

"Well, hello there," I called after it as I checked the hallway for its owner. There wasn't anyone else about, even the elevator remained quiet. Shrugging, I closed the door and went searching for the little intruder.

I found her on the kitchen counter, pawing at a plate of calzones as if I'd prepared them for her alone.

"You like the smell of that, don't you?" I hummed, studying the cat. She gave me no mind and continued her conquest until I sighed and placed the calzone she was so intent on having on a separate plate and cut it into smaller pieces.

"If you get stomach aches after this it's your own fault," I warned her. Her ears twitched, but my words did not stop her from digging in.

"I warned you," I muttered, pulling a bowl out of a cupboard and filling it with water for her. She let me get close enough to check her collar, purring happily at my touch.

Drixie.

The address on the name tag was on the other side of the city, but I knew who Drixie belonged to, and I knew where she lived now. Like the fool I was, I saved the phone number on her tag.

This was Haylee's cat. Of course, it was, because fate would not let me forget about her so easily. Or at all.

Knock, knock... who's there?

There was a knock at the door, and both Glen and I jumped at the sound. We'd just settled onto the sofa to watch another chick flick after the horribly misshapen dinner. Most of it ended up in the rubbish bin and very little in my stomach. I was telling the fat there that we were fasting, but that didn't get the grumbling to stop.

We shared a glance as perfect quiet replaced the knocking. "Did you order anything?" I whispered while Glen shook her head violently.

"No," she hissed as if I'd accused her of something atrocious. "With what money? I'm saving like you told me to."

It was too quiet after that until the knock came again.

Glen nudged me. "Go check who it is."

I nudged her right back. "You go, this is your flat."

She shook her head again, her red hair falling out of the bun high up on her head to slap her across her face with each movement. "What if we're being evicted."

"We are not being evicted," I snorted. "Your bills have been paid."

"But what if—" A longer knocking sequence stopped her mid-sentence, and she gulped.

"They are adamant, that's for sure." I jumped off the sofa, surprised Drixie didn't react to my sudden movement, but a quick glance around the room showed she wasn't here. I tiptoed past the armchair she was usually lying on and into the short hall, Glen right at my heels.

"Be careful," she whispered.

Instead of opening the door right away as I'd been preparing to do, I peeked through the spyhole first.

"Ohhhh." All breath wheezed out from my lungs at that one word as my heart jumped to my throat.

"Oh, what?" Glen hissed. "It's the eviction crew, isn't it. I knew it!"

My hands felt clammy, and my cheeks heated up, but I pulled the door open anyway.

"Luke," I breathed, my voice still quiet from whispering with Glen.

He looked even better without the glass to distort his features, though he'd dressed down to sweats and a regular T-shirt. His green eyes searched mine as a small smile played on his lips.

"I found Drixie here at my door," he said, and my eyes fell to my cat snuggling in his arms. She was rather content on staying there, too. She gave me a hooded-eyed look, as if mocking me for not rushing to be hugged by Luke right away, since that was naturally the best place to be. Almost convinced, I took a step closer to find out for myself.

"Luke?" Glen's voice brought me out of my momentary daze, and she bumped into me while trying to get to the door to confirm it was really him. "With offerings!" she exclaimed, her eyes not on Drixie but a bag dangling from Luke's hand.

I dragged my eyes away from the man to look at Glen, instead. "How did Drixie get out?"

She gave me a wide-eyed, innocent look. "It wasn't me, I swear."

"You're the one who emptied the waste." Right, because if I kept arguing with Glen I could pretend Mr

Umbrella was not standing behind our door staring at me as if I was looking gorgeous again, or something.

He did not let me forget about his presence. "She's back where she belongs now, no harm done."

I swear she purred when Luke spoke, and my cheeks heated further. *I get it, Drixie. We like the man.*

"Ah… Um, thanks," I stuttered, trying to find something else to say. Anything would do. "Love the outfit."

Nope, definitely not everything. That was the stupidest thing I could have come up with. What outfit? The cozy homewear he was rocking? The regular grey sweats girls go crazy over? Shut up, Haylee.

"Yeah?" Luke grinned, stretching one hand out, showcasing his look, while the other still cradled Drixie. "I was trying to match your style."

Glen swooned against me, making me work on my balance, and let out a long "awww."

"It looks better on you," I blurted. Goodness gracious, stop talking. Just take the cat and shut the door.

Glen clung to me like a jacket—only jackets do not keep pulling on your clothes and giggling. She could have been my grounding point but instead messed with my balance even further.

"Are you calling me gorgeous, Red Cheeks? Because I'll take it."

I blushed and chewed on my lower lip. It must've been the nickname. Definitely not the obvious flirtation. Nope.

"She sure is," Glen said when nothing coherent came out of my mouth, not for the lack of trying.

I raised a shoulder and dropped my eyes on my tapping feet, murmuring, "Maybe."

Bored with the conversation, and no prospect of petties, Drixie stretched in Luke's arms, then pushed off, and landed softly on all four paws. She disappeared inside. Without the cat in his arms, the bag Luke was holding became the main focus. At least for Glen. Me? I was staring at my feet and his. Then counted the floorboards between the two. There weren't many to be sure, since they stopped at the threshold where the floor continued in grey tiles.

"Okay, I've got to ask," Glen buzzed. "What's in the bag?"

Luke's right foot slid on the floor, and I raised my eyes just in time to see him drag his hand through his hair. "I was baking," he muttered, a tentative smile playing on his lips. "Too much for me alone."

Glen squealed. "You're a lifesaver! Hallie cooked today, and it was god awful. That's why the waste needed to be taken out in the first place. I'm starving. Hallie is too, even though she wouldn't admit it out loud."

I nudged Glen, who finally stopped hanging on my shoulders and 'humphed' in annoyance. Well, *humph* right back at you; I thought we were rooting for me. He didn't need to know I failed our dinner, an experiment as it was in the first place.

His eyes were burning through me, but I dared to meet his gaze this time. "Thank you, you didn't have to."

"You're very welcome, Haylee. I hope you'll enjoy these." With the bag still dangling from his fingers, he stretched out his hand for us to take whatever baked goods he'd made this time.

"Why not see it for yourself?" Glen grinned broadly. "We're watching The Notebook, come join us."

I opened my mouth, then closed it.

"You're sure?" Luke's gaze flicked between me and Glen, but neither of us expected her to take hold of his arm and pull him across the threshold, the baked goods and all.

"Okay then," he chuckled, "I suppose I could stay a while."

Hearted conversations

I gave Haylee a small smile as her best friend dragged me through the hallway toward their living room. She stood by the front door a moment longer, dumbfounded before she shoved it shut and followed us.

The living room had not changed since I first saw it on the day I brought Haylee's mattress up here. Impressive antique furniture that likely had many stories to tell filled almost every available space, making manoeuvring through the room a dangerous task. One wrong move and something would go tumbling over.

If Glen had been worried about Drixie ruining something, she shouldn't have, because the cat tiptoed through the minefield with impeccable ease. I, on the other hand, felt like an elephant in a porcelain store. Once I sat down on an armchair I was afraid would disintegrate under my weight, I swore not to move an inch more. Glen flopped down on a blanket-covered vintage couch, being much less mindful of her surroundings, and Haylee hovered by the doorway chipping paint off the framework with her index finger.

The image of her uncertain like that hit me harder than I expected. I blamed the videos now stored on my harddrive, as well as safely guarded by the new security I installed for Lewis & Walker law group. I didn't want to even think about anyone else finding those files, let alone having them all over the internet. That must have been horrifying.

I pushed myself back to my feet. "Look, I can leave if you'd like me to," I told Haylee, and Haylee alone. Glen was cool, and she probably meant well, but she hadn't considered how inviting me in would make Red Cheeks feel. "I wouldn't want to intrude if you're not comfortable having me here."

"No." Haylee stepped further into the room, dropping her hand to her side. "No, it's okay. I'm okay." Her lower lip disappeared between her teeth as she dropped her eyes to the floor, avoiding mine when she mumbled almost inaudibly, "I'd like you to stay."

Okay. Be cool. Chill. But I couldn't stop the grin from stretching across my lips. My heartbeat played a rhythm of its own in my chest as she gracefully avoided all the obstacles in the room and sat down next to Glen, pulling her feet up on the couch and hiding them into the blanket. She looked so adorable, I regretted picking the armchair, because I wished I could wrap her in my arms and have her leaning her head on my shoulder. Yeah, I was far from being chill, that's for sure.

I dropped my ass back on the armchair, surprised it held my weight this time around as well and took a deep breath. I couldn't look away from Haylee even when the movie started playing. Her brown curls were wild and uncontrolled, framing her round rosy cheeks. Eyes darting between me and the TV screen, while her hands kept rolling up the blanket from one corner before smoothing it up again. Damn, she was beautiful.

Her eyes flicked to me again, and I turned my gaze to the movie, reminding myself that I didn't want to make her uncomfortable. *Just don't make her feel uncomfortable. Simple as that, right?* Right. *So pretend you're really interested in the movie and not in the prospect of spending time in the same room as her.* Perfectly normal, I'm sure.

"These look really good!" Glen exclaimed, ripping open the bag she'd snatched off my fingers. "What do you call them again?"

Glad to have a reason to look their way again, I discarded my pretense and cleared my throat. "Calzones."

Without further explanation, she bit into one like a starved dog, her eyes rolling to the back of her head.

"Mr Umbrella," Glen mumbled through a mouthful, "these are incredible!"

"Luke," Haylee corrected her before she bit her lip.

"Luke," Glen amended. "Luke Ombrello. Are you Italian? Luke doesn't sound Italian to me. I couldn't find you online."

They both peered at me with curiosity that I could practically touch. I cleared my throat again, tapping at the arm of the chair. "My father's side of the family is Italian, but my mother was American."

"Was?" Haylee asked softly.

"Is," I corrected, rubbing the back of my neck.

"Oh?" Glen chirped in. "I sense a story there."

"Glen, don't—"

"It's okay, Red Cheeks, it's not like it's a secret. My mother left when I was very young. *Nonni* likes to say that the Ombrello men are hopeless at love affairs. My father certainly was. I've still got my hopes up for myself, but it's anyone's guess how it'll turn out."

Glen let out a very long lasting "ooh" that only stopped after Haylee slapped her across her chest.

"I'm sorry you never knew your mother," Haylee said. "Mine is disapproving in almost everything, but at least she's been there… and very loud about it."

Glen shook her head. "Sad topics are not allowed. Why don't you tell us how your Italian family came up with this very not Italian name instead."

"Ah, it's Luca, actually. Luca Stefano Ombrello, but most people call me Luke." Glen had her phone out already, typing my name in the search engine before I could say, "And, you don't need to bother looking that up, I don't have much of an online presence."

"Why not? I have TikTok, YouTube and Instagram. It's so much fun, look!" She pulled out one of her accounts and a clip of her and Haylee outside the apartment building came in view.

"You are tuning in with Hallie and Glen in the middle of a moving mayhem…" the Glen in the video spoke over whatever happened in the movie on the TV screen. Haylee looked all flustered and hot, just as she'd been the day I helped them with her mattress. I smiled at the memory as the clip kept playing before the phone was snatched away, and the Haylee on the couch made it stop.

"Looks like a lot of fun," I murmured. "Haylee, you also have all those accounts, or…?"

She shrugged. "I don't use them nearly as much," she muttered.

"I get it." And I did. I understood better than she could ever imagine. It almost rolled off my tongue how much I understood that. Shit.

"She dances for my videos sometimes," Glen mentioned with a grin before devouring another calzone. "She's really good, too."

"Is that so?" I hummed, studying Haylee as she nudged Glen and mouthed "*stop.*"

Glen clamped her mouth shut at Red Cheeks' request, nodding her head instead. We all stared at the TV for the next few minutes, but in the corner of my eye, I saw Haylee slip her hand into the calzone bag and tentatively pull one out. She relaxed further into the couch after she bit into it and her expression softened. Without having to say it out loud, I knew she liked the taste. One point for me, not that I was counting.

Their TV was an older Samsung model. It did its job, of course, but the longer I looked at it the more faults I found, starting with the picture quality and ending with the sound system. My fingers itched to play with the settings to see if I could improve any of that, but I settled for rubbing the armchair and basically playing peek-a-boo with Haylee. Now if I could somehow let her know of all the things running around in my head without scaring her off that would be great.

I'm not sure any of us actually focussed on the movie, because when I came back from a short trip to the toilet sometime in the middle of it to find that Drixie had stolen my place, Glen had no problem jumping off the couch and disappearing to the kitchen for the rest of it.

I sat down next to Haylee. "So, if it was you, would you wait seven years?"

"For who?" Haylee wiped the tear marks on her cheeks and sniffed, not looking away from the screen, where the final credits continued scrolling after a sad, but very predictable, ending to the movie we'd just watched.

"Ain't that the question," I hummed, my pulse quickening just at the thought. "Someone? The one?"

"I'm not good at waiting."

My lips twitched. "I think you'll find out how good you are at waiting when you find someone worth waiting for."

"Have you?" she asked quietly.

There were so many ways to answer that question. I could go with a flirty reply and have her blush adorably again. I could shrug it off and say I wasn't good at waiting either. Or... I could tell the truth.

"I thought I did once," I replied, hoping this was the right path. "I was ready to run through fire and all for her, give her anything she'd ask for, but she didn't want that. Not from me at least. I've been more careful since."

"I'm sorry." She did look it, too. Like my confession meant something. Like it had touched something within her.

"I didn't mean to make you sad. It's in the past. Three years ago this September." Pointing it out like that made it sound like I still thought about it and counted the days. I didn't.

"We shouldn't have to be careful."

"That would make things much easier, wouldn't it?"

Haylee met my eyes and my hands felt clammy. "Quite a bit."

I told myself it was now or never. Either speak now or forever remain quiet. There couldn't have been a better moment, so why then was my heart stuck in my throat, making speaking so much more difficult?

"Listen Hals, ever since you—"

"Hals?" She interrupted me

"Yeah, it's short from Haylee. You don't like it? I can keep calling you Red Cheeks." We were getting sidetracked, and a small part of me was relieved. I enjoyed teasing her, possibly too much for my own good.

"I've actually grown rather fond of it."

I grinned, "Oh, you have? In that case—"

"Hals is fine," Haylee rushed to say. "Sorry. What were you saying?"

Right. I cleared my throat. "I was just reminiscing on the time you trapped me between elevator doors, is all."

"Oh God, I thought we promised to never speak of it."

"We did? Hmm..." I rubbed my chin, pretending to think about it, and she laughed. "I've grown rather fond of the memory."

Delicious plans

If there was one thing I really disliked about independence it was grocery shopping. Absolutely despised it, really. Glen pushed our trolley through the sweets aisle while I frantically shook my head at her.

"No, most certainly not. That's not lunch nor is any of it dinner material," I grumbled.

"You're no fun!" Glen whined. "The last nice thing I ate was Luke's cooking. Luca's? Mr Umbrella's. Ugh…"

"Which wasn't a sugarbomb, so it's possible to make something nice and still be healthy. We'll just need to learn how."

"So biscuits and gravy?" Glen stared at our basically empty cart that only held ingredients for exactly that.

I huffed. "Well yes."

"You don't know how to make proper gravy." Glen stopped mid-aisle to cross her arms and stare at me.

"And you are not helping one bit," I scoffed.

We had a staredown, blocking a family from exiting the sweets section, the mother holding a wailing boy by the armpit and shooting daggers our way. Glen was an unmovable boulder, however, especially when she decided she didn't want to move.

"Pasta," Glen said. "We could make pasta."

"I bet Luke—Luca?—makes delicious pasta."

"Italian pasta," Glen hummed happily, imagining the taste, while I dragged her into a different aisle, letting the family behind us go their own way, without a thank you, or anything. Typical.

"How difficult could that be? I can make pasta."

"Probably not as good as Luke. Luca. Heaven's sake, you should ask him which he prefers because it's messing with my head."

"He's messing with mine in more ways than that." I kind of liked it but was kind of scared to death of it. There was a fine line between the two. Very fine. Almost impossible to see, truefully.

Glen giggled. "You are enjoying it, admit it!"

I glared at her. "Not as much as you are by the looks of it."

"Not as much as I'd like to taste his pasta," she countered.

I nudged her, and she nudged me right back, still laughing. People in the dried goods aisle rolled their eyes at us, grumbled something under their breath, and let us be silly all we wanted.

"Yes because mine wouldn't be nearly as good as Luke's, I heard that already."

"Luca!"

I shook my head at Glen, "You go ask him how he prefers to be called; this is getting absurd."

She shook her head right back at me, pointing at something I couldn't see and mouthing, "He is right behind you."

I jumped at his voice anyway. "What's not as good as mine?"

I squeezed my eyes shut and took a deep breath before I turned around to face the man who hadn't left my mind ever since he'd departed from our place on Friday evening. Or even before that.

Luke was comfortable in jeans and a sweater that peeked out from his half-open jacket. His new umbrella hung from the handle of his trolley, and I stared at it for a beat longer than necessary. It hadn't been raining when we'd made our way over to the shop. I was wondering if I'd be getting wet again today because that was just my luck. I wasn't wondering anymore once my eyes raised to his face. In fact, I wasn't thinking anything at all since all the words fled my brain for a terrifying second.

Glen didn't even miss a beat, "I could think of a few things."

"We were talking about pasta." I rolled my eyes at Glen because that was easier than continuing to admire the man. "And how it's a given that mine would never compare to yours."

Luke exclaimed something in Italian while waving a hand enthusiastically. He managed to look perfectly comfortable standing out in the crowd, meanwhile in that moment, I wished I could disappear. Then he shook his head and grinned, "I can teach you. Tonight? What do you say?"

I gawked at him. "Tonight? I—ah—I don't know. Glen?" I turned to my best friend for help, as nerves got the better of me. She raised her shoulders in a shrug with an I'm-staying-out-of-this glint in her eyes. Or maybe it was a go-get-'em glint? She was much too smug about it.

"I'd very much like to cook for you, Hals—with you, however you want."

I dragged my eyes back to Luke as my foot started tapping against the floor. "And you just so happened to be making pasta tonight?"

"It can be arranged. Plans change all the time."

Tonight… *That'll leave me no time to prepare mentally.* Prepare for what exactly? I'd been thinking about him since I trapped him between the lift doors. Yet the thrill I thought I'd feel at the invitation turned cold in my stomach, freezing me from the inside out. I wasn't ready.

Luke waited so patiently as I struggled to come up with an answer, my cheeks heating up as embarrassment settled in for my inability to just say yes. To say something, anything at all.

"Okay, what if it's casual? Just friends. You cook with Glen all the time, right?" Luke asked.

I opened my mouth, then shut it again. His words rang in my head. The very same head that had conjured all kinds of fantasies that will never happen because I was too busy freaking out. "You want to be just friends?"

Luke's eyes softened, and he gave a slight shake of his head as if he was trying to figure me out but couldn't quite comprehend where I was coming from. "It's not about what I want, Red Cheeks, it's about what you are comfortable with. I hope you realise your consent matters to me, and I would never have you do something you weren't unwilling to do." Something I couldn't quite read crossed his face as he cleared his throat. "Just cooking, Haylee. You say no, and we'll leave it at that."

Perhaps he comprehended more than I'd thought. Too much.

"I enjoyed Friday night," I mumbled.

"Me too," Luke agreed.

"It could be nice."

He murmured, "Yeah."

My hands trembled at my sides, and I squeezed them into fists. "Maybe...ah... maybe next time?"

You coward!

Glen looked as disappointed as I was. Luke, however, nodded solemnly as a smile died on his lips. Stupid. Stupid. Stupid!

A series of fake coughs pulled me out of self-loathing, as my best friend worked her magic to diffuse the rejection I basically gave myself.

Glen to the rescue! Bless her. "How about we make it a competition? We make pasta at our place, and you make pasta at yours. Then we'll share ours, and you'll share yours. It'll be fun."

"Yeah, sure." Luke's voice came out raspy and slightly flat. "That could be fun."

"Brilliant!" Glen's exclamation sounded just as forced, far from her usual enthusiasm.

"Okay," Luke nodded, regaining some of his composure. "We'll do that. How about we follow the same recipe to make it fair for you. And I'll show you which ingredients I'll use. First off, tomatoes."

He started moving away from the aisle we met and towards vegetables, talking about tomatoes like they were something magical when it came to proper pasta. As if he hadn't been turned down and offered a sloppy deal in return. I had to pull myself together, too, and act like everything was divine. This was my doing after all, and Glen just tried to make the best of it.

"I was just going to use canned sauce." The words scratched my throat on the way out.

If Luke noticed, he didn't mention it. "Insane! We'll be using fresh tomatoes, you'll never want to look at the canned stuff again once you've tasted it."

His ease got me to relax my shoulders, and some of the tension in my chest loosened. "I'll take your word for it. Lead the way to the freshest goods, why don't you."

I was relieved to see a smile gracing Luke's lips. "This way, ladies. Our haul is waiting."

"Why didn't you say yes?" Glen reprimanded me when we were safely out of the lift and behind our front door where Luke—who'd taken my rejection surprisingly gracefully—couldn't hear us.

Surprisingly? No, nothing about him should surprise me. He was perfect in every way, as far as I could see. And I was an idiot.

"I panicked."

"I saw that. Hallie, you've got to get over it. Men like Luke—Luca—are not easy to come by. He is gorgeous, kind, funny, and patient. I'd take him, if he'd have me, but he is really into you. Don't mess it up!"

"I know! Don't you think I know that?" I wiped angrily at my wet cheeks, hating how unstable I was acting. The rest of the shopping trip had been really nice, and I'd almost forgotten about my failure until we'd been in the lift going up. That's where the tension returned. The damned lift, with its damned hum and the tightness of its space that ruined everything somehow.

"Oh, Hallie. I'm so sorry, I didn't mean—You know I'll be here for you no matter what, right? And I'll be rooting for you all the way, but if you're not feeling it I'll chase him away."

"I really like him." I sniffed. "I thought I was ready, you know. I thought I left it all in the past, but the way he said it—the part about consent—it's like he knows. It's absurd, I know it is. The internet was wiped from all evidence of what happened, but I froze anyway."

"The internet never forgets," Glen whispered.

"The internet never forgets," I agreed.

"Come here." Glen didn't wait for me. Instead, she pulled me in for a hug, and I clung to her as if my life depended on it. "I don't think Luke cares about any of that. He doesn't even have an online presence to speak of. It's more likely he's reading you like a book. You're conflicted and it shows."

"I'm not conflicted," I denied into Glen's shoulder. "I'm terrified."

"Potayto-potahto, same thing," she murmured into my hair, rubbing my back and getting me to burrow deeper into her embrace.

"It's not always. It's when I'm expected to decide on something. When I'm put on the spot, like when he asked if I wanted to cook with him. I do, but then I start doubting myself. Like I couldn't possibly make good decisions after the few very horrible ones I've made."

Glen clicked her tongue. "Oh, Hallie. Luke is a very good decision."

"He seems like it, but how can I know for sure?" I mumbled pathetically.

"He is. And you'll have proof. Tonight."

I pushed away from Glen to look at her. "I will?"

"Yes, you most certainly will. If you want to, of course. We wouldn't want to have you doing anything unwillingly. Consent and all that."

I snorted and slapped her shoulder. "Shut up!"

"Oh, I will, but not until you hear my plan. Which is brilliant, by the way."

"Ugh, oh? Let's hear it then." I stared at her intently, willing it to be as brilliant as she promised, because I needed brilliant just about then.

"Okay, here's what we'll do," Glen said. "We'll put those groceries in the fridge, then let Drixie out into the hallway. Twenty minutes after that, you'll knock on Luke's door, looking all pretty and innocent. Then you'll be eating that pasta he's making, and I'll order something for myself."

I wrung my hands in front of me, chewing at my lower lip. "I don't even know where he lives exactly."

"If that's the part of this plan you're disagreeing with, it'll be very simple." Glen laughed. "There are only four apartments on the tenth floor. You'll knock on them all until you find the right one."

We took our perfect pasta ingredients to the kitchen. Then Glen went over my wardrobe for the best casual wear that wouldn't be too casual but wouldn't be screaming 'scheming bitch' the moment Luke laid eyes on it either. What was wrong with my current attire, she didn't say.

After she was happy with the way I looked, she practically dropped Drixie into the hallway, whispering, "You better play your part in this. You know where to go," and closed the door in her meowing face.

"If she gets lost, you'll be searching for her," I warned Glen.

"She won't get lost."

"But if she does—"

"Yes, yes, I will be searching for her."

Gorgeous, kind, funny and patient

I was way too nervous to even look like I was searching for Drixie when I knocked on the second door on the tenth floor, after the first one had opened to an elderly woman who hadn't seen any cats. Didn't own a cat of her own, nor did she want anything to do with the furballs whatsoever. I'd asked her just to stay in character, and she babbled away for quite some time before she left me standing in the corridor. I felt the lie slipping away when Luke opened the second door, drinking me in like seeing me was a pleasant surprise, but a surprise nonetheless.

"Haylee," he greeted with a soft smile that did all kinds of strange things to my stomach. "You can't possibly be ready with the pasta yet, even if you're using dry spaghetti."

He was searching for the obvious—a plate of pasta to taste—which I didn't have because Glen's plan didn't involve actually making any pasta ourselves.

I swallowed hard, trying to make room in my mouth for the words to come out. "Oh, um...no?"

"No?" Luke studied me while I fidgeted on his doorstep, his smile turning into a look of concern. "Haylee, is something wrong?"

"Why would—" I stopped, swallowed again, and as practised said, "I'm looking for Drixie. I thought she'd come here again."

She hadn't, though. I saw it on his face that she hadn't. If I was jittery before, my stomach made an horrified somersault that left me nauseous now.

"It's okay," I whispered. "I'm sure she's somewhere. I'll find her."

"Give me a minute, I'll come and help you look." He rushed back into his flat, leaving the door wide open.

I heard him talking to someone in the other room, and despite telling myself to wait outside, like was proper, I couldn't help myself. Curiosity got the better of me, and I stepped inside, pulling the door closed behind me, and sneaked closer to the noise.

The short hallway opened up to an open-plan living room. There wasn't anyone else in the room that I could see, but the conversation continued, and not all in perfect English.

Luke was by the kitchen island, a red kitchen aid in the center with half-shredded noodles falling out on one side that momentarily caught my attention. He wasn't focussed on that task, however. He was leaning over a tablet that showed the image of a different kitchen, where an older woman stood next to a man who could have been his father. Probably was his father, come to think of it. Something about the nose...

I stopped in my tracks. He was in the middle of a video call, and now I was intruding. Then my name was said, and my heart stopped.

Luke peered over his shoulder and met my eyes. "Yes, that's her," he told his family, because that was who he was talking to. It couldn't have been anyone else. And they knew about me. They knew something about me, at least, because the way my name was said sounded like they'd talked about me before.

Luke had told his family about me.

My heart pounded in my chest, and my stomach did an anxious swirl as he beckoned me closer. I stumbled my way over to the countertop.

I'd barely even talked to my family since I moved in with Glen. Dad checked in a few times. To see if I was still alive, I'm sure, but that was it. Only Glen knew about Luke. If I'd told my mum anything about my lovelife, or a potential threat to the lovelife I didn't have, she'd go bonkers. After the online catastrophe she helped to patch up, she had every right to be wary of any relationships I might get into. I was wary, too, but I couldn't let one bad experience stop me forever. Okay, one absolutely horrifying experience.

Irredeemable, detrimental... nasty? There were too many words for it, and none that I wanted to share with anyone. I knew if I told my mother anything, the first thing she'd do would be bringing it up and having me live through the utter embarrassment of it all. Hoping that would keep me from searching for companionship. It had certainly kept my clothes glued to my body for this long.

"She's very pretty," the woman on the screen said, speaking in English for my benefit with an obvious accent. Her dark hair had streaks of gray in it, and her once youthful face had wrinkled, highlighting laugh lines most of all.

"Yes, *Nonni*." Luke smiled, not turning away from me. "Yes, she is."

My cheeks burned, and I sucked my lower lip into my mouth.

"You might not be hopeless after all, *Fagiolo*," *Nonni* said affectionately. "Now, go find her *gatta*. We'll talk later."

They said their goodbyes, the tablet screen turned black, and Luke and I were now alone in his kitchen.

"Sorry about that," he said, scrubbing his face. "I might've told them a few things. Like how I seem to lose my head whenever you're around. Asking for advice, really."

My heart skipped a beat at the confession. It was one thing to realise he'd obviously told them something about me; it was a different thing entirely for him to confirm it out loud. "And did you get it? Advice, I mean."

Luke's lips twitched, and crinkles appeared at the sides of his eyes as he recalled the conversation. "My grandmother said, and I quote, 'be yourself, boy. There's nothing else you can do. She'll either like you for who you are or she won't be worth your time.'"

I blushed and dropped my eyes to our shoes. "She sounds like a wise woman."

"I've learned to trust her judgement in most things."

Luke led me back to the hallway, not that it was hard to find. The layout of his flat was rather straightforward. The hallway led to the open plan kitchen and living room, while his bedroom must've been the door just on the other side of the sofa—I wasn't thinking about his bedroom, or anything.

In sheer contrast to now mine and Glen's decor, his choice of furniture was minimalistic and modern. Simple. Nothing cluttered anywhere that I could see, at least. I couldn't see a lot during my very short stay, but it felt warm and cosy like the man himself. Very unlike the corridor that was gray and gloomy and hiding Drixie somewhere in its dark corners.

"I suggest we check all the floors first and then start knocking on doors, if we don't find her in the corridor," Luke said. "You cool with that?"

I nodded. "Okay. I kind of already knocked on that one." I pointed to the door to the left of Luke's.

"You did, huh?" he hummed. "We can skip that one, then."

I shrugged. "Thought it might be yours. It wasn't."

"Well, you found me, and we will find Drixie. Come, let's start from the top."

After a long downward climb that somehow reminded me of the time he carried my mattress upstairs, we ended up on the ground floor, and I was growing increasingly more worried. The only thing different now was the continuous 'pspspsps' that carried through the corridors and was supposed to call Drixie toward us. And the worry. And perhaps I wasn't as sweaty as I had been then. Okay, a lot was different, but Luke wasn't. He somehow remained calm throughout the search. He even attempted to raise my mood with banter that I responded less and less to the lower we reached. It wasn't his fault that I was beginning to lose hope.

"Luke, she's not here." My lips trembled, and I hated Glen just then. This whole thing was her idea after all. Some grand plan of hers—brilliant, as she called it. "What if something's happened to her?"

We'd looked by the mailboxes, which was the last place Drixie could have gone if she hadn't somehow gotten outside altogether. It was raining, so the chance of that happening was slim at best, but who knew? She might've been in the mood for a shower. I certainly didn't know anymore.

I'd dragged my hand through my curls too many times, and it felt like they were wilder than ever. I did it again, just to give my hands something to do other than shake at my sides.

Luke took a step closer, his hand reached out. "Hey, hey. It'll be okay, we haven't checked the apartments yet." His brows furrowed as he flexed his fingers, dropping his hand before he could actually touch me, and cleared his throat. "We'll find her, okay?"

"Okay," I whispered, but I didn't know if I believed it.

"Okay," Luke repeated. "Yeah. Okay. From top to bottom again. There's a better chance that Drixie ended up on a higher floor."

"Okay," I said again. "Thank you."

He looked at me like there wasn't anything he'd rather be doing.

I stammered on, "For helping me. I don't know anyone who'd take the time to carry mattresses up twelve flights or search for a cat. Well, except for Glen, but she doesn't really count."

"That's what friends do," he replied. "Right?"

With a lump in my throat, I nodded. *Friends.* He had friendzoned himself for me.

"Still, thank you."

Luke called the lift, and the signature hum of it descending broke the silence that had fallen between us. Luke was staring at the numbers above the lift slowly trickling lower as if content to give me the opportunity to uninterruptedly study him. While the silence was kind of comfortable, I still felt the urge to say something. Explain myself and the earlier dismissal of his invite to hang out. How would I even go about it? In the most awkward fashion... So obviously, I clamped my jaw shut and drank in Luke's handsome face for as long as he'd let me.

The lift opened with a ding, and his face lit up, making my heart skip a beat. He was gorgeous when he smiled like that. Genuinely smiled. Gorgeous, kind, funny and patient like Glen had said. And he was interested in me a little, at least. Enough to tease and flirt. Enough to invite me over to see if it could go somewhere. Certainly enough to help me look for Drixie.

"There you are, you little trouble maker." Luke's voice took a higher tone, like he was talking to a child—or an animal.

I flipped my head to find Drixie, all smug, in the corner of the lift staring back at us.

"Oh, thank God, I was really starting to worry." I rushed inside, and to Drixie's annoyance picked her up, pressing my nose in her fur. She purred despite herself.

"Well, that's that, then." Luke joined us in the lift much slower and pressed both tenth and twelfth floor buttons before sliding his hands in his pockets and resuming his staring into space. It was accompanied by a quiet tapping of his foot.

As the floors flew by, somehow faster than ever before, nerves plagued my stomach. This wasn't Glen's plan. Nothing had gone according to her plan at all. I was supposed to end up in his flat, so I could get to know him better. I wanted to get to know him better! But now that we'd found Drixie, we'd be going our separate ways. He assumed my earlier 'maybe next time' was forever, and he wasn't going to push it. He'd made it clear on several occasions that he didn't want to make me uncomfortable, and I'd obviously been uncomfortable when he asked me out. If he wasn't going to say anything, I would need to. Before it was too late.

With Drixie pressed to my chest and my eyes flicking from the dial to Luke and back, I couldn't swipe at the sweat that I felt dripping down my forehead.

"Haylee." Luke cleared his throat. "I'm glad you came to me. For help. I'm glad you came to me for help."

"Me too," I replied quietly, my heart in my throat. Time was running out. That was all we were going to say to each other.

The dinged sounded final when it pierced the space between us, and I squeezed my eyes shut. Breathe. Just breathe. But gasping for air did nothing to calm my nerves. Luke didn't move for a beat, and the swirling in my gut intensified.

"Okay." He met my eyes, rubbing his palms against his trousers as if they were as sweaty as mine. "Yeah, okay. I'll see you around, Red Cheeks."

He moved then, slowly stepping off the lift, hands fisted on his sides. Blood rushed to my cheeks as if to be worthy of the nickname, but he didn't look back as the doors started closing. *Shit.*

"Luke," I breathed, taking all my courage and unwrapping it in one long stammering gasp. "I would very much like to learn how to make proper pasta if you're still willing to teach me."

He turned around then, searching my face for something. What? I didn't know. He seemed to have found it, though, because he slid his foot between the closing doors just before they could slide shut, purposefully trapping himself between them.

"You mean it?" he asked through the crack.

I squirmed under his intense stare. "I do. I really do."

Next thing I knew, Luke's fingers slipped into the space his foot had reserved, prying the doors open, and I rushed to press the 'open doors' button. Luke grinned victoriously when we won the battle with the lift.

"I would very much like that too, Hals," he murmured.

Roll them balls

First thing Luke did when we were back in his kitchen was take out a small glass bowl and fill it with water for Drixie. I melted right then and there at his thoughtfulness.

"Do you mind if I let my family know that Drixie is all right before we start cooking?" he asked after he'd placed the bowl on the ground, slightly out of the way so we wouldn't accidentally trip it over.

Shit! Glen! She hadn't gotten an update from me either. "No, it's okay. I should tell Glen."

I fished into my pockets for my phone and shot a quick message her way, while Luke fired up the tablet again. I looked up just as his grandmother appeared on the screen.

"*Fagiolo*," she exclaimed happily in the midst of sizzling and clattering, obviously still in the kitchen cooking. "We didn't expect to hear from you again today, thought you'd be busy."

"Just wanted to let you know we found Drixie," Luke said, then pointed a finger at the meatballs she was frying. "I see you didn't wait for me. Smells good."

"You think yourself a comedian." She waved a spatula at the camera as Luke chuckled. "You can't smell a thing."

"I know your cooking, *Nonna*. It smells good whether I'm there or not."

Their good hearted banter, sometimes mixed with Italian, went on a few minutes longer. The smile interacting with his family brought to Luke's face was priceless but left a void in my heart. My parents and I were never like this. Neither were my grandparents and I. Dad joked sometimes, but it was often short-lived, and any such occasion was clouded by the countless times Mum frowned at me in disapproval or outright lectured me for the choices I made. Or the ones I didn't make. There wasn't this level of affection expressed in my family, and I didn't know how much I'd been missing something this simple—this essential—until I saw Luke on that video call.

I didn't even realise I was crying, which I seemed to be doing way too often lately, before my sniffles caught Luke's attention, and his sole focus turned on me as his grandmother stilled on the screen.

"Haylee, are you all right?" He touched my shoulder carefully. "What happened?"

It was stupid, so stupid, which is why I closed my eyes and shook my head, even as the tears kept flowing down my cheeks. My mouth pressed into a tight line to keep the words in.

A warm thumb caressed my cheek, wiping at the wetness. "I can't even begin to fathom what goes on in that lovely head of yours, but know that I'm here to listen if you want to talk about it."

I opened my eyes to find his green ones really close. He dropped his hand but didn't otherwise move as we stared at each other. I gathered my thoughts and said, "Your relationship with your family is beautiful."

Luke quirked an eyebrow.

"You're crying because you think my relationship with my family is beautiful?" he asked gently.

I closed my eyes again. "I know it's silly. I'm sorry."

"Haylee, it's not silly. Nothing you say or feel could ever be that."

"You really think that?" I sniffed.

"Of course," Luke replied without missing a beat.

The conviction in his voice assured me it was safe to look at him, so I did. He still stood very close, but his presence felt comforting, and he wasn't doing anything to make me feel crowded. In fact, after the soft caress on my cheek, he kept his hands to himself. "It feels stupid. I'm not usually emotional like this."

"Is your family okay?" Luke asked carefully.

"They're fine. It's fine, we're not that close. I wanted to get out. Moving in with Glen was possibly the best thing I've ever done. I'm happy here." I wiped at my cheek furiously. "I am!"

"I didn't say anything."

"My family never felt like this." I pointed at the screen, where his grandmother pretended not to listen to us. "It is complicated. We shout at each other more often than we show affection of any kind to each other. It just got to me."

"We've had our fair share of shouting too. Trust me, that's all part of it."

I wiped at my cheeks again. Somehow, I didn't think it was the same, but instead of pointing that out, I just nodded.

"I want something like what you have," I whispered.

His eyes softened, but he didn't respond. What did I expect him to say anyway? That he'd give it to me? And then what? Go have a freak out at the implications. Him not saying anything was for the best.

Once I had gotten myself somewhat together, and the tablet connected to the speaker system instead of the voideo call, Luke showed me how to use the kitchen aid to cut the pasta dough. He set to mixing the seasoning into the minced meat all the while explaining each step he took. I realised his grandmother had been making the same exact meal.

Luke grinned when I asked about it. "Sunday is for family dinners. It's a tradition to always cook together on

Sundays. We have been doing it a bit differently during my time in Egland, but we've made it work."

"That sounds lovely." I thought about my family traditions—something solid and unbreakable—but couldn't come up with anything. "Do you miss them?"

"A little, but we talk every week. And once my work here is done, I'll be going back." He stopped mixing the minced meat, eyes glazing over for a moment before shaking his head and smiling at me.

He'd be leaving. Maybe not tomorrow or next week, but nonetheless, he had no plans to stay. I shouldn't have latched onto that revelation, but now that he'd said it, a playlist with the same name was made in my brain, and someone pressed 'play.' *Leaving*.

"And what is it that you do here, exactly?" I was finished with the pasta dough. It was all cut up in strips and placed in a bowl to wait until we could cook it. My hands now fidgeted around without purpose as I watched Luke fold over the roll of mince, press down on it with his palm, and repeat the motion several more times. His entire biceps flexed along with the movement, mesmerising me.

"Programming, mostly. Internal systems."

My mouth fell open, and he grinned at my reaction. "Impressive, but couldn't you also do programming from afar? It's not something that needs a personal approach."

"This company was very adamant on seeing me face-to-face onsite. A security measure I fully understand." He got a faraway look again, and furrowed his eyebrows at whatever he was thinking about. "Let's not talk about work unless you want to tell me about yours?"

I shrugged, tapping my fingers against the countertop. "Not much to tell. I give a few dance classes and do a little waitressing. Pretty standard stuff."

"Is that where you met—" he stopped mid-sentence, slight shock registering on his face. He took a deep breath and pushed the minced meat bowl to the center of the kitchen aisle. He turned toward me, meeting my eyes as I waited for whatever he'd left unsaid. It never came. "Wait, you give dance classes? There's nothing standard about that."

We watched each other for a nerve-racking moment, both wondering if I was going to call him out on the swift change of direction. I dropped my eyes and shrugged again, letting him off the hook for now. "It's nothing like programming."

"But you like it?" he asked.

"I love it." Thinking about dancing brought a smile to my lips. I'd been working on a new choreography that I couldn't wait to show the class on Monday. It made me bounce on my toes.

"Then it's much better than programming," Luke said in a raspy voice.

A quick flick of my eyes confirmed he was still staring at me. "It doesn't pay as much as programming."

That was my mum talking through me. I swear she had repeated this same sentence, switching programming with law, often enough to make my ears hurt. Definitely often enough for it to become my standard response—my mantra—since here I was, tearing down my own profession, which I loved more than anything.

"Okay, would you rather do something you love and get paid a little, just enough to get by. Or would you choose to be filthy rich, stuck doing something you despise?" Luke asked.

"I don't care about the money."

"You're the one who brought it up."

I sighed. "It's conditioning. I would be stuck in a pantsuit in some well-esteemed law firm if I hadn't fought this hard to do what I love. I'll choose dancing over anything in a heartbeat."

"Law firm," he echoed slowly. "Yeah, I don't see you stuck in a pretentious place like that."

I snorted. "Where do you see me, then?"

A smile tugged at his lips. "In here with me, making meatballs. Now here's how you roll them."

My stomach did a perfect pirouette as he snatched a handful of mince. His hands worked to form it into a decent-sized ball. He showed it to me between his thumb and index finger once he was satisfied with it.

"Not too small, and not too big. About this size so they cook well and have a decent bite to them. You got it?"

I knew how to roll meatballs, it wasn't science, but Luke seemed to have switched into teacher mode again, and I enjoyed the presentation. And listening to him talk. His voice had this perfect rumbling pitch to it that felt safe and thrilling at the same time.

"Not in the least. How do you roll them again?" I bit my lip, trying hard not to grin.

Luke raised his eyebrow at me. "Do you need another demonstration, Red Cheeks?"

"Yes, sure," I giggled.

"Okay, then."

Instead of picking up another handful of mince, he ran his hands under water at the sink. All the while his green eyes never strayed from mine. Then he thoroughly dried his fingers on the towel hanging over his shoulder, biceps flexing with every movement. Once satisfied, Luke walked over to my side of the kitchen island.

"Let's try it this way," he said from right behind me, raising the hairs on my neck just by his nearness.

He took a step forward, and his warmth seeped through the back of my very casual Glen-chosen shirt. One of his hands snaked around me and slowly slid across my arm, stopping under my palm. Goosebumps spread in its wake, and my breath hitched.

"Luke," I gasped, not sure if I wanted him to stop or me to press much closer against him.

"I don't ever give special one-on-one meatball-rolling instructions, Haylee, so you better pay close attention," he whispered close to my ear. "Are you ready?"

I swallowed, my mouth feeling far too dry for it to be any use. Not trusting my voice, I simply nodded my head 'yes.'

Luke's free hand reached out into the bowl and scooped up a decent-sized haul. He brought it over to our joined hands. "Now this will feel a bit cold," he said before he dropped it onto my palm and covered it with his much bigger one.

The meatball mix might've been cold, just like he said, but I didn't feel it through the warmth of his hands sandwiching mine and the insurmountable heat building up in my stomach.

"Do you feel the size of it?" Luke murmured and my heart literally stopped. "That's the way it should feel."

It was definitely warm. Very, very warm. And Luke's comment about size wasn't helping the matter.

He guided my hand against his, rolling the initially shapeless mixture into a perfect sphere.

Despite the texture of the warming mince, the sensation of my hand between both of his was thrilling. I don't know if Luke intended it to become this intimate—who am I fooling, he possibly planned it this way. It was the oldest trick in the book. Done countless times with billiard cues and baseball bats, and apparently meatballs, although this might be a first. You know, step behind the girl and guide her into scoring a hit, or ah, making a meatball. 'I'll show you how to do it' and all. Either way, he certainly knew what he was doing and he'd reeled me in effortlessly.

I liked his proximity. I liked it a lot, but I didn't understand why he would want to be this close to me. I didn't comprehend why he'd been giving me attention, calling me gorgeous, showing me how to make meatballs.

Because the one time I thought someone liked me for me had proven how very wrong I was to assume such a thing. I was spiralling deeper into my thoughts right then and there in his embrace. I wanted nothing more than to simply enjoy this one piece of solicitude he was offering me without worrying what his scheme might be. Not everyone was a scheming dickhead, right? Right. *Get out of your head now before you mess this up!*

"Do you teach any other classes after this?" I asked before I could catch the words behind my teeth.

Luke's chuckle vibrated through my back, and his breath brushed against my cheek. "Only if you want me to, Hals."

I turned my head, and his lips almost grazed my cheek. I was overheating for sure, and even if there was a fan right in front of my face, I don't think that'd been enough for proper air circulation to get my brain working.

"So there are other things you're good at?" I asked breathily, getting stuck in his green eyes. "Good enough to teach."

The longer he stayed near me, the more intoxicated I became. His musky scent and warmth thoroughly encompassed me. I was ready to combust into flames by the intensity of his gaze alone. The speedy thumping of his heart tried to outdance my own. I wasn't certain I could take the tension much longer, but I didn't want to move.

"What is it that you're asking me, Haylee?" he murmured. "I want to be sure we're talking about the same thing."

We probably were, but I wasn't brave enough to point it out, so instead I took the coward's way out. "Pottery, or yoga, or clarinet?"

"Ah," Luke hummed. "Clarinet? Just so we're clear, that's not slang for anything sexual is it?"

Combust I shall. "The musical instrument?"

"So not an euphemism for playing the flute?"

I blinked. "Do you play the flute then? They're similar, right?"

"Okay, that would be a no then." Luke cleared his throat, untangling our hands and stepping away from me. "I wouldn't be much of a teacher for any of those, I'm afraid. Flute, the musical instrument, included."

I blinked again, not sure why the specification was necessary, but I sure as hell wasn't going to ask. No, I let him take his warmth all the way to the other side of the kitchen island and let him admire my perfectly red cheeks.

Three unsaid words

Haylee had the most incredible smile, and every time I managed to coax it out was a small victory I celebrated by saying something even more ridiculous to keep it there a while longer. Haylee's laugh? Even better than her smile. Like chimes swinging in the wind. Like a long-lost melody that was there one moment and gone the next, the sudden absence left you empty and longing to hear it again and again. Her laughter was taking my heart and wrapping it up like a gift basket. Hers for the taking. It took my soul and breathed life into it, warming me up inside out. I could have survived off of her laughter alone.

When she looked at me, eyes bright and unguarded, my heart soared, and she did look at me that way more often as the night went on. Longer than she'd dared before, especially as she fully relaxed into the playful dynamics I vowed to uphold. And I? I was dumbstruck, staring at her the entire time. I admired the softness of her curls, all the while wishing I had the sense to touch them when I'd been close enough. The rosy flush on her cheeks was a canvas I wanted to trace my fingers on. Lips that teased with playful phrases beckoned me to plant a kiss on them. I stood with the kitchen island between us to behave and keep my distance. I was not to be trusted to keep myself in check.

I was buzzing like I'd been drinking a little too much, and the words 'drunk on you' finally made sense. I was drunk on Haylee. All it took was an hour of cooking to pull her out of her comfort zone, and another to introduce her to mine. She now looked cozy as hell perched upon the barstool, elbows resting on the kitchen island, while she leaned towards me with a twinkle in her eyes that I was afraid to misinterpret. I didn't want this night to end, but I knew sooner or later she would be leaving, so I took it as my mission to make her laugh as much as possible before that time came.

I knew better now to steer clear of topics about her family and let her talk about her dancing lessons, once we were clear pottery nor yoga really interested either of us and my other expertees weren't going to be exploited. At least not tonight. We skirted around the topic, sure. Toyed with it every now and then, and it was always Haylee who drifted back towards safer subjects. To pottery, yoga and clarinet—the musical instrument. I let her. She could pick the pace as long as she kept smiling at me sweetly.

I was under her influence; she could do whatever she wanted, and I'd go along with it. Like a fool. A lovesick fool.

"There's a few more meatballs left if you want them," I said, nodding towards the pan between us.

"Oh no, I couldn't possibly," Haylee laughed. "I wouldn't fit out the door if I did."

She'd been making similar comments about her body here and there, each conflicting with my image of her and leaving a stale taste on my tongue. I'd tried to diffuse each and every one of them but wasn't sure she registered my attempts.

"All the better," I hummed. "Then I could keep you."

She tilted her head, wetting her lips. "And then what? I'd become a perfect meatball in your collection?"

"Haylee, I am going to say it as many times as it takes for you to start believing it. When I look at you, I see a masterpiece sculpted with precision and utmost care. Every part of you is perfect, and I have been trying to memorize them all night. My offer to keep you is incredibly selfish since simply looking at you could never be enough. I have no collection to speak of, you'd be the only one and yes, you are absolutely perfect."

Her mouth fell open and the color on her cheeks deepened. She also avoided my eyes so I hoped she heard the sincerity in my voice.

"You're just saying that to—"

"I'm not just saying that, Red Cheeks. I'm not trying to flatter you, nor get you to bed with me. I wish you could —"

"You're not?"

"—see what I see when I look at you. And I have been looking at you all night, Haylee. You are absolutely stunning, and there is not a thing that needs changing. Not a thing, do you hear me?"

Her lower lip disappeared into her mouth, and she remained quiet. I'd already said enough to leave no doubts about the way I viewed her. Surely, she'd realize I wasn't playing around?

"And yes, I wouldn't say no, if you wanted to—" I cleared my throat. "Frankly, I've been thinking about it the entire week, but sex is not my end goal. It either happens or it doesn't, I just want to spend time with you because I really like you."

Everything was out on the table now. My heart thrummed in my ears and the earlier fuzziness I'd felt faded. Now alert, I waited for her response.

Slowly, Haylee raised her eyes from her hands. I gave her time to study me, gave her time to digest my words. It felt like forever, seconds dragging by as we stayed still and the air thickened, poking and nudging at the playfulness that had previously occupied the space.

"I want to believe you," she finally said.

It didn't take long after my confession for Haylee to realize how late it was getting. Drixie, who had fallen asleep on my couch, narrowed her eyes on Haylee when she picked her up but settled in her arms regardless. I walked her two floors up to her door, and we stood there in that slight awkwardness that tends to carry into the end of a first date.

"I hope you had a good time, because I really did," I said, fidgeting my keys around in my pocket.

Haylee nodded. "I did."

"Despite my lame jokes and teasing?"

"Yes." She laughed. I loved the sound of it.

"Despite—"

"Yes, Luke." She laughed again.

"Good. Feel free to invite yourself over any time."

When I took a step closer, she tensed, yet her chin raised up in expectation. I breathed in the scent of her, something sweet and enchanting, and raised my hand to push a stray curl behind her ear. It was as soft as I'd imagined.

Haylee's breathing quickened, her eyes falling closed even as a slight tremble went through her. I threaded my hand deeper into her curls and pulled her forehead to my lips. An audible sigh escaped her as the tension in her shoulders released. One of her arms came up around me while the other continued to cradle a rather annoyed Drixie, as I lingered for much longer than I intended.

"Good night, gorgeous." My voice came out raspy.

She tilted her head to look at me, her lips almost brushing my chin. "Good night, Luke."

I smoothed her hair, enjoying the feel of it against my palm before I took a step back and away from her gentle embrace. She leaned towards me as if to keep me from moving. Her lips parted, and her eyes reflected a mix of disappointment and relief that I hadn't actually kissed her. I had half a mind to trap her between my body and her front door to do just that and find out if she would reciprocate or push me away.

I'm falling in love with you.

I escaped the hallway before that left my lips.

My forehead pressed against the cool metal of my front door once I'd closed it behind me. The deep breaths that were meant to calm my frantic heart did nothing of the sort, as my brain kept running in circles around everything I said or almost said or didn't quite say at all. I was moving fast, coming on too strong. Way too obsessed, already.

Haylee was moving at a different pace. I needed to slow down for her. I needed to stop blurting out everything I was thinking and give her time to figure out how she was feeling and what she wanted—if she even liked me the same way and what her expectations were. I only had a month, though. Just one more month. I had to let her know I was leaving, not that I was becoming crazy about her. It wasn't fair to reel her in and then go.

I slammed my palm against the door. *Fuck!*

Deep breaths. I had to keep my cool. I had to go and bake something for the sake of getting my shit together. I could figure this thing out, long distance was a thing, right? Not a favorable thing, but if this was meant to be, we could make it work. I was jumping way ahead of myself again. I was in over my head. I wanted to head back up to her apartment and give her head. Wait no. Well, yes, but also no.

I wanted to hear her say that she was feeling the connection the way I was. That there could be more to whatever this thing was. That it wasn't just wishful thinking. That I wasn't imagining things, and we could—we could what? Live happily ever after? *Porco Dio,* as if that was in the cards for me.

I dragged myself away from the front door and into the kitchen. Our plates still scattered the bar, and when I slid my hand across the stool she'd sat on, it was still warm to the touch. Insane as I was, I lowered my face to the seat and inhaled the leathery scent of it. Her perfect bottom had perched here just a moment ago. Right here. It didn't require much of an imagination to picture her in front of me, flushed but ready. Oh so ready.

Didn't want to get her in my bed? Those couldn't have been my words less than an hour ago. That'd been someone else, someone more noble, because if Haylee had still been here right now, she'd probably be squirming under me.

Yeah, baking wasn't going to fix me, this tension required a different type of release. With one hand leaning on the barstool, my other gripped my dick through my pants. The warmth was already fading, but I was burning up with need.

Fuck it. I released the devil and did what needed to be done, smearing the seat with my cum when I finished. It didn't help much. Did it help at all?

Monday morning arrived like a trainwreck I wasn't prepared for. Not that anyone can ever truly be prepared for accidents. Still thinking about Haylee, obsessed as I was, I decided to try something different and fired a text to the number I'd saved off Drixie's collar. Nothing crazy, though my mind came up with several inappropriate options.

It was a simple: *Good morning, Red Cheeks*. Good thing too, because what I received back wasn't a variation of the same, but a very confused: *Who is this?*

I stood in my kitchen, staring at the barstool from the day before while gripping my phone and telling myself I was going to be fine. This was different from the time I got my heart wrecked. Haylee was a different girl. And even then, if it wasn't going to work—fuck—I'd be fine, because I'd survived once before.

Just don't go all in, I told myself.

Too late for that, jackass.

I opened the text, tapping at the screen harder than was necessary, and sent: *It's Luke, but you would have recognized me by the greeting if you were Haylee. Who am I speaking to?*

Three dots appeared, then disappeared.

I shook my head. The phone number was a dead end. I needed a different approach.

Fairy Tales

"No dad!" I shouted into my phone. "Luke is not like that."

He'd called me this morning concerned for my well being and asking about any men that I might have troubles with, because why else would I give anyone his number instead of my own? I hadn't given Luke his number, but when I told Dad that he became twice as concerned as before.

"You should be careful, Haybear. Not all men have good intentions, you should know that by now," Dad said on the line.

I expected that shit from Mum. I'd been pleasantly buzzing last night after Luke left me to recount every single detail to Glen. We giggled like teenagers. I knew the high would come down eventually; I just didn't expect it to be this soon.

"He's a neighbour. He carried my mattress up the stairs, let me borrow his umbrella, and never asked for it back. We ate pasta together. That's all. I might be bad at reading people sometimes, but I'm not outright stupid."

Dad sighed. "I didn't say you were, honey. I just told you to be careful."

"Fine," I huffed.

"Do you want me to respond to his text? Shoo him away?"

"No!" I replied perhaps way too loud. "I mean, I'll take care of it myself."

"Be caref—"

"You said that already. Twice. I'm not a child anymore."

"No, I suppose you're not."

The line was quiet for a moment. Long enough for me to be able to stuff my mouth with a sandwich.

"Will you tell me if something is wrong?" Dad eventually asked. "If you need help with... anything."

I chewed on the dry bread before I swallowed. "There's nothing wrong, but if there is, you'll be the first to know."

I wasn't sure how truthful that was, since Glen would always hear everything before anyone else, but it was the only thing I could say that would get him to drop it. He was worried about me, I got it. But all of that carefulness was making me angsty. What if I missed out on a once-in-a-lifetime opportunity by worrying about everything that may or may not happen?

Last night was special. I felt special. Luke was enchanting, charming, and funny. Somehow, he'd wanted to spend time with me, and the intense focus he directed towards me made me feel worth the attention. He wasn't afraid to express his mind and the things he'd said—I really liked him and hoped there was some truth to all of it.

Hoped? Pshh... that's what all the being cautious did to me. Last night, I had simply hoped and buried my head into my pillow—not *his*. I bet that would have been incredible. If his attention to detail was anything to go by, he'd likely be very... all-consuming. But no, I'd been careful. I'd run back to Glen's and hadn't even managed to receive a goodnight kiss, not a proper one at least, because somehow he knew. Somehow Luke had figured me out and melted a little more of the walls around my heart that I'd thought were impregnable. And then he'd fled as if the fire had been too hot to touch. As if he'd been afraid to cause a collapse if the fortress crumbled all at once. As if the force of it falling could leave me buried underneath, more damaged than I already was. That was the man I had to be careful of?

I'd dressed for my waitressing job this morning and was running later than usual due to the unexpected phone call. Monday mornings weren't all that busy at the restaurant, but I hated being late. I was brushing my hair in the lift, staring at my reflection in the dirty mirror at the back of it, when the thing stopped and dinged only two floors lower to mine.

"If it isn't Little Red-Cheeked Dancing Girl."

I dropped my hands, still gripping the brush. I blushed at the sound of his voice. The deep amused tone of it caressed my ears.

What had he said again? I whipped around to face him, getting caught in his wide grin as his words registered.

"And you're what? The Big Bad Wolf?" I asked, my cheeks blazing ever more.

"I was hoping to be one of the hunters since the wolf didn't fare all that well at the end of the story."

"The wolf was well fed. There weren't even any hunters in it."

Luke stepped into the lift, eyes drinking me in before stopping on the brush in my hand. His fingers pried it out of my grip, leaving tingles behind. Then he resumed combing my hair as if it was a perfectly normal thing to do. His brushes were soft and careful as he coaxed knots out.

"I like my version of the story more," he said.

I closed my eyes, enjoying the way he touched my hair. "How does your version of the story go?"

"The hunter saved the girl, obviously."

"And they lived happily ever after?" I could feel my pulse in my neck, so close to where Luke's fingers were threading through my curls.

Luke grinned. "Her gratitude knew no bounds, but she had nothing to thank him with, so he asked for a dance. So she did for him."

I bit my lip but couldn't stop the smile. "Is that so?"

"Mhmm," he hummed. "It was the most enchanting sight."

I snorted and pulled my brush out of his fingers, only to drop it in the bag I was carrying. That was enough, thanks.

Luke didn't step away, however. He was content standing so close I had to tip my head to be able to see his eyes. So close I could almost feel his body heat against mine. And even though I'd taken the brush away, his hands were still in my hair.

"Dance for me, Red Cheeks," he murmured so close to my ear I could feel his breath tickling my skin.

I could hear his breathing. Or maybe it was mine that started to become irregular. "Right here?"

He wet his lips and nodded. "Right now."

Okaaay, that was a hot thought, but it wasn't going to happen.

"We're in the lift," I gasped.

"So what?"

"There's not enough space."

Luke chuckled. "You could dance really close."

We stared at each other for a heartbeat, possibly longer while my head swam. His gaze was all-consuming, mine was baffled. Eventually, he nodded and backed away, his hands ending in the pockets of his dark jeans, and his eyes roamed the ceiling.

"I'm full of foolish ideas, in case you were wondering," Luke said.

That's when the lift announced the end of our descent. I was running late, but I didn't want to go anymore. I wanted to stay in this strange bubble with Luke and hear all about his ideas.

I dragged my feet out of the lift anyway. "Like texting my dad 'Good morning?'"

He shifted awkwardly. "Ah, that's who it was. I didn't expect it to be anyone other than you, to be honest. The number was on Drixie's collar."

"You're lucky it wasn't my mum."

"I would've told her all about my honorable intentions."

"And she would've given you a restraining order."

"I'm sure it wouldn't have been that bad. I can be pretty charming."

Oh, I knew he could. I'd fallen for his charm already. "You could be Prince Charming himself and not make an impression on my mother."

"I'm not trying to impress your mother, but if it comes to that, I'll do whatever it takes to convince her that her daughter is safe with me."

I was starting to believe that.

When we stepped outside a car was already waiting for Luke. The same one I'd seen before.

"A colleague," he shrugged. "Can we give you a ride somewhere?"

I chewed my lip and checked the time again. "That would be great, actually."

The way Luke grinned was as if he'd won the lottery, or something. It was just a lift and a short one at that, but the shine never left his face.

Unexpected Visitor

After a long day of that included no dancing but generous tips instead, I got back to the mansion block. A very lonely trip on the lift left me longingly thinking about Luke.

He'd weaseled himself through the cracks of my crumbling fortress and wrapped his careful fingers around my heart. Not yanking it out of my chest but embracing it instead. Keeping it safe. I hoped he was keeping it safe.

There was a red rose on the welcome mat when I stepped out, and the heart Luke was wrapped around kicked in my chest as my insides turned into hot lava.

A little note accompanied the stem, and I rolled it out with shaking hands. In a neat handwriting the message read:

> Red like your cheeks. I thought it was fitting.

I giggled, then inhaled the sweetness of the rose. The scent made it all the more real. I rushed inside, ready to show Glen, so we could gush about how sweet Luke was. As I entered the living room, however, I ended up hiding the flower behind my back instead as my joy faded.

I stumbled to a stop. "Mum?"

The woman sat on the Victorian lounge set next to a rather sedate Glen. Still wearing a pantsuit that I found uncomfortable to look at and couldn't even think about trying on, she clashed with the interior in a hilarious way, but I would never point that out to her. No, when she was around, I was better off eating my words. Nothing good ever came from speaking my mind.

Mum turned to look at me, her eyes narrowing. "When were you going to tell me that you were moving here of all places?" She shook her head distastefully, not expecting me to answer as she continued, "Don't you think I had the right to know? I've been doing background checks on real estate agencies and going through all the recent sale and rent records not finding your name on any of them. You don't call to let us know you're all right. I'd thought the worst had happened!"

I just stood there by the door, clamping my mouth shut. She'd rather go searching through records than ask me about it herself. She could've asked Dad. She probably did eventually, but I was still the one to get an earful.

"And then what do I hear? Men texting Arlo trying to reach you!"

Of course, Dad would have told her about that, too, if they were already talking about me. Just once, I wished he'd be on my side.

Glen looked like she'd bitten into something sour but was unable to spit it out. I squeezed the rose behind my back, thorns biting into my palm.

"Who is he?" Mum demanded.

"That's none of your business." I considered that a polite answer, but she didn't take it that way. Oh, no, she went on about background checks and all manner of other things nobody else's mother was able to threaten suitors with. I simply set my jaw and counted seconds in my head.

"See?" I finally huffed, unable to keep quiet any longer. "This is why I couldn't stand to be under the same roof as you. You can't possibly think controlling every aspect of my life is going to help me in any way."

"All I've ever done is try to help you, Haylee," my mother said harshly. "When those horrible videos of you were going around—"

"That was two years ago! We are done talking about it."

"...it was me who got them taken down. You wouldn't be dancing in a studio but a strip club if it wasn't for me! I am only trying to look out for you, because we both know you can't do it on your own."

I gaped at her as a firestorm took root in my stomach, raging with the ferocity and heat of a giant-ass dragon straight out of a fairy tale that wasn't meant for me.

"I am twenty-five," I said very slowly, gritting my teeth. "You should go look after Henry, who is twelve and actually unable to look out for himself. Just leave me alone."

"Henry doesn't get his tits blasted all over the internet." Glen slapped a hand over her mouth, her eyes wide, but my mother didn't even notice her reaction. "Of course, I'm worried when a new man comes into the picture. I will not leave until you tell me who he is."

Tears pricked my eyes. I was pretty sure my palm was bleeding from the force I was gripping the rose with. I'd been so happy to receive it just moments ago. Now I wanted to snap it in half.

"The problem with you is that you don't trust me, and therefore, I have never learned to trust myself. Now, I am going through life doubting every single decision I make, worrying about every single little thing. You know what that means? You no longer have to worry since nobody does it better than me. Nobody is getting through those walls that you've built around me. Nobody. I am going to die alone and unhappy. Congratulations, you've gotten what you came for."

I wanted to be wild like Glen and free to express my feelings the way Luke was. I wanted to jump head first into love. Get wrapped up in this short-lived dream, but that just wasn't for me, it seemed.

"Haylee, you haven't told me anything yet." My mother's voice was beginning to sound like a fire alarm that kept blaring no matter how fervently you tried to make it stop. Taking out the batteries wouldn't change a thing. Nothing would.

"I need you to leave right now."

"You don't mean that, Haylee."

"Don't you tell me what I do or do not mean. Leave now, or I will have you removed by force."

"Very well then." She stood up from the sofa, smoothing a pant leg as if it had gotten dirt on it. "But don't come running to me if this man means trouble."

I stepped aside when she marched past me and made sure the rose stayed hidden from her until she was out of the flat. I wasn't quite able to breathe. My legs shook as hot and cold tremors ran through my body.

"I'm so sorry, Hallie." Glen's voice sounded distant, and her hands on my shoulder tugging me toward the sofa barely registered. "I thought she was here for my situation with A&R's. I wouldn't have let her in if I'd known she'd go at you like that. You've got to believe me."

I nodded absently. I hadn't even told her about Glen's situation with A&R's. I'd told Glen we could get at least her last paycheck from the antique's shop, but after today, I doubted my mother would help us with that. I wasn't quite sure I wanted her help with anything at all, but Glen deserved some support in the matter.

"Would you please..." I brought my hand up, still clutching the rose. It was definitely bleeding.

"Oh my god, Hallie." Glen carefully pried the rose out of my fingers. She guided me back through the hallway and into the kitchen, where she pushed me onto one of the barely-used dining chairs.

The rose ended up on the counter as Glen pulled tissues out of a kitchen paper roll and pressed them to my bleeding palm. It stung, but not as much as the entire encounter with my mother had.

Glen's rush of words went in one ear and out ther as she hurried about the space, bringing over an emergency kit I didn't even know she owned and starting to wrap my hand. Her babbling was comforting despite me not registering a word. Once she was done with my injury, she brought over the rose, reading the message on it out loud.

"Yes, that sounds like a total stalker," Glen huffed bitterly. "Should do a background check and all to see he's not totally insane."

I didn't have energy for sarcasm.

Glen wrapped me in a hug, rocking us back and forth. "Do you want me to go get Luke?"

"No."

"Okay, but you should talk to him about this."

"No."

"Maybe he knows how to deal with overprotective mothers."

"I said no, Glen."

"Will you talk to him about other things?" Glen tried one last time.

I shook my head before I buried my face in my arms on top of the dining table.

Don't run

I *found another red rose* on my doorstep the following morning, and another one when I got back home from the dance studio. Glen pried them both from my fingers before I could drop them in the waste bin and gathered them into a vase that now decorated our coffee table.

"I think it's cute," she insisted when the next day more flowers joined the ones already there. "You should leave him a note back."

"I don't think it's a good idea," I sighed.

"Hallie, we've been over this. Luke is not a good idea; he is a *great* one. And you shouldn't let your mother, who doesn't even know him, dictate who you spend your time with."

You have the most beautiful smile.

I picked at the note on one of the roses with my finger, chewing on my cheek. Luke's handwriting was neat and careful, as if he'd taken great care to spell each word out. Or perhaps he'd had several previous tries before he'd perfected the sentence. I didn't allow myself to imagine him wrapping those notes around the roses. I couldn't.

"I'm not going to write him a note back," I said stubbornly.

By Thursday—four more roses later—my resolve had dissolved, and I was smearing a piece of paper with scrawls of my own. I wasn't worth Luke's time, he should be romantic to someone who'd be able to reciprocate his affections. My life was too messed up.

I tried to put that in a letter, while Glen did her best to change my mind.

"Hallie, you're not really serious about giving him that, are you?"

I read over the letter, wincing internally. It wasn't great. I wasn't a wordsmith by any means.

"You're running. You always run," Glen huffed. "You said it felt right last Friday."

I set my jaw and folded my imperfect letter into a small square.

"Hallie, stop and think about it for a second. You don't really want Luke to stop flirting with you, that's the highlight of your day!"

"I thought you said you'd be on my side," I snapped.

"I am on your side," Glen retorted. "So is Mr Umbrella. After that forehead kiss, you must realise that. You've never looked more blissful than when you told me about it. Hallie, it's meant to be."

    I don't do pottery or yoga, but I'm
willing to try dancing if you'll teach me.

I squeezed my eyes shut trying to stop the butterflies that came with the memory. He surprised me. He seemed to always surprise me. I hadn't expected the tender gesture, or the way he'd lingered.

"This isn't about any of that. My mum—ughh!" I marched past the roses as Glen shouted after me.

"It is about all of that!"

ELEVATE WITH ME

I miss your gorgeous face. Elevate with me?

My heart thrummed in my chest as I skipped waiting on the lift and took the stairs down to the tenth floor. I was just going to leave the note on his welcome mat, so the nerves had no reason to bugger me. Yet, I couldn't calm the mayhem in my stomach. By the time I reached Luke's door, I was shaking like a leaf, which was silly. It was just a note, not a love letter or anything. In fact this one said I'd be better off alone, and Luke had nothing to do with the reason for it.

I was about to drop the message on his doorstep when his door opened, freezing me in my tracks. I was not ready for it. I had not prepared to actually look him in the eyes while I gave it to him. Those eyes always made me feel seen in the best possible way, but right there and then, I did not want to be seen.

I rose my gaze from his feet to the five roses in his hand, to the genuine smile on his face that got my heart to kick in my chest like a feral horse.

"Red Cheeks," he said cheerfully. "What are the chances? I was just coming up to see if you'd like to have dinner with me, and here you are."

I swallowed and fumbled with the offensive paper in my hands.

"H-hi." Goodness, I was hopeless.

"What's that?" Luke's eyes crinkled as he caught sight of the note. I couldn't quite hide it behind my back fast enough.

I opened my mouth. Then closed it again. I really did come underprepared.

He raised an eyebrow, and I almost drooled. Oh, this was going brilliantly, indeed.

"Was that for me? Because those are for you." Luke wiggled the flowers gently before stretching his hand out with them. "Maybe we can do an exchange?"

"Ah... yeah. Okay?"

Eeek! This was exactly what I didn't want, but here I was now, taking the roses from him with his fingers grazing mine as the note switched hands. My heart thrummed harder. He was still smiling, but I was sure that would change the moment he read what was inside. I was going to be sick.

Luke took such care folding out the letter I handed him that I was sure he wouldn't notice me backing away from his door, roses and all. I needed to leave this second. It was going horribly. I just needed to go.

When his eyes pulled away from the paper, I was already on the second tread, making my way up the stairs, clutching the roses for the support they couldn't possibly give.

"Haylee, wait! Please." Oh, he was definitely no longer smiling. His voice was strained, almost panicked.

That's what stopped me on the third tread with my heart in my throat as he ran after me. His front door hung wide open, all but forgotten.

> Here's a secret. You make me nervous,
> too.

Luke cleared his throat. "You like me but—? That's no way to start a letter."

"I can't do this." My own throat was too tight, and it came out as a whisper.

"Red Cheeks," he basically begged. "I thought you had a good time. You were warming up to me."

"I did. It's just..." I trailed off, not sure how to explain. I was protecting myself. Wasn't that enough? Bringing my mother into it wasn't going to aid this conversation, even if she had gotten me to doubt myself again. To question everything. As if happiness wasn't meant for me at all. Relationships? No, they were for someone else completely, for everyone else, really. Just not for me.

Luke's eyes roamed my face, trying to understand. Hoping to find something he could work with. "What changed? Is it the roses? Are they too much?"

```
Roses are red, violets are blue

More often than not, your cheeks are red,
                 too.
```

"It's not the roses. It's complicated, okay?" I worried at my lower lip, not quite able to look him in the eye. My head was swimming, but that might've been due to the overwhelming scent of sweetness wafting from the roses now squished against my chest.

"Maybe if you talk to me about it we can uncomplicate it."

"I... I'm no good at talking. It's one of the reasons I didn't follow my mother in the career path to being a solicitor." There it was, I brought her up anyway. She was supposed to stay out of it, but how could she? Once she put her head somewhere, she never really left it alone.

"I just want to know what brought this on. Is it something I said or did? Because I never meant to pressure you."

"No, you're perfect. You're—" I gasped, slamming my hand over my mouth and squeezing my eyes shut. That was definitely not meant to come out.

"So it is something outside of my control that makes you pull away from me?"

I bit my lip and stayed quiet.

Luke took a step closer and reached for my hand. I didn't stop him. And I didn't stop him either when his fingers wrapped around mine to tug me down the step I'd stopped on.

"Why don't you let me be perfect for a moment and make you some tea? Then, I will tell you what I think about outside forces coming between you and me. Is that okay?"

I focussed on the warmth of his hand and his thumb circling around the back of my palm. The simple touch eased some of the tightness in my throat.

"Okay," I agreed quietly.

"Okay. Good." Luke's hand squeezed mine.

When I braved a glance at his face, a gentle smile replaced the desperation. He guided me out of the corridor and into a much warmer flat. The door shut behind me with a soft click, shutting out the grey tiles outside and highlighting the brightness of Luke's personal space.

"Come, gorgeous, time for tea. English style." Luke hummed, tugging me forward until we stood in his kitchen. I'd spent several hours around that island last Friday, yet the unexpected familiarity surprised me and comforted me at the same time.

Instead of the kitchen aid on the central island, a large vase full of even more roses took the spot. Luke appeared to be sheepish about it but let me place the ones in my hand back into the water with the rest of them.

Don't forget your umbrella today.

It's raining, but your smile will prompt the sun to come out.

Apparently Luke owned a kettle; not an electric one but an actual, real kettle that he filled with water and placed on a stovetop. I watched him bustle about the kitchen, pulling out two cups, placing herbs in an infuser, and dropping that in one of the cups.

"Sugar?" he asked.

I bit my lip and nodded. "Can't say no to sugar. Big weakness of mine. Glen keeps exploiting it repeatedly."

"Weakness, hmm?" Luke took a small container off a shelf and placed it next to the cups. "Say I had chocolate pudding on my chin, would you lick it off?"

My eyes widened at the straightforwardness of his question. His eyes didn't waver from mine even as the kettle wheezed its readiness.

"I wouldn't call it a weakness then," he replied to my reaction when no words left my gaping mouth. "Or maybe we should experiment? That could be fun."

"Do you have chocolate pudding?" I wondered, licking my lips.

Luke poured steaming hot water into both cups, placing the kettle on a trivet before he stirred the infuser in one of the cups in lazy circles.

"We could always get some. Would that make you happy?"

I shook my head. "No. I mean, I don't need—"

Luke switched the infuser over to the second cup and slid the first one in front of me, along with the container of sugar. Then, he leaned over the central island and reached out with his index finger to dip my chin up higher and urged me to look at him.

"I didn't ask if you needed it, Red Cheeks. I asked if it would make you happy."

The air grew heavier as we looked at each other. I sucked my lip into my mouth, avoiding the question. His eyes focussed on the movement.

"I don't know," I said at last. "Momentarily, perhaps."

He let go of my chin and nodded before going back to stirring his tea.

"I think you should allow yourself to be happy," Luke said.

"We are no longer talking about chocolate, are we?" I mumbled, dropping my eyes the moment he pulled away from me.

"No, I suppose we're not." He took a sip of his tea and nodded in approval. "I'm not going to push if you don't want to talk about it, Haylee, but spending time with you last Friday made me very happy. I would very much like to keep seeing you."

I fumbled with the sugar and dropped a spoonful in my tea as my heart hammered in my chest. "I like the idea of it."

"But?"

"I don't want to pull you into my drama, and there's a lot of it. It's not fair on you, you're perfect." There, I said it again. "My life is far from it."

"You assume I'd shy away from a little bit of drama."

"A lot."

"I think you're worth it, Red Cheeks. Hit me with it. Nothing you say will make me change my mind."

"You can't know that for sure."

"I can." He looked so serious. "Besides, what do you have to lose?"

My dignity.

Must be the pheromones

Haylee was wringing her hands on the table about as much as she sipped at her sugared tea. She looked absolutely adorable while at it, but also made me wish I had a reason to join her on her side of the kitchen island and still her fidgeting with a kiss. I'd start by kissing the backs of both of those hands, the top of her head, trail kisses down to her cheeks, and to the tip of her nose.

I kept telling myself not to make her uncomfortable. She clearly was, though. Flustered and uncomfortable. She probably thought I'd belittle whatever made her embarrassed to speak up or think less of her. If she was thinking about her incident with Jay, the fuckface, she could've also felt insecure and vulnerable.

Fuck, I didn't really know what went round and round in that beautiful head of hers. I did know, however, that simply having her back in my kitchen eased my soul. Despite whatever plagued her, she'd agreed to have tea with me. She liked me, but—I would be supportive throughout whatever secrets she may reveal, because the thought of her walking away the way she almost had in the hallway terrified the living shit out of me. It was just like me to fall this hard.

"When you accidentally texted my dad, he must've told my mum, because she showed up in my flat Monday evening," Haylee finally said.

I knew she didn't like talking about her family. I noticed that on Friday. There was tension in her shoulders whenever they came up, and I'd agreed to steer clear of all of that.

"So my text stirred suspicions? Were they worried about you?"

Haylee raised her eyes from her teacup. Her sorrow was like a rainy day. Sticky, wet, and clinging to me with a cold embrace. I did not have an umbrella efficient enough to protect me from such downpour.

"She came guns blazing," Haylee said very quietly. "Telling me I was bound to be reckless and stupid, and would most likely get into trouble. She'd need to fix it for me. She demanded your name, so she could run a background check. She trusts my judgment *that* little."

I raised my eyebrow. "Did she find anything?"

She probably didn't, since they'd ran a background check on me before I could start working with Lewis & Walker Law Group. Hell, it was probably her mother who'd done it then, too, since why else would Lisa Walker have the video files of Haylee's assault? I was surprised she hadn't confronted me about courting her daughter. If all of that happened on Monday, she had plenty of time to pull me aside and give me an earful. Or a warning. Or an outright smack in the face if she disapproved of me that much.

"I didn't tell her. It is none of her business."

Debatable, but I could understand where she was coming from.

"What happened after that, Haylee?"

"I... ah... started doubting my judgment," she murmured into her cup.

That was it. I was done standing on my side of the kitchen island. This woman needed a hug, and I damned well was going to give it to her. I might have not understood her relationship with her family, but I saw how it ate at her.

I left my cup in its place as I walked over to where she sat on her barstool and pried her hands off hers, turning her towards me in her seat.

"What are you doing?" she gasped.

My lips twitched as I stepped between her legs and wrapped my arms around her. Even sitting on a barstool the way she was, her head came up to my shoulder, and I decided kissing the top of it was a safe enough thing to do.

Soft curls smelling faintly like coconut met my lips. I inhaled deeper, unwilling to move away just yet. Her breathing grew rapid, but after a few rather quick heartbeats, her hands came resting around my back, too. Damn, that felt satisfying.

"I don't think your judgment is lacking, Red Cheeks," I murmured into her hair. "But if it makes you feel any better, you can have your mother do a background check on me. I have nothing to hide."

"I don't want her anywhere near you, Luke." Haylee was definitely breathless.

I squeezed her tighter to me. "*You* can do a background check on me then. Ask me anything you want to know."

She buried her face on my shoulder, her breath warming up more than just the spot it touched. "Why do you smell so good?"

I chucked, taken aback by her question. "Do you want the scientific or simplified answer?"

She shifted, and I was pretty sure she was shrugging.

"I think we can blame the pheromones for that." I dropped my face to her neck and made a show of inhaling her scent. The coconut was less obvious there, instead a sweeter fragrance greeted me, and I sniffed a few more times. "Yup, most definitely the pheromones."

Haylee giggled, and the sun peeked out from behind the clouds. I really did love the sound of it. Just hearing it brightened my day. My heart soared because that laughter was for me, ignited by me, and that brought a grin to my face. God, she made me happy. Just having her in my arms and laughing. She felt so right I almost blurted out I was falling for her. Outright speeding down, heart first.

Tempted by the tender skin of her neck now so close to my lips, I gave it a small peck, halting Haylee's laughter in a gasp.

I took a deep breath, but all I could smell was her. I needed to put some distance between us before I crossed a line. I had no idea where that line stood exactly, but I did know that there was one. I pulled away just enough to still keep my arms around her, and she raised her chin to look up at me.

"So you like me but don't want to pull me into your drama, and I like you enough to thread through any drama you throw at me," I concluded. "Can we compromise?"

"What would that look like?"

"You let me decide if the drama is too much."

"And what do I get?"

"Anything you want, Red Cheeks," I murmured. "Anything at all."

She gaped at me, her lips enticingly parted. "You want my drama so badly you're offering anything?"

"I want you." I smoothed her wild locks, unable to keep my hands still. They wanted to explore every part of her, but I restrained them to this safe motion. "And everything that comes with it."

Haylee's eyes widened before she shook her head and clenched her jaw. "You are not real. Men our age don't want drama; they steer away from any kind of commitment. They're just playing the field. Toying with girls before they throw away whatever's left, and the circle begins again."

Her ghosts were at the forefront of her mind, but she circled around, admitting what she was really afraid of. I knew, of course. I'd seen the toying she mentioned recorded, but I couldn't comment on it without admitting I'd been snooping around in places I shouldn't. That wouldn't go down well, especially since our relationship was fragile to begin with. I hated lying to her.

"I would hope men my age have learned their lesson and are tired of stupid games that lead nowhere. I am not playing with you, Red Cheeks." I wrapped one of her hands that had fallen from around me to her sides in mine and guided it to my heart. It beat frantically in my chest, trying to reach hers. "I'm also not afraid of commitment." Long distance or otherwise. *Shit.*

She blinked. With brows furrowed and pouty lips squeezed tight, she studied me. Her hand was trapped between mine and my chest, and she didn't move to amend that. At least she wasn't pulling away. It meant something, right?

"Men your age," she whispered at last. "I suppose we never talked about age."

My stomach hollowed out at that.

What if— No, don't assume. She moved out from under her parents. She was no longer studying. She was giving dance lessons for God's sake; she was not underage. But her mother's protectiveness would make sense. Fuck, I was stupid.

We stared at each other for a terrifying heartbeat that seemed to last forever.

"Ask," I rasped, my throat clenching.

Her soft lips parted, and a warm herbal puff of air drifted out, but she didn't say a thing.

"Ask about my age," I repeated softer, still running my fingers through her velvety hair as if that was the last time I would be able to touch it.

"Luke." Her eyes dropped to our hands still locked against my heart.

"I'm thirty-two," I said in a rush. The tension was too much. I had to know if I was going to scream into my pillow tonight.

Haylee sat frozen for a moment, before she sagged and exhaled another puff of herbal warmth. Her fingers gripped my shirt.

I couldn't read her reaction. Didn't know what it meant. "Red Cheeks?"

"Seven years." She blushed. "What are the chances?"

I ran the numbers in my head real quick and allowed myself to relax. "You don't have to wait seven years for me, Gorgeous. I'm here now."

Happiest with you

I don't know how I got from hoping Luke wouldn't question my letter to wishing he would never let me go, but as he smiled down at me, I wanted nothing more than to stay wrapped in his embrace. The world disappeared. My worries disappeared. There was only Luke, his admissions, and the warmth of his palm against my cheek as he stared straight into my soul.

"Anyone who says you're not worth the drama is a fool," he said with such conviction I almost believed him.

"Did you just call me a fool?"

Luke's eyebrow raised. "You will be educated accordingly when I show you that you're worth it, Gorgeous."

I snorted. "Educated and all?"

"You bet."

I sucked in my lower lip when a smile brightened his face. He was calling *me* gorgeous? I was looking okay today, but that was the extent of it. Just okay. Luke, on the other hand, was hot every single time I saw him. And he saw something in me, something he wanted. I would be a fool if I kept pushing him away. An unbelievable fool. But then again, he promised to educate me.

"What do you say, Red Cheeks? Are we going to try this?"

My stomach swirled with butterflies, and I still gripped his shirt right where his heart beat almost as fast as mine. I couldn't help my lips spreading into a tentative smile as I nodded.

"Thank God." Luke pulled me into a tight hug that left me breathless.

His face found the nook of my neck again, and hot breath tickled the delicate skin there. The man knew how to hug. I'm sure he also knew how to kiss. Judging by the soft brush of his lips earlier and the tingles it had elicited, I was going to be in big trouble when he decided hugging wasn't quite enough.

My heart was going to be in big trouble. I wouldn't be able to hide it from the man for much longer if he kept being this perfect. Maybe it was also safe with him?

"You'd better start delivering on anything that you've promised," I spoke to his very solid chest.

"Mmmmhm." His hum vibrated through my body, heating up much more than my already flaring cheeks.

Trouble. Trouble. Trouble. So much trouble. My mum had been right after all. I didn't mind it in this very moment, however. I didn't need help getting out of Luke's arms. If his kiss was going to be stupendous, then his touch —*Haylee!* He would be careful and considerate, wouldn't he?

Oh God, stop thinking about sex.

Much good did it do to try and avoid thinking about it, with his most-likely talented hands crushing me to him and every hard surface flat against my softer curves. Trying *this* would include sex, wouldn't it?

What if I froze? What if I panicked right in the middle of it? I would not be living up to that. Time to switch gears right now.

Luke pulled away and smirked as if he knew exactly why my cheeks were blazing this time. "Lay it on me."

You lay on me—top it!

I cleared my throat. "I've yet to have supper. Perhaps we could eat together?"

His smile widened. "I will make you dinner, Red Cheeks. I can make you dinner every day if you so wish."

"Every day? Really? I am already sold."

Luke chuckled. "If it means I can keep looking at you, yes."

He kissed my forehead before he stepped away from me, taking his warmth with him.

I rubbed my lips together. *Don't say it. Haylee, don't—* "Just looking?"

He was already all the way to his refrigerator and threw a grin over his shoulder. "Beggars can't be choosers."

"You're hardly a beggar."

Luke pulled several ingredients out and placed them on the central island. I had no idea what he was going to make, but my mouth already watered.

He hummed. "Would you be here had I not begged you?"

I blushed. "Once I got my head out of my arse."

"You know you can still ask for anything, Hals. This offer is indefinite. If just looking isn't what you want, feel free to let me know."

"I'll be sure to remember that."

Luke sure knew how to cook. I tried to help him but mostly felt like I was getting in the way. He didn't complain when I dropped the salt shaker, and it shattered against the floor tiles. Only smiled, kissed my forehead and cleaned it up.

I kept apologising like a broken record and resigned to stay still on my designated barstool even though Luke didn't seem mad at all. Staying out of the cooking process was for the best. It gave me plenty of time to admire the chef.

We talked about all the things we hadn't yet talked about and, somehow, the heaviness I had brought into his kitchen when I first stepped in here faded, until it was completely replaced by light banter and laughter.

We'd just finished eating possibly the best meal I'd ever had, and Luke was looking at me—always looking—from across the kitchen island. His elbows rested on the countertop, and his body leaned towards me.

"What makes you happy, Sunshine?" he asked out of the blue.

"Sunshine?" I snorted.

"What makes you happy?" he repeated seriously.

I worried at my lower lip, considering it. I wasn't going to say chocolate. That would sound stupid, even though it was partly true. There had to be something else that better fit the answer.

"I want to make you happy, Haylee."

I giggled. "I think you're doing pretty good so far."

"Oh yeah?" His palms patted a rhythm on the countertop, giving me the impression that he was nervous. Somehow that made me less nervous.

I'd been worrying about myself and how opening up to someone left me vulnerable, without even considering Luke's perspective. He'd been making confessions left and right, throwing caution to the wind. He'd done it again by wanting to make me happy. Who said things like that? Luke, that's who. Every time he opened his mouth, he offered up a piece of himself, while I'd been hiding myself behind walls higher than Big Ben.

"What about you? What makes you happy?"

"You didn't even answer me!" Luke protested.

"I need time to think about it. You go first."

"You need time to think about what makes you happy?" he asked incredulously.

I hid behind my hands, and he reached across the counter to pull them away from my face.

I smiled and shrugged sheepishly. "Other than you and chocolate custard? Yes, I need to think about it."

Luke's lips twitched. "Now you're just flattering me."

"And you're far from just looking at me."

To be fair, he was only holding my hands in his, which was much less contact than our hug had been. His touch wasn't unwelcome, either, and I tried to convey it with a shy smile, but he cleared his throat and shifted back to his side of the counter.

"Hmm... What makes me happy, huh? Certainly good food, my family, seeing you smile. A sunny day, hearing you laugh, cooking. What else?" He tapped a finger against his chin, thinking about it. "Good conversation. When something succeeds. Hugging you felt pretty darn good. Should I go on?"

I opened my mouth, then closed it.

His eyes were drawn to the movement. "I bet kissing you would be total bliss."

"I bet you would be really good at it." Was I playing with fire? Sure. But if he was willing to speak his mind, so should I. It didn't mean I would blurt out absolutely everything I was thinking, though I had most definitely been thinking about kissing him, too. I just wanted to offer him reassurance that, even though I was as awkward as a baby foal in showing it, his advances were not totally unwelcome. Luke's smile was worth it.

"You'll have to be the judge of that."

"When is the trial? I might need to go over my law books to be fair and just in the verdict."

Luke laughed. "I'm ready when you are, Haylee."

"It probably doesn't work like that," I mused. "There are rules and such that one must follow. Set dates. I don't really know."

"We can set a date if that makes you feel any better."

I shook my head. "Oh no, please no. That would only serve to make me nervous. It's best to be spontaneous with such things."

"Is it safe to assume I have the permission to be spontaneous about such things?" he asked with a grin.

"Are we still talking about kissing or—" I tapped my fingers against the now empty tea cup, not sure why I had to say 'or' at all, since no words came out after that anyway.

"I was, unless there are other things I stand on trial for." His cheeky grin made sure I knew he was joking. He was joking right? "Maybe you can enlighten me about what else you'd like to give me permission for."

Oh my goodness. I did talk myself into this one, for sure. Maybe I was the only one thinking about sex. More like worrying about it. How many dates did one go on before that became a thing? We'd had supper twice now, plus all the times I'd run into him accidentally. We hadn't even kissed yet, but he said he wanted to, and I kind of wanted to, too. After that there was only one place this could lead.

"You're not really on trial," I said to get out of answering.

"Good, because I'm rather terrified about what the punishment would be should I not pass the evaluation."

I shook my head and giggled. "We are preposterous."

"I'll be ridiculous all day long if it makes you laugh, Haylee. It makes me happy, remember?"

Staying in the moment

"Dancing!" I blurted on a Sunday evening after cooking with Luke and his family on the other side of the world. He'd even made his own chocolate custard, and I was avoiding the fact that he had purposefully smeared some across his jaw.

I was becoming rather familiar with Luke's kitchen. And his living room. Even ventured to his bathroom once or twice and found it as clean and organised as the rest of his flat. The one room I hadn't seen yet was his bedroom, and I sure as hell wasn't going to ask for an invitation.

Instead of leaning over and licking the chocolate off Luke's chin, I came up with an answer to a question he'd asked a few days ago. Even though he had cooked for me every evening since, we still hadn't kissed. He'd given me many opportunities to initiate something myself, as shown by the dripping chocolate custard on his chin, but I was too chickenshit to do anything about it.

Avoidance, my best friend, here we are.

He raised his eyebrow, not moving to wipe the brown splotch away either. "I've heard that word before. It's when your body moves to the beat. I hear you're pretty good at it, but you've yet to show me how good."

I laughed. "It's something that makes me happy," I disclosed. "Remember you asked?"

"Aah. I see. And it took you this long to figure it out?" Luke teased. "Maybe you do need some refreshing. Why don't you show me just how happy it makes you?"

I'd danced in front of an audience before. Plenty of times. This felt different somehow. Luke's undivided attention on me, as I took centre stage right there in the middle of his living room, was so much more different than my students studying my moves or a crowd at a performance. Dancing just for him was intimate in a way dancing hadn't been in a long while. I was opening myself up to him better than any words ever could.

The song from his speakers changed, and he increased the volume as I stood there, listening to the beat with my eyes closed. Everything else faded, it was just me and the beat, with Luke somewhere in the kitchen watching. I swayed to the melody, and timed my steps to the beat. The music took over. I barely even registered what my hands were doing or the movement of my feet. Me and the music, we were becoming one for the duration of the dance. It was always freeing to become something bigger than myself. I wouldn't be able to explain it if I tried.

The song stopped, and another one came on, but I didn't even pause. I'd been hiding from this freedom for days. It eased all worries, made me feel as gorgeous as Luke kept saying I was. It made me think I was worth it.

Worth the attention. Worth the trouble. Worth being loved.

When I danced, I could see it so clearly. I could relay all of it with a series of steps and fluid movements. A choreography that was born in the moment and was meant for Luke's eyes only.

I searched the kitchen, but he no longer stood by the island. He'd left? How long had I been dancing? Slowing my steps, I whipped my head around the room, catching a sight of him just before I collided with his chest. His arms came around my back to steady me, but I stumbled awkwardly anyway.

I stood frozen in place until Luke began swaying us gently to the melody that still played through the rush of blood in my ears. His hands stayed firmly around my back, and mine were awkwardly trapped between our bodies. I couldn't even shake my hips in fear I'd rub against something I wasn't supposed to. He was that close.

"You are so incredibly beautiful, Haylee, and you have no idea," Luke whispered into my ear as if sharing a secret. "Stunning."

I swallowed. "Not cute, though. That's good. You're learning."

Luke chuckled. "Cute is reserved for Hello Kitty and girls in cat-patterned PJ's. I thought you knew that."

I hid my smile against his shoulder and slipped my arms around his neck, as he kept swaying us around his living room. I was much stiffer in his arms than I'd been out of them. Telling myself to relax didn't seem to work, either. *Relax, for crying out loud!*

"So you decided to use the words I offered you instead?" I asked. Stunning. Beautiful. Gorgeous. I'd laid them all out for him.

"How about breathtaking?" he suggested. "Because you're that, too."

I raised my head from his chest and met Luke's eyes. They glinted happily.

"Absolutely magnificent," he continued.

I blushed. Good thing red seemed to be his favourite colour. "Now who's not trying to flatter me?"

"It's the truth, Haylee."

"I'm starting to feel like I don't give you enough compliments," I muttered.

"You compliment me every time you grace me with your smile."

My lips did just that at his words, and his eyes shone brighter.

The song changed again, replacing a soft tune with something more upbeat, but instead of matching our swaying to the new tempo, Luke stopped.

"I hope this is spontaneous enough, Haylee, because I am going to kiss you now."

My stomach somersaulted, but I couldn't otherwise react to his words as he leaned in and softly brushed his lips against mine. My heart thundered so loudly I could barely focus, but I didn't want to miss this.

I inhaled sharply, trying to calm my nerves while Luke's mouth lingered just a breath away from mine. One of his hands left its position on the small of my back and threaded into my hair. If he was waiting for me to pull away he'd be waiting a long time. I wasn't going to.

"Then kiss me," I whispered against his lips.

That was all the encouragement Luke needed. He captured my mouth more firmly than the initial brush, all the while pulling me closer. Soft but insisting, his mouth overpowered me, and I melted against his chest, letting the sensations become my entire world.

I held onto his shoulders for dear life as he became my music and our lips danced their own secret choreography.

"Haylee," he groaned before kissing me again, capturing my lower lip between his teeth and tugging gently. "Seven years, beautiful. I would wait seven years for this."

I couldn't respond even if I tried when he deepened the kiss. All I could do was moan and hang onto his lips, like they were going to save me if I was to fall. I barely even registered moving until my heels hit the sofa, and he lowered me on it, not pulling away from my lips for even a second.

His weight hovered over mine, and his mouth was reassuring and soft, but the moment I registered that I was now lying under him and wouldn't be able to get out if I wanted to—not that I wanted to—the entire moment tasted entirely different. My heart didn't only thunder; it roared and bucked in my chest. I didn't only grip his shoulders but tug my nails into them as my body prepared for a fight it had no reason to expect. My head swam and swarmed with memories I'd much rather keep confined.

Stay in the moment, Haylee. It was harder said than done when I felt Luke's erection through our clothes rubbing against my lower stomach. I couldn't control my reaction even if I tried. I froze.

I'm not sure how long it took for him to realise I was no longer into it, but when I opened my eyes a while later, he was looking down at me with his hooded eyes marred by a creased brow.

"I'm sorry," I croaked. "It's okay."

I tried to prove it to him by pulling him back for a kiss and awkwardly nibbled at his lips. His eyes did not leave mine as he let me make a fool of myself with that pathetic attempt.

"What scares you?" he asked gently.

I slumped against the pillows, squeezing my eyes shut. That most definitely didn't count as staying in the moment.

"I'm not scared," I denied.

He didn't buy it for a second. "Do you feel confined, Red Cheeks? Because that's an easy fix."

Without waiting for my answer, he wrapped his arms around me before rolling over, pulling me with him. I ended up on top of him, pushing him against the pillows that had pressed against my back just moments earlier.

My breath hitched as his unmistakable bulge now rested more prominently against my stomach. I wasn't able to move, even as Luke's arms around me loosened and lowered to rest on my hips.

Pushing myself off his chest so that he wouldn't be crushed under my weight, I tried to make space for my knee between his body and the back of the sofa without rubbing against him. No such luck. He groaned underneath me, and I stopped moving altogether.

"I relish all control to you," Luke said, his gaze intense as he searched my eyes. "Whatever you want, you have me."

I took a deep breath meant to calm myself. It didn't work, of course. One thing that made this all a little less embarrassing was Luke's rapidly beating heart under my palm. If he was nervous, too, we were two peas in a pod.

"I'm sorry," I said again. "It wasn't your fault."

He waited as if expecting me to tell him what exactly happened that wasn't his fault. I couldn't bring myself to do it. If my earlier freeze hadn't yet ruined the moment, talking about it surely would. I couldn't tell him about it, even under different circumstances. All I wanted was to forget the past, keep on kissing Luke, and hopefully not make this moment any more weird than it already was.

"I don't know what to do with the control you gave me," I admitted pathetically, still perched on top of him. Still absolutely unmoving. So much for not making things weird.

"Anything you want, Red Cheeks. You can take us back to the kitchen, and we'll have another desert. Or you can kiss me. You set the pace. Anything, Haylee. Anything, and it's yours. I told you."

He said that, but the way his eyes were flicking between mine and my lips said enough about what he was hoping I'd choose. Kissing him had been amazing, and I didn't want it to stop either. Most certainly not like that. With me running away from him.

I shifted in Luke's lap. His hips bucked involuntarily—I think— and he moaned. My cheeks had flamed at this point, and my stomach had imprisoned a bundle of nerves, but that sound touched something in the core of me. Still, I almost apologised again. For what? The accidental friction he seemed to enjoy? That would be silly.

I bottled up my anxiety and focussed on the warmth pooling in my belly. I was in control, he said. I could do anything I wanted. Anything at all. So I leaned closer to his lips. He wet them expectantly as I hovered over him. His breath smelled like the chocolate we'd eaten; he'd tasted like it, too. Sweet and enticing.

The first brush of my lips against his was as tentative as his had been. He let me take my time deepening the kiss, giving me control just as he'd told me he would. I cupped his face, exploring his lips like they were a new music track and I was to choreograph a dance to it. I learned what made him let out guttural sounds and chase my lips if I pulled away to take a breath. He learned things, too, like the fact that his tongue would make me squirm even as I tried my hardest not to rub against him too much—or at all, really. He kept teasing me with it, until he was drinking my moans like they were fresher than water.

We were just kissing. His hands rubbed up and down my back a few times and got tangled in my hair, but that was the extent of his exploration. My own hands didn't venture any lower than his chest either. While I did not intentionally create any extra friction between our bodies, he was stiff in every sense of the word. Not frozen like I had been under him, more like forcefully still. As if he didn't want to bring any attention to how much he wanted to do more than just kiss me. We both pretended not to be turned on by each other, and it was getting more difficult by the second.

Luke practically vibrated with unreleased tension, and I felt hot, oh-so hot all over. Our kisses grew more hurried than tentative. All consuming in every way, and his arms caged me in against his chest as he forgot who was supposed to be in control, and I forgot all the reasons why he had given it to me in the first place.

At that moment, he had all of me. Every single facet in my body, heart and soul. He could have taken that 'anything' he'd given me the power of, and I would have let him. No boundaries applied to us at that moment. Nothing could stand between us and not be burned to crisp by the heat urging us onward. That undeniable flame that sparked whenever he was near. Fire that ravaged the walls around my heart until they crumbled, leaving me completely and utterly at his mercy.

Right then, I knew: I was in love with Luca Stefano Ombrello.

Excitement. Expectation. Exploration.

The kiss on Luke's sofa unleashed something within me. I was uncharacteristically reckless and a whole lot attached to his side every moment we weren't working or sleeping. We did both of those separately. The first was set in stone and unchangeable; I didn't know a thing about programming. I was getting more and more interested in changing the latter, however. I couldn't quite find a way to express it, which was why I kept that little fact all to myself. And to Glen, of course. That girl knew every single secret I kept.

"Oh my Goood, Hallie!" she screeched when I got back from my failed attempt at keeping Luke at a distance with the entire vase full of roses, which he had on the countertop the other day. None of them had little notes around their stems, but I didn't need those to know how he was feeling. We'd pretty much established that. "What did he say? What did he say? Tell me!!"

I giggled. "That he doesn't care if my mother is the Devil incarnate. He'd rather eat sawdust than let me walk away like this."

"Oh my God!" Glen exclaimed again. "You have to tell me everything!"

I took the roses to the ones on the coffee table and arranged them around in the vase. "He kind of kissed my neck."

Kind of? He had most definitely done that.

"What!" She squealed and jumped around the living room, making so much noise that Drixie scattered off into my bedroom.

I giggled.

"I need details. Like right now!"

I was still floating from the experience and stroked the petals of a rose adoringly, thinking about it. "He is incredible."

"That's not a detail, Hallie! That's more like a conclusion." She ripped me away from the roses and sat me on the Victorian sofa, gripping my hands in hers, buzzing with excitement so much that I swayed to the same jumpy rhythm with which she bounced up and down.

"Okay, well. I told him he could kiss me if he wanted to."

Glen squealed again, making it impossible for me to say anything further.

I snorted. "Do you want the story or not?"

"Yes, yes. I'll be quiet."

"Doubtful."

"So he kissed you. Go on! Wait, how did you get from the break -up letter to kissing?"

"It wasn't a break-up letter."

"Semantics."

I shook my head, grinning like a fool. "He was coming out from his flat with the flowers when I dropped the letter off. I couldn't do anything. I tried to run once I handed it to him, but he came after me and dragged me in for tea."

"Of course, you tried to run." Glen clicked her tongue.

I rolled my eyes. "He made tea. We talked. He said he wants all my drama, no matter what. Wait, before that, he hugged me after I told him about Mum and kissed the top of my head."

"That's a lot of kissing." Glen squeezed my hands and kept on bouncing.

"Well, it was only that and the one on my neck. It was more like a brush than a kiss, but I said he could kiss me for real."

"Okay, did he?"

I cleared my throat. "No."

Imagine our conversation after Sunday—when I came home with swollen lips and several markings on my neck that I was unable to hide behind my hands. She gave me no rest until I'd spilled every single detail, down to how hard he had felt against me and how I almost thought I could go further than just kissing. It was a squeal-party in our living room.

"When are you going to see him again?" Glen demanded. "You need sexy lingerie. I'll take you shopping tomorrow."

"Oh my God, no."

"Oh my God, yes!" Glen insisted.

When she got an idea, it was almost impossible to convince her otherwise.

On Monday, after my shift in Turtle Bay, we hit the shopping centre.

"Look at those, aren't these hot!" Glen exclaimed, pulling a bra-and-knickers set off the hangers and holding it in front of me. That particular one was black and had straps going every which way, barely hiding anything at all.

"No. Most definitely not."

"You have to try it on before you refuse."

Yeah. When Glen got too insisting, I could not win. Five minutes later, I stood in the changing room with my mouth gaping open, wearing only straps across my breasts, unable to cover the underwear I wore with what little the knickers had to offer. If I'd thought my cotton bras needed an upgrade, this most definitely didn't suffice as an appropriate replacement. Finding me wet and in this— well, that would end up with much more than just staring. Which I supposed was the entire point of this shopping trip.

"How does it look?" Glen asked from behind the curtain.

"Umm… a bit uncomfortable."

"I'm coming in!" Without waiting for a response, she slipped through the curtain, and I rushed to make sure there was no gap left for anyone to peek through.

"Glen!" I crossed my arms over my chest after I was certain nobody could see me.

"Come on, Hallie. I've seen you in a bra before."

"Not in this bra." I pouted but, once again, had no choice but to relent.

I dropped my hands, chewing on my lower lip as Glen grinned like a lunatic. "This is perfect! You look ravishing. You have to buy it."

"I will never wear it in my life."

"You most certainly will. For Luke."

I mean, it did look hot. It looked way more than just hot, but thinking about showing up at Luke's place wearing this made me want to melt through the floor and disappear. It wasn't my style.

What about those cotton bras you own? I cringed internally. *They were both unpretty and ineffective in actually covering stuff up when you most needed it. And the sports bras? Yeah, not quite the image you'd like to plant on any man's brain.*

"Isn't there anything else?"

Glen shook her head solemnly. "Nope. This shop only sells these, I'm afraid."

I snorted, despite myself. "What a lousy business plan."

"So are you getting it?"

I chewed on my lower lip and checked my reflection in the mirror. Even uncertain as hell and more awkward than ever, I looked... well, sexy. My curls fell a little lower than my shoulders, stopping just before the several lines of straps began, doing absolutely nothing to hide my perked nipples. He wouldn't be able to look away. It might even distract him from the few folds on my stomach.

"I don't know," I mumbled.

"Come on! If you won't buy it, I will."

"And what? Wear it to bed."

"For you, dummy. I'd buy it for you."

I shook my head no. "You are not supposed to spend any money, remember?"

"You'll leave me with no other choice. It's a matter of life and death."

"It definitely isn't."

"For you maybe." Glen had her arms crossed in front of her and lips set in the most stubborn pout anyone has ever seen. "For me, it is."

"Let me get this straight. It is a matter of life and death for you if I have sex in sexy underwear or not?"

"Yes!" she insisted. "Very important."

"As opposed to unsexy underwear?"

"He will not be able to get it out of his head," Glen said.

"If you are to believe him, he thinks about me whether we have sex or not," I muttered.

"Of course, he does. You're gorgeous."

I wave Glen out of the changing room after a few more minutes of admiring my reflection and change into my own clothes. I'm unable to leave the store without the pair of little-to-nothing tangling from my fingers, and it is not entirely Glen's fault, either. I just didn't know if I would actually ever put the set on again or leave it hidden in my closet.

I did hide it in my locker before the dancing class that evening, but couldn't get it out of my mind for the duration of the class, even as I let the students do a short warm up and, we learned new steps for the entirety of the lesson. I imagined Luke's eyes watching me dance. I imagined wearing nothing but the lingerie as I danced for him. Yes, I had officially lost my mind.

If I thought I'd get some room to clear my head that evening and slow down my raging imagination just a little, I was wrong. I looked rather decent when I joined Luca Stefano Ombrello to wait for the lift after my dance class. I'd showered, my wet curls bound up in a bun. I had a clean pair of jeans and a sweater that was flawless. Impeccable, really.

The lingerie set burned a hole through the duffle bag hanging at my side when Luke's eyes met mine in a mischievous smile.

"If this isn't my lovely Little Red-Cheeked Dancing Girl. I was wondering when I'd be seeing you again."

Those red cheeks he kept pointing out made their appearance effortlessly.

"Does the hunter have any requests other than the dance he already received? You know, for saving me from the wolf and all."

Luke chuckled. "The hunter has way too many requests, none of which are appropriate to discuss in such a public place."

I grinned like a fool. "Sounds scandalous."

Luke hummed for an answer, eyes glinting. My stomach swirled in the most incredible way as we stared at each other. Excitement. Expectation. Exploration. Wait, what?

It wasn't surprising to either of us that when the lift arrived, and we were locked in together, I dropped my gym bag and pulled Luke in for a kiss. Actually, it came as a surprise to me. I baffled myself for about three seconds, but then Luke was all over me, pushing my back against the dirty walls and devouring my mouth the way he had on his sofa.

"Fuck, Haylee," he groaned against my mouth, before he slammed his lips on mine again.

Fuck, indeed. I was insane and reckless, and I should've stopped after the first three kisses, before it became impossible to count. Probably seven now, or maybe just one very long and very passionate kiss. Either way, I was clearly not thinking straight, because all I was thinking about was the basically-nothing-covering lingerie set in my duffle bag and how much fiercer Luke's kisses would become if he were to see me in it.

The tenth floor came faster than we expected, and Luke slammed the "Close Doors" button, panting as he leaned over me, with his other hand skimming my cheek on its way to my hair, which had somehow loosened from its bun. I was breathless, and light-headed.

"I think it's safe to say that the jury has approved your kissing endowment. You are very, very good at it."

Luke let out a full belly laugh. "I'm glad. There's no way I can go back to just looking at you now."

Parched

Bliss. Total bliss, like I'd known it would be. Kissing Haylee was everything, and after the first time, I took every chance I could to get my lips on hers. In the elevator on Monday evening, on her couch on Tuesday before Glen interrupted us, with her perched on my kitchen counter on Wednesday. Best. Meal. Ever.

Thursday came and went in a blur, and Friday had us sitting on my couch, listening to the rain tapping on the living room windows. She shuddered and burrowed deeper into the pillows, letting the steam of her hot chocolate whiff into her face and bring a grin to her lips. She'd stopped denying herself things that made her happy.

"The rain is such a nuisance," Haylee sighed, giving the window a side-eye. "Some days, I wish I was born in the desert."

"Really?" I hummed. "Did you forget your umbrella again today?"

"I didn't forget—" Her lips formed an adorable pout, but I wasn't allowed to say she was cute, so I kept it to myself.

"It's okay, you can tell me. I won't judge." I had my own steaming cup between my palms, which was the only reason I didn't reach out and poke her playfully.

"It has become a more decorative part of my room rather than something I use," Haylee mumbled.

I laughed.

"No judging!" A blush colored her cheeks a stunning hue. She hid it behind her cup.

"I'm not, I swear." I raised one of my hands in surrender, while the other kept my cup from spilling its contents all over my lap. That'd be one way to get out of those jeans. Moving on. "Just wondering if there's anything I can do to change your mind."

"About the rain?" Haylee scrunched up her face adorably. "Why?"

"There's a certain charm to rainy days."

Haylee snorted. "Charm? Maybe when it doesn't rain every other day. Or maybe when you're staying inside, sitting next to a fireplace, reading a book. When you look at it from afar and don't have to trudge through it daily."

"I suppose I see it a bit differently, but then again, I don't forget my umbrella when it rains." I winked to make sure she understood I was teasing. Her face reddened further when I called her out on it. Time to stop making her uncomfortable. "My appreciation for the rain comes from the family farm. You can't grow corn in a desert, now can you? Let alone grapes."

"I doubt it rains as much in Colorado than it does here. Makes it easier to appreciate."

"Sure."

Haylee stared out the window, eying the gray sky and the never-ending droplets misting the glass. "Well, I don't have a family farm, and here the rain is only good for romantic kisses."

"Romantic kisses, huh?" A jolt of jealousy surged through me and settled in my stomach. I arched my eyebrow to hide my forming scowl. "How often exactly have you done that?"

The eyebrow didn't work. I still sounded like a jealous prick. Haylee's thinning lips were a clear sign that I should've likely left it alone, but I was now thinking about her, dripping wet in the elevator the first time I saw her, and how the rain had highlighted all her delicious curves.

"Have you ever kissed someone in the rain?" I asked when she stayed quiet.

Haylee shook her head, and the curls framing her face bounced around more joyfully than her detached expression afforded. "No," she said quietly.

My eyes flicked between the window and her lovely face, making up my mind. That wouldn't do. If romantic kisses were what rainy days were made for, then we should make use of this opportunity. I placed my drink on the coffee table and pried Haylee's away from her fingers, too. Then I pulled her off the couch and towards the door.

"What are you doing?" she gasped, resisting me a little.

I stopped pulling her, to look her in the eyes. "Amending the situation."

Haylee's eyes widened. "What?" she gasped.

"I will be your first." *And only*. But I wasn't going to say that out loud. "If romantic kisses in the rain is what you want, of course."

Her hand in mine squeezed tightly. I wasn't sure she was aware of the reaction. Caressing the back of it with my thumb, I hoped to reassure her as she worried at her lower lip nervously. "But it's very wet outside."

"All part of the experience, Red Cheeks. Don't worry, I'll protect your dignity. If this shirt turns transparent, I'll be the only one seeing it."

"I—" She turned beet-red. "I don't know."

"Come on," I urged gentler this time and got her to cross through to the hallway. "I promise it will be all right."

Her nervous energy was enough to fill the elevator with static. I wanted to tell her I found it adorable—and a little amusing—how she seemed to not know what to do with the hand I wasn't holding onto. Her eyes jumped around the metal box, and she swayed from her heels to her toes and back. She didn't want to be called adorable, though, so I kept it to myself.

"You didn't take the umbrella," she blurted out of the blue and pulled us toward the dials to get the elevator to stop and go back up to fetch it.

"We're not going to need the umbrella. Getting wet is part of the experience."

"Luke—"

I pulled her against my side, rubbing a hand up and down her back, feeling knots forming in her shoulders as we rode down to the first floor. "I see now what you meant about not setting a date for our first kiss. You are tense. I might need to give you a massage."

"I'm fine," Haylee muttered.

I pressed my thumb on one of the knots between her shoulder blades, and she sagged against me, muffling a moan against my neck. "Are you declining the massage?"

"N-not exactly."

I bit back my grin. "Are you declining my offer to kiss you in the rain?"

She wiggled in my arms, undoubtedly from the nerves she confessed having. "No," she whispered.

I searched her eyes, but she stared intently at the collar of my shirt. I tipped her chin up with my finger to get her to look at me. "It is all right if you are."

Haylee set her jaw. "But I'm not. I want to do this."

I hummed happily. "Then we'll do this."

Once we were out of the elevator, it took a little encouragement to coax Haylee out into the downpour. She held her arms protectively across her chest, and I did my best not to assess the situation. My own shirt drenched and stuck to my skin in a heartbeat, cooling me down considerably until my limbs felt chilled. Haylee shivered across from me. Perhaps she was hugging herself to keep warm instead of modesty. We would both catch a cold if I didn't get us back inside. This was a terrible idea, but we were outside now so better make the best of it.

It wasn't just raining, it was pouring. My shoes splashed on the wet pavement of the parking lot as I closed the distance between me and Haylee, since she still stood much closer to the entrance. The whoosh and splatter of the droplets attacking the ground rumbled around us, and there was nothing gentle in the way they slammed on my bare forearms and the top of my head. Rivers ran down my face, dropping off my chin. Even more collected in Haylee's hair before escaping down her back and between her breasts. Her shirt clung to her like a second skin just like mine, only I had nothing to hide, and her jewels were drawing my attention more and more. We were here to kiss, not grope. Kiss romantically. How the fuck was I to do that exactly?

I slid an arm around Haylee, drawing her against my chest. The wet squelch and her hardened nipples through our shirts were a turn on. Her half-lidded eyes and expectantly parted lips were a turn on. Fuck, the coconut scent of her wet hair was a turn on, too. I was such a goner for her.

I traced the outline of her rain-kissed lips with my thumb, and her breathing grew rapid. "Now, what would make this more romantic, Red Cheeks? Oh, I know."

I made sure my arm around her was secure as could be and that my balance wasn't any way compromised before I dipped her. She yelped at the unexpectedness of losing her gravity, but my hold around her was firm, and I trailed my other hand across her thigh, tugging her foot off the ground so I could lower her further. When her nails jabbed into my back I leaned over her and pressed my lips on hers. She tasted like raindrops, which wasn't surprising seeing the amount of water that dropped off my hair down to her face and trailed down between our faces. I drank it off her lips as if I'd been parched for days, stuck in that desert she so willingly wished to be born in.

I wasn't cold anymore, and Haylee was no longer nervous. I knew it because she kissed me back fervently as if she was as thirsty for my touch as I was for hers.

"Do you like the rain now?" I asked huskily after I'd pulled her up straight again and let her find her balance.

"No, not really." Haylee laughed. "But I like you."

That was even better.

Like a broken radio

With every passing day, I was falling deeper in love with Haylee. It was impossible to forget how little time we had together when the weekend came, and my grandmother reminded me of it during our video call.

We were making *braciole* and rice, and Haylee was rather happily pounding on the sirloin slices to make them equally thick before I filled them up with a breadcrumb mix and rolled them up. That was when *Nonni* quite accidentally dropped the news I should've had the guts to relay weeks ago.

"*Fagiolo*, this time next week we cook together here," she said with a bright smile on her face while wrapping her own breadcrumb mix into sirloin pieces.

My stomach hollowed out. It couldn't have been this soon. Where had the time gone?

Haylee's mallet stopped mid-strike, and she turned to look at me.

"What did she say?" she asked tentatively.

My face gave it away. I gripped at the meatroll in front of me hard enough to squish it in half as Haylee's expression began to match mine.

"Luca is coming home next week," *Nonna* said cheerily, not paying attention to the screen and the way I shared a pained look with Haylee.

Her eyes glittered, but she set her jaw and swallowed hard. "When were you going to tell me?"

"Red Cheeks—"

Haylee shook her head. She placed the meat mallet carefully on the counter top and stepped away from it. "Luca, when?"

She'd taken to calling me that when we were with my family or after a heated kissing session. It would come out breathless then and drive me absolutely insane. Now though? It sounded chipped, harsh. I deserved it.

I dragged my fingers through my hair. "I thought there was more time."

"This is not—I can't—Please?"

My family was now most certainly focussed on their screen, but all I cared about was the desperation on Haylee's face and what I could do to make it go away. My own emotions were tumbling towards heartbreak real fast, and I had to stop that line of thought while I still could.

I took a step toward Haylee, and she stumbled backward as if my proximity would make whatever she felt worse. Much worse. I would make it better. I would show her I could make it better.

"Haylee, I love you."

She stopped in her retreat, staring at me, dumbfounded. Then she shook her head again.

"No," she whispered.

"Yes, I do."

"You can't just say it like that."

"Yes, I can, because it's true."

Tears rolled down her cheeks, but she didn't step away from me when I breached the space between us and pulled her into my arms.

"I've wanted to tell you I'm in love with you for a while now," I murmured against her curls as she buried her face in my shoulder. "It wasn't supposed to be like this."

"But you're leaving." She hiccuped adorably, and I squeezed her tighter in my arms.

"I don't want to go."

I had no idea I'd want to stay this badly until I started spending all my evenings with Haylee. I figured leaving would be hard, but getting to know her proved to me just how hard it was going to be. Her crying was absolutely devastating, further breaking my resolve.

"But you will go," she said quietly.

I swallowed. "I have the plane ticket."

Haylee nodded and pulled away from me. I released her with a heavy heart. "Were you going to tell me?"

It would've been better if she was angry, if her question was biting. I could have dealt with that. But she asked it quietly, her voice hitching. It outright wrecked me.

"I was working up the courage."

I know I should've said it from the get go. I knew I was leaving before Haylee was even ready to step into a relationship. I knew it before I kissed her. From the very start. I should've put a stop to this and told her we were likely not going to work out, not because I didn't want her, but because I would be across the ocean. In a week. In only a week.

"You are the bravest person I know," Haylee whispered.

Meaning: How come I didn't have the courage to tell her I was leaving? She was right, of course. Not telling her was one of the dumbest things I could've done, but I wasn't lying when I said time got away from me. It moved too fast. I hadn't realized I'd be gone *this* soon.

I rubbed my face. This was not the way love was supposed to go. Yet somehow, I always ended up here, on the side where bliss turned sour. Falling always ended with a crash and broken limbs.

"I need to go." Haylee wiped her hands in her skirt and began backing away again.

"Please, don't go," I begged. "We can talk about this. Please. I don't want to lose you. I love you. Haylee, I love you."

She stopped. "Would you stay if I asked you to?"

I should've said yes in a heartbeat. It was the only right answer, but I hesitated. I'd be starting a new project back home. I'd signed that contract before I even knew Haylee. My rental agreement would end together with my employment in Lewis & Walker Law Group, so would my visa. None of it changed how much I wished I could stay.

"Anything." Haylee sniffed. "You said anything I asked."

"I want to stay. I want it more than anything."

"But you won't."

It hurt to see her like this. Her shoulders slumped, resigned. Tears running down her face. It had been raining endlessly this week, but no downpour ever hit me this hard. In fact, after Thursday, I'd looked at the rain with a new appreciation. Not today.

"Can I please come and hug you?" I asked.

Haylee didn't reply, but she didn't move away when I approached her either. I stopped in front of her, wiping tears from her cheeks. She didn't react at all. It's as if she was building a wall, and with every brick, her resolve hardened, and a bit of numbness replaced the hurt splayed all over her face.

I pulled her into my arms gently. She sighed and leaned into me.

"I love you," I repeated. I couldn't seem to stop now that I'd said it. I needed her to understand.

"What was this all for, Luke?"

I kissed the top of her head, smelling the now familiar coconut. "You are so special, Haylee."

"Why did you do this to me?"

I squeezed her tighter to me as my vision blurred. "We can make it work."

"I fell for it," she whispered. "Somehow I always do."

"I am not playing," I said tightly. "I love you. We can make it work. Haylee, we can. If you want, please, listen to me. I want to give you everything, but I need to go back to Colorado. My lease is expiring, and I have a project there—Haylee?"

Her fist pounded against my chest as if it was the mallet and I was the sirloin. "You already knew. Before you asked me out, you already knew!"

I'd thought her anger would be easier to take, but when she raised her voice it pierced through me even worse.

"Why?" she cried.

I did not let her escape my embrace. I needed to feel her warmth, I just hoped deep down she wanted me to hold her, too. She was fighting me, though.

"Because I knew I would love you," I told her. "I knew you would steal my heart, and I couldn't not be with you."

"But you're leaving!! No matter what I say, you're leaving anyway."

"And I'm telling you, we can make it work. Long distance. Please, we can make it work. I love you."

Fuck, I was a broken radio. I would be broken, period, if she refused to hear me out. She struggled less, so I repeated it again, "I love you, Haylee."

She slumped against me, sobbing. After much too long, she finally whispered, "I want to believe you."

Somehow, I managed to get Haylee to stay, but she didn't hammer the meat happily any longer. She was hitting it as if she wished it was my face. I wished it was my face, too. Getting pounded at would've felt better than the stiff shoulder she was giving me. But she was still here. At least, she was still here.

My grandmother gave me a lecture when we settled back to cooking together. I deserved that.

"*Fagiolo*, are you even listening? That's why you have a problem now. You don't listen to your *Nonni*."

I sighed. "I heard you."

She clicked her tongue and kept muttering under her breath.

I turned my attention to Haylee, who was living her emotions out on a piece of meat. "I think this one has had enough already."

She kept hitting it.

"Red Cheeks?"

She gave the sirloin another thump, then dropped the mallet.

"Sorry," she muttered. "I don't like feeling this way. Distract me."

"Okay." I reached out and took her hands in mine. Her skin was so soft I rubbed my thumb over it to memorize the feeling. Then I brought them up to my lips and kissed the back of both of her hands. When she didn't pull away, I leaned in and kissed her lips.

Kissing her was bliss. I could forget all the time we didn't have. And when I came up for air, she gave me a small smile, which was better than a frown. I'd take any kind of smile any day over a frown.

Haylee licked her lips and gave her head a slight shake. "You're not a master distractor, that's for sure."

"No?" I asked, slightly amused. "I'll show you."

I wrapped my arms around her and hoisted her up on the counter right next to the meat rolls. She squealed when I found a ticklish spot on her neck and blew air on it before planting a kiss there and trailing more kisses all the way up to her lips. She was panting by the time I reached her mouth and sucked her lower lip between mine.

I looked her straight in the eyes and said, "I love you," again.

Haylee closed her eyes and squirmed a little before replying so quietly I almost didn't hear it at all. "I love you, too."

My heart soared. Those four words were everything.

"Thank you." I hummed, pulling her in for another kiss.

"For what?" she asked breathlessly after I released her lips. "I don't have much of a choice in the matter to be honest."

"Thank you anyway."

"After all, you're perfect, Luca."

I shook my head. "I'm far from perfect."

"But we will make it work," she whispered my own words back to me. "Right?"

"Yes, we will."

Knuckles and pain

"What does *fagiolo* mean?" I asked as we sat down to eat our hard-earned meal. Four hours was way too long to be in the kitchen, no matter what the Ombrello family said about the best things needing time. Our argument didn't help, of course.

I wasn't quite over being mad at Luke about leaving so suddenly, but there was nothing I could do about it just then. Or at all, really. He'd clearly shown that his offered 'anything' did not apply to that situation. I either trusted that he meant it when he said he loved me or prepared for my stupid lovestruck heart to get hurt. I couldn't quite make myself rush out of his flat when he begged me to stay so here we were.

"Ahh," Luke chuckled. "It means 'bean'."

I attempted to raise my eyebrow at him but didn't quite succeed. He laughed, reaching out to rub his thumb over the back of my hand, before he settled back in his stool.

"There's a story for it, of course."

I stabbed my fork into the meat roll before looking at him again. "Will you tell me, bean-boy?"

He laughed again, harder this time. "God, I love you, Haylee."

Every time he said it my heart tried to sprout wings and flap around like a bird. My stomach tickled with butterflies. Everything else stopped as if needing me to hyper-focus on the words and the way his expression softened as he pronounced them. The more he said it, the easier it was for me to believe it.

The first time, it had come out rasped, then desperate. He'd said it softly. He'd whispered it in my ear. He'd given those three words depth each and every time as if the emotion itself was carried in his voice. I believed him because I wanted to. I believed because I needed to. Because if it wasn't true, I would not come back from this unscathed.

"I was ten when the nickname stuck," Luke said, bringing me out of my reverie. "We were making *Pasta e Fagioli*, a bean and pasta soup. It's an easy recipe and usually doesn't take too long to make."

Which in Luke's dictionary meant it wasn't a three-hour cooking party, but likely still took longer than the thirty minutes I tended to dedicate to meal making.

"*Nonni* sent me to grab the beans from the pantry while she prepared the vegetables. Neither of us realised that the bag of beans was on the higher shelf, and while I was tall for my age, I couldn't quite reach them without climbing on the lower two shelves and balancing on my tiptoes. Even then, I barely grazed the sack with my fingers. The act of even trying dipped the entire shelving unit, and it fell over with the beans scattering all over the floor. I was lucky to not get crushed under the weight. While we cleaned up most of the mess, we kept finding beans in the pantry, and some even around the house for weeks afterwards. The nickname never went away after that. Haven't managed to outlive it since."

I bit at my lower lip, trying to contain my smile. "So, would you say you are full of beans?"

Luke raised an eyebrow. "How long were you waiting to say that one?"

I grinned. "From the moment you said 'bean'."

We shared other childhood stories after that. Me and Glen getting in trouble together ever since we met in kindergarten, and Luke growing up at his family farm. We were so different in every level. He'd grown up fast, while I'd been a bit of a brat for the longest time. He followed rules and always listened to his parents, while I dodged being grounded by sneaking out and staying at Glen's until my mum organised a search party in her panic. He went after the girl he thought he loved, while I avoided all of my highschool crushes like the plague. Luke getting his heart broken, me getting myself broadcasted all over the internet when I finally thought I was ready for something— I didn't tell him, of course. It would've been the perfect opportunity, but I didn't tell him. I just couldn't.

While we talked for hours after we'd finished eating, we focussed so deeply on the past that we said nothing about the future. Not a thing. And while I was avoiding bringing up Luke's leaving again, I expected him to at least offer his ideas about making it work, because I saw the distance as an unbreachable obstacle.

Talking to Luke was nice, don't get me wrong. It was very, very nice, but each and every time I got worried, or scared or lost in my stupid trauma, it took touch to bring me out of it. Luke brushing my tears away, hugging me, kissing me. And distance made all of that impossible. How was I to cope with any irrational fears—that were bound to become my constant tormentor—if I couldn't look at him across the kitchen island and see the spark in his eyes when he stared back at me? Urghhh.

"Let me walk you to your apartment." Like every evening since we first kissed, those were the final words from Luke, right before a kiss goodnight at the door and "I will dream about you."

Tonight wasn't really a night to change that habit either, even if I felt braver after our love confessions. He wasn't going to take advantage of me, knowing all too well he wasn't going to be here by the end of next week, and I wasn't going to throw myself at him for the same exact reason. I just hoped we would have a chance to talk about it before he left.

I also hoped that the heartache I already felt would go away and let me enjoy the kiss goodnight. For in that moment we were breathing the same air. We were as close as we could be without ripping each other's clothes off. His lips were worshiping mine, slow and needy, before he pulled away and rested his forehead against mine.

"I love you," he rasped. His eyes were hooded, and his breath tickled my lips. His fingers gripped my hair, keeping us locked in this moment.

I shivered against him and wrapped my arms tighter around his back. "I don't want you to go."

For a moment, we just stood in the hallway, wrapped in each other.

"The day I leave you, I will be a dead man walking. I will not leave you, Haylee."

It is safe to say that Glen and I were not squealing on the couch together that evening, even after I recounted all the times Luke had said 'I love you' to me. It was exactly ten, if you were wondering.

"What are you going to do?" Glen asked.

I shrugged pathetically. "I really don't know."

"Maybe you can make it work."

I laughed dryly. "Maybe you're right."

And then I fell asleep, crying on her shoulder.

I avoided Luke on Tuesday. I wasn't quite sure what I would say, and my emotions were unbelievably unstable. It was better to eat ice cream for dinner and mope on the sofa with Glen while watching Dirty Dancing. Okay, maybe it wasn't better, but it's what I ended up doing anyway.

I was more than ready to take the world by its horns on Wednesday, but a girl in Turtle Bay called in sick, and I got stuck with the late shift. I'd already punished myself with a bloody good workout before I heard the news and stood behind the counter, wobbling on my feet when the time came.

The restaurant was buzzing with activity, as was normal for that hour, and the bar side was beginning to get rowdy. I counted the minutes in my head until the end of the shift, with my tip in my pocket.

I didn't enjoy waitressing. That fact became clearer as I was waiting for the food for table five and checking the progress of tables seven and ten. Table six had just sat down and stared at their menu with boredom. My feet hurt from standing, and my stomach growled since I'd yet to have my own dinner. It would likely be something gross either way. Who knew I'd become so dependent on Luke's cooking in such a short time? Thinking about fixing something up for myself made my stomach roll, because I knew—I knew!—nothing I made would ever compare to his meals.

That train of thought got depressing really quickly, so I headed over to table six to see if they'd decided on what they wanted. I stood there blabbering out the specials when the door to the restaurant opened, and a group of men pushed through. Five of them. They weren't big or anything, but they were cocky and loud. In fact, they walked in as if they owned the place, but that wasn't what got me hiding behind my notebook. Very small, very uncovering notebook. It was only meant to scribble down orders, after all.

Smartphones in their hands pointed every which way, capturing the buzzing restaurant on camera, because why the hell not? Snickering followed them to table nine, and I squeezed my eyes shut while taking deep breaths. I already hated today with vengeance, now I wished I was the one who had called in sick, not the girl I covered for.

I rushed to take the order of the couple by table six and hurried to the kitchen as if the room had caught fire.

Ripping the scribbles out of my notebook, I slipped it among the previous ones.

I hid in the midst of clanking utensils and dishes and shouted commands longer than was totally necessary while trying to get my heartbeat to slow down. No real luck with that, but at least table five's food was ready by the time I finished my breathing exercises.

I walked back into the restaurant, carrying three plates, with my head held high, hoping to manifest the confidence I didn't really feel. It was hopeless, really. By the time I placed the plates down and grabbed menus for the group of influencers, my stomach was tied in knots.

I gripped the booklets between my fingers and kept telling myself to breathe. I would survive this. Worse things happened in the world than serving the person who had ruined my life. This was fine. He probably didn't remember me anyway. It was two years ago, and we hadn't seen each other since. While Jay had been a pretty significant incident in my life, I most likely was a little bit of fun in his, and he'd probably moved on to tormenting some other poor girl. Yeah, that must've been it. It would be fine.

When I reached the fateful table, my knuckles had turned white, and my face was likely just as pale. I swallowed hard and placed the first two menus down without anyone paying much attention to me. When I handed Jay one, his eyes widened, and my lungs stopped working.

He remembered me after all.

"Haylee? I didn't know you worked here."

Perfectly normal reaction. Shrug it off.

I started to do just that when one of the other men raised his phone at me, and I froze. Not a normal reaction. Not normal at all!

"Haylee?" he snickered. "I remember this one."

I didn't remember him, but I hadn't really known the entire group. Oh no, I'd been pretty focussed on Jay alone, a lot of good that did me.

"Tell us about your life after fame," the man behind his phone said.

The rest of the group took greater interest in me after that, and even when Jay tried to push the one pointing his camera at me to stop filming, there was no way that was going to happen.

"Her mother is a solicitor," he gritted through his teeth, but even that was brushed off as not important. Jay would know. He had to deal with my mum quite a bit after the disastrophe. I'd dealt with my mum often enough to know it wasn't a pleasant experience. Especially when you lost every single argument with the woman. Jay had most certainly lost. His friend with the camera had no such close encounters with my mother, however. He also had no care in the world, it seemed.

I dropped the rest of the menus in the corner of their table, backing away from the scene. I had to go. I couldn't do this. I needed a moment, or seven, to breathe and hide. Or better yet, run. I just had to get out of here. Out from the limelight. Bloody hell!

"I—I will be back for the drink order," I croaked.

I hadn't even paid attention to the door while stuck in my irrational fear, nor did I notice it was Luke who'd entered, or that he was standing right behind me before I stepped right into him, and his arms came around to steady me. All I knew was that I was locked in a tight embrace now, and there was no way out. All I knew was that I was going to be embarrassed all over again, and there was nothing I could do to stop this situation from unravelling. This would be so much worse than the previous time; we were in a public place this time.

I yelped, shrill and clipped. Now, I held the attention of more than just table nine. Now, every single table I'd served—and the ones that weren't mine—turned their gazes my way.

I had to hide. I had to hide. I had to—but the camera was still pointed at me, and the snickering only grew more prominent in my ears.

The man behind me leaned closer to my ear, his breath brushing against my neck. I shivered.

"Relax, Red Cheeks," he murmured against my ear.

Luke. It was Luke. He wouldn't do any of the things I imagined happening just then. Luke was safe. Goodness gracious, he was safe right? I didn't know anymore. All I knew was that no words would be able to make me relax. Even after I recognised him, I was tight as a bow string.

"Luke," I gasped. "What are you doing here?"

He was better in the kitchen than any chef in town. I didn't think he ate outside at all. I couldn't see his expression, but the longer the influencers kept laughing the more worried I became. Was this a set up? Was this how my heart would get ripped apart?

Breathe. I just needed to breathe through this.

Luke turned his head to whisper "I missed you" in my ear, then nudged me behind him, and all I saw was the back of his jacket.

Somehow, it was easier to breathe with Luke standing between me and my past.

"I suggest you delete whatever video you just recorded, and we will not have a problem." Luke's voice came out in a growl a second after he'd been all but gentle with me.

"Chill, mate, this has nothing to do with you." Jay held his hands out and gave a fake laugh. So much for being afraid of my mother. "We're just joking. Right, Haylee?"

I stayed silent and rested my forehead between Luke's shoulder blades, taking deep breaths and pretending to be anywhere else.

"That's where you're mistaken," Luke drawled out slowly, his voice dropping an octave. I gripped his jacket and kept gasping for air. "You see, Jay—is it?—wherever Haylee is concerned has everything to do with me."

"Do I know you?" Jay's humourless chuckle reached through the bubble I was trying to create around myself.

"No, but I know you, and to be honest, I really do not like you. If you don't want this to escalate, I suggest you do what I say."

"What are you going to do? It's five against one," one of the other men pointed out.

"Why don't you test me and find out," Luke growled.

I squeezed my eyes shut. "It's okay. I'm fine. Let's just go."

Luke didn't hear me or chose not to hear me. He made a go at the phone in the cameraman's hands and managed to take the influencer by surprise.

"Cunt!" the man shouted, but Luke's fingers were already expertly sliding over the screen and deleting any video evidence of me.

He was quick, too. Very quick. The man hadn't even gotten out of his seat when Luke dropped his phone on top of the menus I'd left behind. But the phone owner was not going to leave it at that. The moment he got his feet under him, his fist was heading right at Luke's face. I saw it happen, because despite having gripped Luke's jacket with all my might, the moment he grabbed for the phone, he'd stepped closer to the table and away from me. Now, I was gripping at nothing but air and letting out another silly yelp.

Luke dodged the blow effortlessly, driven by either skill or a sense of justice. His responding blow smacked against his opponent's nose, and a crack resonated through the entire silenced restaurant.

I backed away further as the other four men all rushed to their feet to retaliate on behalf of the one now gripping his bleeding nose and shouting curses left and right. I bumped into one of the tables. Twelve or eleven, not that it mattered. I rocked it hard enough to spill a pint of beer and drown a woman's meal in the residue. The glass itself rolled off the table and shattered on the floor.

I wasn't the only one yelling after that, but I was the only one crying. I was sure of it. A wave crashed over me, and I sagged against the table, gripping at its edge as it took me under.

Through my blurry vision, I could see Luke decimating the four men fighting him, catching one in the cheek and knocking him out cold, right after his elbow left another crouched over and gasping. He took a hit to the stomach from the third before the man ended up splayed over their table. He grabbed around the top of it, fingers closing around a salt shaker before the thing went flying across the restaurant, missing Luke by a long shot. The pepper followed suit, much closer to the target, but not by much. The next thing to fly was the candle from the centre table, and that came out of nowhere, slamming into my face like a rocket before shattering at my feet. I didn't see how exactly things stopped flying with my hand slamming up to my face, as if that would somehow stop the burn of the impact. When I did manage to look over at the scene, only Jay was left standing, his hands up in surrender the instant Luke's wrath focussed solely on him.

"Okay, I catch your drift, mate. We're cool."

Luke stepped over the man he'd elbowed in the stomach, now kneeling at his feet, to get closer to Jay. He grabbed him by his collar, and Jay's eyes widened, but he kept his hands up in surrender.

"Wanker," the one with a broken nose gritted but didn't move to help his friend out.

"We are not cool," Luke said, low and threatening. "We will never be cool after what you did to Haylee. And while violence is unbecoming of me. You. Deserve. Worse."

Before Jay could move his hands to protect his pretty face, a fist slammed into his eye socket. Jay swung away from Luke, only to be pulled back by his collar and meeting another blow, lower against his cheek this time. He swayed on his feet but didn't quite fall fast enough to avoid a third hit, splitting his lips.

"I fucking wish I could feed you your own balls," Luke spat, letting go of Jay's shirt to watch him collapse to the ground. "Stay away from Haylee."

Sweat and beer

My fist throbbed. I shook it, taking in the damage I caused. My eyes caught on Haylee pressed against a dripping table, its occupants throwing tissues at the mess in an attempt to contain it. One of her hands gripped the edge of the table while the other held onto her cheek like it hurt. Tears ran down her cheeks, leaving wet lines in their wake.

I forgot all about my own pain as I strolled across the short distance. Haylee shuffled away from me, shards of glass crunching under her feet.

"Haylee." I softened my voice. "Red Cheeks, I won't hurt you. You know that, right?"

Her eye, the one that wasn't covered by her hand, was wide. Her lips trembled, and she whimpered.

I had gone to their apartment after cooking today to see if Haylee would like some dinner. It hurt to think that she was avoiding me. Glen was more than happy to take the food I'd brought before announcing Haylee wasn't home. I wasn't fully certain what exactly stopped me from going back to my apartment and eating in solitude, but here I was.

Taking a step closer to a shivering Haylee, my hands held out carefully to show I wasn't a threat. I pulled my jacket off when I was close enough and draped it across her shoulders. Her shivering didn't stop. It wasn't likely to be from the cold.

"Hey, beautiful," I whispered. "Let me take you out of here."

She gave the slightest of nods that had relief washing over me, and I wrapped an arm around her, guiding her away from the glass shards and prying eyes.

A woman called after us. "Excuse me! Is anyone going to clean this up?"

I didn't fucking care.

I wanted to march Haylee right out the door and get her as far away from here as possible, but she steered us toward the counter, then behind it and through a personnel-only door.

A chef looked up from placing a plate under a heat lamp. "What the bloody hell is going on at the front of the house?"

Haylee shook her head.

"Ice," she said quietly, dropping her hand from her cheek. "I need ice."

Underneath her eye, a blueish, raised patch was working on welding her eye shut. A roar I was barely able to contain rose from my throat, and my hands balled into fists. Fuck, I wanted to punch the lot again.

"Bollocks," the chef cursed. He shuffled around before a package of frozen peas flew across the kitchen. "Catch."

I caught it without a hitch and moved in front of Haylee to apply it gently to her bruise. Her sharp inhale and a whimper had me gritting my teeth.

"I'm sorry. I'm so sorry," I muttered over and over again, pressing the peas to her cheek with one hand and smoothing the hair with the other.

Standing this close to her, the smell of sweat and beer assaulted my senses. Despite that, I leaned in and brushed a kiss on Haylee's forehead.

"There was a fight," I told anyone listening in the kitchen. "It's resolved now, but I am taking Haylee home.

Make whatever arrangements you need, but she is not staying."

"I get you," the chef replied, already calling someone over to take care of the plate he'd finished and whatever else needed to be done. "Feel free to take the peas with you."

I nodded. "Thanks. I think we will."

After Haylee had regained a semblance of calm, I took her out the back door, heading straight for the subway station. It was on days like today that I despised the traffic here the most. Look left, look right, all in the wrong order, cars in the wrong lanes, everything just wrong in definition. I didn't drive here for that exact reason; it was messing with my head, even after six months. Tonight, it was infuriating me.

I had to stay calm for Haylee's sake. I'd already lashed out once. It wasn't a good look, and she was clearly scared, whether it was me or the situation itself. I didn't need to give her a reason to decide it was me, after all.

When we were seated on the subway train Haylee finally looked at me. Her voice was so quiet and fragile; it shouldn't have cut through me, but it did anyway. "You know."

I thought back to everything that had transpired in the restaurant and what I'd said exactly. She must have meant what happened with Jay all those years ago.

I let out a shaky breath. "I know."

"How?"

I rubbed my face. "It's a long story. One where I become the culprit and break like a dozen company rules just because I was curious. I shouldn't have looked at those files. I know that, but I can't unsee them now. I'm so sorry, Red Cheeks. You shouldn't have had to endure any of that."

Haylee dropped her eyes to her lap, and we listened to the female voice welcoming us to the next station.

"Company rules," she muttered.

"Lewis & Walker Law Group. That's where my current project is. Or well, ends." I swallowed. Haylee was still staring at her lap, but she gasped at the name.

"When did you see the files?" she whispered.

I squeezed my eyes shut, taking a battered breath. "Before The Notebook."

Haylee's head whipped my way, and she moaned in pain when her bruised cheek got pressed harder against the bag of peas she was holding to it.

"What?" she gaped at me.

I searched her eyes, or the one that wasn't covered by the ice bag. Was it bewilderment? If so, I could work with that.

"When I'm angry or frustrated, I tend to bake. Seeing what he did to you—" I took a deep breath and pried my fingers loose from the fist they formed of their own accord. "I was very angry and very frustrated, hence the calzones."

"Oh my God." Haylee hid her face in her hands—well, what wasn't already hidden by the bag of peas, that is. "Shoot me!"

"It's okay, Haylee. Or well, it isn't, really. Fuck." I groaned, covering her hand with mine and trying to pull it away from her face to get her to look at me. She didn't budge, so I wrapped my arms around her instead. "What I mean is, it doesn't change anything for me."

"Is that why you've been so forbearing?"

"Forbear—Haylee, I would've waited for you whether I knew it or not. I saw how you reacted to my teasing. I felt your heartbeat and heard your raspy breathing. I might've not understood why, but I would not have pressured you, either."

She was still not looking at me.

"I'm sorry about the way I found out. I'm not sorry that I know. It doesn't change the way I feel about you."

Several more stops passed by, and Haylee didn't say a word. She had shut down completely, barely registering that we were on the subway to begin with. I resigned to staying quiet, as well. When our stop came, I coaxed her gently to her feet and helped her off the carriage. I kept my arm around her as we approached the apartment building, avoiding the stupid traffic as best we could. Haylee wasn't paying attention to it at all; it was up to me to get us safely inside.

I didn't even bother pushing the button for my own floor when we reached the elevator. She might not argue with me, but it was clear she would rather go home than to my place. We rode up in complete silence.

Once behind their door, I looked at Haylee, but she didn't make a move to get her keys, so I knocked instead. Of all of the times I'd stood here waiting for the door to be opened, this one must've been the worst of all. Not nervous. Not jittery. Scared for my heart—that was more like it. Scared for Haylee's, too.

I'd screwed up already before today. I just kept screwing up.

The door opened to Glen in a t-shirt and pajama bottoms. "Why are you knocking when you have the key?" she asked before taking a proper look at us. Her tone changed immediately after that. "Hallie! What happened?"

She pulled us across the threshold and sat us down on the vintage couch.

"My bag is still at Turtle Bay," Haylee muttered, and I cursed myself. I hadn't even checked if she had everything when I rushed her out of the place.

"That would be my fault. I will go get it for you." I stood to do just that, but Glen pushed me back on the couch.

"Nay, you're going to tell me what the hell happened."

I settled down, pulling Haylee into my arms. She didn't resist. Much. I breathed in the scent of her, mixed with still very prominent beer. We needed a shower. I couldn't quite convince my brain that us having it together would never happen before I imagined just that.

"Jay happened," I said softly. "And then I mopped the floor with him and his camera-wielding friends. I didn't even see Haylee get hit. Which one was it, Red Cheeks?"

She melted into my embrace and pressed her unharmed cheek against my shoulder. She trusted me enough to relax. That was good. That was better than nothing.

"The one throwing things off the table," she murmured.

"Shit."

"It was the candle."

I tightened my arms around her and dropped my face in her hair. "I should've stopped him before he got to that."

"You had four more to worry about."

"Two were already taken care of at that point. Plus the one with the broken nose. I should have got to him before he hit you."

"It's not your fault."

It felt like my fault. My failure. "I'm sorry," I said again. It was either that or "I love you." I had them both on repeat at this point.

"Let me get this straight," Glen said, seating herself on the coffee table in front of us. "You were at Turtle Bay with Jay the arsehole and his friends, and now they are what? Black-eyed and bleeding?"

"They were filming Haylee. I could not let them go," I admitted.

"You told him?" Glen exclaimed, looking at Haylee, who kept hiding her face on my shoulder. "I didn't think you would."

I cleared my throat. "Not exactly."

"Ugh, oh?" Glen crossed her arms in front of her, giving me a pointed look.

"Look, it doesn't matter how I found out. I'm just glad I was there."

"I think it matters," Glen threw back. "Doesn't it, Hallie?"

"He told me already," she mumbled into my shirt. "Besides, he saved me."

I kissed the top of her head. "You forgive me?"

She didn't reply right away, and I thought she never would. "You did save me," she repeated after a while.

"You're my Little Red-Cheeked Dancing Girl. I will always save you."

Escape the world

I called in sick on Thursday, both to the dance studio and Turtle Bay. I definitely looked it. I felt more dejected than ill, but I suppose depression was an ailment of its own.

Standing in front of the bathroom mirror, I prodded at the black eye still clearly visible. As if it would fade away during the night and make me forget my latest horror. Definitely still there and throbbing painfully. My poking made it sting even more.

Getting hit by candles was terrible. Thursdays were awful. Luke leaving in three days was outright rubbish. Ughh...

It wasn't only seeing Jay and the freakshow that made me feel so utterly miserable. I'd not handled it well, true. But Luke hadn't either. Hell, he'd gone berserker on the men to protect what? My honour? Nobody had ever stood up for me like that except for Glen.

I wanted to hate him for finding out about Jay, but it was impossible. I wanted to hate him for leaving, but I couldn't muster that either. Now I just wanted to be wrapped up in him and forget everything else. Three more days until that wasn't possible anymore.

I drew a heart on the misted-over mirror after my shower and wrote his name in it. Then stared at it for an eternity before I managed to snap out of it and wiped it away with a huff. My reflection hadn't gotten any cheerier since my previous peek at it, only cleaner perhaps.

Luke talked to his family across the ocean every week. Every single week, like clockwork. We would exchange phone numbers and do the same. We could text daily and have a video call on Sundays before they started cooking. It was not quite like an embrace or a kiss, but if we were both serious about it, we could make it work.

We could make it work, couldn't we? Yes, we could.

The distance between us would be measured by miles, not the level of intimacy. In the end, intimacy would win. God, he knew my best kept secret and didn't care. He'd seen through to the bottom of my heart—every broken piece—and still wanted me. I would not let him walk away without a fight.

I blow-dried my hair, rubbed oil into my curls, then stared at my black eye again. Not pretty, not even close. It looked horrific. Glen agreed once I came out of hiding and joined her in the kitchen.

"Yuck! That'll stop anyone from luring you into their bed," she commented. "That's still the plan, right?"

She was the one at the stove this time, since I'd given up on trying. Nothing healthy on the pan, either. It was pancakes. Knowing Glen, they were most likely sugar bombs, too. Today, I didn't really mind.

I huffed. "That was never the plan."

"Of course, it was. That's what the sexy lingerie is for, remember?" Glen gave me a pointed look. "The one that made you look like a goddess of desire and virtue."

"It did not."

"Oh, it did, trust me. And Luke will agree with me once he sees you in it."

I shook my head. "Only, I'm terrible at flirting and now also horrible to look at."

"We could try to cover that up a little."

Because that didn't scream: insecurities! Luke knew I had a black eye, hiding it would be—I don't know, it just didn't feel right.

"Um, no. Just forget about it. I just need his phone number, or email, or something." I rubbed my face—the side that didn't hurt to touch—and stuck my lower lip out like a child. "Actually, I haven't a clue what I'm doing."

Glen flipped a pancake before she turned towards me. "Yes, you do. You're going to put that lingerie we bought on and show up on Luke's doorstep tonight, and then you'll blow his mind."

"Or he'll blow mine."

"As long as someone gets blown, I think it'll go great."

An hysterical laugh bubbled out of my throat. "There are so many things wrong with this plan."

"You'll be brilliant." Glen dropped the pancake on my plate and started another one.

Tentatively, I ripped a strip from the corner and nibbled at it. Definitely sweeter that you'd expect, but edible. I squeezed some lemon juice on the rest to counter the sugar, then rolled it up, and bit into it like a sandwich.

"I should let you cook more often," I mumbled while chewing.

"No," Glen refused. "This is a one-time service because you are down. Once you're up and well again, you'll be back to making woks and whatnot."

"And whatnot," I parroted. "You hated all of those."

"You just need some practice. Just like with flirting." She flicked her hair over her shoulder and tapped a finger against her lips, then licked it. "And other things."

"Stop it!" I groaned. "I am not even in the same league as you when it comes to *other things*."

Glen laughed. "Like I said. Practice. I bet Luke will allow you to practice on him."

"What will you bet?"

Glen ignored my scrunched-up, focussed face as I tried to morph it into a semblance of raised eyebrows. It wasn't working. "Next month's rent?"

"I'll be paying for it anyway."

"Okay, fine. Cooking for the entire next week."

"Two," I countered.

"Fine," Glen huffed. "But you'd better work for it. Because if I hear you didn't even try, the deal is off."

"Fine."

When the clock hit six p.m., I was fidgeting behind Luke's door. The bra straps dug into my skin under my shirt wherever they touched it, and my knickers kept slipping between my butt cheeks, making me squirm even more. This was a horrible idea.

I knocked. Then bunched the edge of my skirt up in my fist as if that would help with the nerves. The skirt was Glen's idea. Easy access, she'd said. The breeze that touched my lower parts told me just how easy.

I released my fingers from my skirt and smoothed it out hurriedly when the door opened, and Luke stood on the other side. He was still wearing a button-up and slacks as if he hadn't had time to change yet. With his five o'clock shadow and hair ruffled up like he'd dragged his hand through it numerous times today, he looked like a wet dream. I'd had one of those. Or two. Maybe five. But now that I stood in front of him with the intention of making them true, I lost any semblance of confidence I might've gotten from Glen's peptalk.

"H-hi," I said, raising the hand that had just smoothed my skirt in a very unnecessary wave.

"Red Cheeks." Luke's mouth tugged up in a grin.

"Blueish," I sputtered, gesturing at the mark Glen didn't convince me to hide.

"Aah, you might be right." Luke opened the door wider and stepped aside. "Would you like to come in?"

I bit the inside of my cheek, nodding. His smile widened.

I shuffled closer, not sure what to do with my hands, or my eyes, or anything at all, really. *Just raise your feet*, I reminded myself as I stepped over the threshold. *Also breathe.* That was a pretty important one.

Do I kiss him now or later? I wasn't certain, so I faltered at the entrance, preventing the door from closing. *Do it,* I decided, breaching the gap between us and inhaling sharply before I planted a kiss on his lips. Luke's arm snaked around me instantaneously, pulling me closer as he took over and deepened the kiss. He manoeuvred us around enough to be able to close the door, then leaned his back against it, pulling me with him.

I could totally seduce him if that was how we said hello to each other. It would be a piece of cake just like Glen said. We'd need to talk at one point, but we could start with this.

I pressed closer to him, running my hands down his chest, to his sides, hoping to sneak my hands under his shirt. I didn't quite get that far when he flinched and grunted. I broke the kiss, attempting to step away as my stomach already filled with hot coals of embarrassment. Luke's hands still caged me in to his chest and held me firmly.

"What did I do?" I gasped. I needed to slow my breathing before I fainted.

"It wasn't you," Luke responded in a low rumble. "It's a bruise of my own."

I gaped at him. "What? Are you hurt? Why did you not tell me?"

"It's nothing."

"Clearly." I untangled myself from his embrace and crossed my arms. "Where is it?"

He held my gaze while pulling the hem of his shirt out of his slack and tugged it upwards. I meant to do it myself and lose the shirt completely, but his hands stopped as soon as they revealed a bruise on his otherwise smooth skin.

I bit my lip, flicking my eyes from his face to the bruise and back.

He dropped the shirt and shrugged. "It's nothing."

"Okay." I wasn't here to argue.

The moment had passed, and I backed away towards the kitchen, wiping my hands in my skirt.

Luke pushed away from the front door and followed me. "Will you be staying for dinner?"

"If that's all right. I wouldn't want to intrude."

"You are more than welcome, Haylee. I wasn't sure if we were good after...everything. I'm glad you're here."

We reached the open living room, and I stood in the middle of it, wringing my hands in front of me.

"I wanted to ask for your phone number," I mumbled. "Before we forgot and never heard from each other again."

"I wouldn't have left without a way to contact you," Luke replied, pulling out his phone, unlocking it, and dropping it into my fidgety hands. "I still have your dad's, though I doubt he'd be of any use after last time."

I smiled, typing my number into his phone, then hitting the call button to have his. "I don't know. You can be quite charming if you want to."

"Is that so?" Luke leaned against the kitchen island, studying me.

"I would know."

Luke hummed, and I looked up from saving his number onto my phone.

"I'm so glad you are here," he repeated his earlier statement. Amusement faded into something deeper and softer. If I had to put a name to it I'd call it love.

I gripped both of our phones in my hands and rubbed my lips together. "You're not getting rid of me that easily."

"I would hope not."

Silence. Staring. Shuffling feet. Mine, of course, since Luke didn't drag his across the floor but walked with confidence. I stood in front of him again, handing his phone back to him.

"Will you call?" I asked quietly, feeling more nervous than the question required. It wasn't even 'Will you strip for me' or anything. Yet, I felt more vulnerable asking it. I probably would have choked on my words had I asked him to lose his clothes.

"Every day," Luke responded without skipping a beat. "For as long as you want me to."

"I really want you to."

Luke reached out and brushed a strand of my hair away from my face. "Then I will."

I nodded and swallowed. The following silence was heavier. Luke's fingers skidded gently across my cheek, thumb caressing my lower lip until it parted. I closed my eyes, memorising the sensation.

"You are so gorgeous, Haylee."

"I look terrible."

"No, you don't."

I peeked at him through half-lidded eyes. "Make me believe it."

Luke's lips twitched, and his arm slid down my neck, over my shoulder, trailing across my back. All the way down until it stopped on my hip, his other hand joining on the other side. He hoisted me up and swung me onto the kitchen island, nudging me to stand between my legs.

His breath tickled my lips. "Believe it, Haylee. I've never seen anything more beautiful."

I blushed and gripped his shoulders. "You've never looked in the mirror, then."

Luke nipped at my lower lip, and my breath hitched. "Every day," he said between kisses. "Doesn't even—" more small kisses, "— compare to—" he slid his tongue into my mouth for a long, slow taste, " —the sight of you."

I wasn't even sure what we were talking about at this point. It was a good thing there was a lot less talking and a lot more kissing after that. I allowed my hands to wander while his remained on the worktop on either side of me. He didn't stop me when I started unbuttoning his shirt or pulling it open and off his shoulders, which I achieved with a lot of fumbling several reassuring kisses later. I didn't stop him when he allowed his hand to rest right where my shirt met my skirt and trailed a line on my skin. Then, a while later, his hand slipped under the fabric and caressed its way up my stomach.

My heart hammered in my chest and thumped in my neck and echoed in my ears. It was everywhere all at once. Everywhere. *Everywhere.*

I kissed Luke harder, hoping to distract myself when his fingers stopped at the thin layer of my bra. He couldn't feel the lacy straps yet—just the wire keeping it all in place— but he already groaned my name through our next kiss.

"Is this okay?" he gasped. "Can I touch you?"

"Mmmmhh."

His fingers didn't move; his lips did, pulling away from mine. I swallowed and wondered if I had done something wrong already.

He searched my eyes, looking for that confirmation. "Was that a yes, gorgeous?"

"Yes," I gasped.

Slowly, he trailed a line over the curve or my breast, eyes widening and mouth falling open. "Are you wearing this for me, Haylee?"

"Yes," I gasped again, burning up under the intensity of his gaze.

"You know I'm leaving on Sunday," he murmured. "I didn't think we'd—I wasn't sure it would be right for you." He cleared his throat and tried again, his hand now cupping the entirety of my boob. "I don't want to take advantage of you, Red Cheeks."

"You won't." My head was swimming, and he hadn't even laid his eyes on the laces yet. All I'd done was rub my hands over his bare back and chest. "You'll call me every day, remember."

He kissed me again, more firmly this time. With fire. Passionate and deep, like he was trying to leave his mark on my lips. I moaned against his mouth when his fingers did something incredible around my boob. His other hand, missing out on the action, began tugging my shirt up until it was bunched up under my chin. Luke shifted and dropped his eyes to what he'd uncovered.

"Haylee," he groaned. "Oh God, Haylee. You're incredible."

I squirmed under his gaze.

He met my eyes, his now hooded with lust. "Gorgeous," he whispered. "Absolutely fucking gorgeous."

Oh God, indeed.

Ohh... what... again?

"Luk-ahh." That's what. Or who. Or why. It was all him and his lips and his fingers rubbing circles across my skin. And he wasn't quite everywhere I wanted him. Everywhere. *Everywhere*.

We jerked apart at a loud pounding on the door, our heads flipping towards the noise. I froze. Luke smoothes my hair and kissed the top of my head, pulling my shirt back in place before he stepped away completely.

"I'll go see what that's about," he said huskily.

I remained frozen on top of the kitchen counter, telling myself to breathe. Once Luke disappeared into the hallway, I ran a hand over my chest, checking if everything was truly covered. Then, for no other reason than my unfathomable fear, I scanned the room for cameras. There weren't any that I could see.

I heard the click of the door opening.

"Shit!" Glen's unmistakable voice exclaimed from the other side. "I'm sorry, very bad timing I see. But I freaked out and need to talk to Hallie."

I slid myself off the counter, stepping on the shirt I'd rid Luke of. True, he wasn't wearing one now.

"It's okay. Come on in, she's in the kitchen."

Glen rushed past him and into the living room. Her eyes scanned the place, and her mouth did a little inaudible 'whoa' before she saw me. Even after that little scan, her eyes looked worried. Her fingers danced around her thigh, crunching a piece of paper between them.

"Are you all right?" I asked as she stopped almost exactly where I had earlier, but kept bouncing on her feet.

Glen shook her head, narrowing her eyes on me. "Are you?"

"You scared me," I said quietly, trying to loosen the stiffness out of my shoulders. "You know how it is."

My eyes flicked to Luke hovering by the entrance, still gloriously shirtless. I hadn't really had a chance to look at him before, but his muscled chest looked as good as it had felt under my fingers. The bruise under his ribcage appeared bigger than he'd shown and was the same colour as my black eye.

Glen shook me out of my admiration. "God, Haylee, I'm sorry. I didn't meant to—"

"I'm okay. I really am. Tell me what happened."

Glen's hand shook as she raised it to hold the sheet out to me. I snatched it from her fingers and smoothed it out so I could read what was on it.

My eyes widened as I took in the words, and I gasped. "No, they wouldn't. That's blasphemous!"

I didn't even notice Luke coming to stand next to me to read over my shoulder.

"I don't know what to do," Glen said. "I need your mother's help. I wouldn't ask if it wasn't critical, you know that. I also know you're not really on speaking terms right now. But who else can help me with this?"

"What's A&R?" Luke asked, and I almost jumped out of my skin.

"Antiques & Restoration," Glen explained.

"She used to work there until they went bankrupt. Didn't even pay her last salary."

Luke's low hum vibrated through my back. "And now they're accusing her of stealing something."

"I didn't do it!" Glen exclaimed. "I swear I didn't."

"They probably know you own several antiques," Luke said.

"Hey, whose side are you on?" Glen huffed.

I looked over my shoulder at him, but instead of looking accusing, he was deep in thought.

"If they do, it wouldn't be a long stretch for them to jump to thievery. But you have proof of ownership, of course," Luke continued.

"They belonged to my grandmother. My parents can vouch for it. There's probably paperwork, but only God knows where it is. Haylee's mum can find out, though, if needed. Can't she, Haylee?"

I pressed my teeth in a tight line, squeezing my eyes close, too. I didn't like this. I didn't want to be part of this. I just wanted to go back to kissing Luke and pretend the rest of the world didn't exist.

"She probably could," I muttered.

"What was it? A vase?" Luke studied the letter again, his arm coming around me and pulling me to his chest.

Glen, not able to stand still, started pacing the living room. "That's what it says. I haven't even seen the thing. Chelsea Porcelain? I would have noticed that around the shop if they'd had it."

Luke nodded. "Sounds like they're trying to get some money out of the business before it closes. They're desperate."

"Again, Haylee's mum can help with that. Hallie?"

"I don't—" I pinched my thigh and gritted my teeth. I didn't want to. Okay? I really didn't want to, even though I knew it was the right thing to do and Glen needed me. I just wasn't quite ready to ask for her help after the last time I'd seen my mother.

"Would it be easier if I called her instead?" Luke's breath tickled my ear and rose goosebumps all over my skin.

It would be easier if this entire situation disappeared. "You would do that for us?" I croaked.

"Anything, remember? Anything I'm able."

I nodded. "Okay."

"Lisa Walker, right?" Luke asked.

Glen stared at him wide eyed while I simply bit my lip and nodded.

"Okay, give me a second." Luke fished out his phone and scrolled through his contacts.

He had my mum's number? The solicitors' firm worked at all hours, but surely, they wouldn't patch anyone through to her if it wasn't something extremely important. Mum would be home right now, cooking. She no longer worked overtime.

Having found what he was looking for, Luke cleared his throat and raised the phone to his ear. I gripped at his other hand still around me as we waited for anyone to pick up. Eternity passed by until someone finally did.

"Luke, it is unlike you to call this late. Don't tell me you ran into a problem this close to utilising the system," my mother's voice rang out through the speaker, and I flinched at her strict tone.

"Nothing of the sort Mrs Walker. I've got a rather personal request, actually."

"And it can't wait until tomorrow?"

Luke sighed. "It probably can, but I wouldn't sleep well knowing it was still hanging by a thread, unresolved."

"What can I do for you, Luke?"

It made me feel only a little better that she talked to everyone in the same clipped tone. Just a little, though.

"I assume you know Glen Buckley, so I'll jump right into the matter. She is accused of stealing from the antique company she worked at before they went bankrupt. They are very serious about the charge and threaten to go to court."

"And how does that affect your sleep quality, exactly?"

"She's a friend."

"Is she the friend who's made you come in late these past few weeks?"

"No," Luke said. "That would be a different friend."

"I see," my mother said. "I wouldn't happen to know that friend of yours as well, would I?"

I tried to step away from Luke, no longer wishing to hear the conversation. He rubbed his thumb against my side but stepped forward together with me, keeping us attached.

"I'm sure you do. You are a well-connected woman."

I squeezed my eyes shut and took deep breaths.

"Do I understand correctly that Haylee is not the one in trouble, but Glen is?"

"Yes, that's right."

A long silence filled the line, and for a moment, I feared that she had hung up. Then finally, she said, "I'll be there in thirty minutes."

Then, the call ended.

Luke dropped the phone and looked at Glen. "She's coming."

"Wait, right now?" Glen gasped.

"Yes."

We exchanged a nervous look, then she gasped again. "Haylee, your eye! She can't see you like that, she'll freak!"

That's when the mayhem started. Luke rushed to change out of his slacks and threw on a shirt. Glen dragged me upstairs to our bathroom to cover up my bruise as best she could after all. I fidgeted under her ministrations and winced more than once when she hurriedly tapped powder on it too hard. This was going to o so bad, I just knew it.

Good riddance with a scoff

Haylee stepped out of the bathroom, Glen right behind her, urging her forward and toward her bedroom. I studied her face as she stumbled to a stop regardless of her best friend's efforts.

"How does it look?" she asked, chewing on her lip nervously.

The skin around her eye was still considerably raised if you knew what to look for. What must've been layers upon layers of makeup covered up the discoloration. It was strange seeing her like this, since she never wore any as far as I'd noticed. Now this... this was very noticeable indeed. Almost crusted, most certainly like a second skin, the foundation or whatever it was they'd used contrasted with Haylee's natural skin tone even with the added shading; they must've used quite a bit of it, considering how long they'd been stuck in the bathroom together.

"I like you better without," I said honestly. "It looks... fake."

Glen scoffed. "Fake? You think you can do better?"

I raised my hands defensively. "Haylee doesn't need makeup."

"Except, today she does. Trust me." Glen began pulling her toward the bedroom again. "You need to get into your waitressing uniform, or she'll wonder why you're wearing makeup. You heard Luke, it looks fake, but it hides the bruise. We will have to say you just got back from Turtle Bay when we found the letter."

I watched them disappear behind another door with an uneasy pile growing in my stomach. They were going through a lot of trouble to cover up something that hadn't been Haylee's fault to begin with. I didn't understand the need to lie to her mother. I just... didn't understand. There must've been a better way to handle whatever worries she had. Then again, my family was very straightforward when it came to communication. We shared everything, and Haylee hadn't even told hers my name.

I rubbed a hand over my face. Was I prepared to lie for this girl? I didn't really get a choice in the matter. I didn't like this one bit, but again, I had no say in it.

I pulled Haylee in my arms the moment she came out of the bedroom, and some of my restlessness settled when she hugged me back.

"I have a request." My voice came out gravelly, and I cleared my throat.

Haylee stiffened in my embrace. "What is it?"

"Never lie to me," I begged. I rubbed my hands up and down her back, trying to loosen the tightness in her muscles. Then pulled away enough to look into her eyes. "No matter what it is, you can always tell me the truth. No covering up things, just talk to me."

"I don't—It's not like—ugh." She sagged against me, closing her eyes.

My stomach prickled uncomfortably, but there was nothing to scratch that itch with.

"Red Cheeks, I admit I don't get why you're doing this, and I'm not going to say anything if you don't want me to, but please just never lie to *me*."

There was no flush on her cheeks, or if there was it was efficiently covered up. A flash of something registered on her face, and her lower lip trembled slightly before she gave a slight nod. I didn't feel much better, but there was no time to talk about it as a knock sounded on the front door.

Glen nudged us out the short hallway we stood in, mouthing *go go go* and waving her hand frantically. I sighed, moving around their minefield of a living room to sit on the couch with Haylee. She shook her head and pointed at the armchair. A charade it was, then. Fuck, that hurt for some reason, but I'd promised to play along.

I heard the door open and pleasantries being exchanged before a click-clack of heels followed Glen's shuffling slippers to the living room. Lisa Walker's sharp gaze pierced through me the moment her eyes landed on me, and her eyebrows furrowed.

I didn't expect to be meeting this way either, boss. Trust me.

I took a deep breath and leaned deeper into the armchair. No escaping whatever judgement came now. I wasn't going to leave Haylee alone with the woman. My Red Cheeks had basically curled into a protective ball around the pillow she was gripping to her chest. Her eyes downcast and lips set in a firm line. Fuck, I wanted to comfort her in some way, but she'd forced me into this separate seating. Moving now might ease my gut, but I doubted Haylee saw it the same way. Shit, I really didn't like this.

I'd been on Mrs. Walker's disapproving side a few times when arriving late, but it had never truly affected me. We both knew my work ethics made up for any lost time, and nobody else could take over the programming of their new system without messing up my code and losing even more time. This look was different, more personal, and the longer her scowl remained on me, the more I wanted to squirm in my seat.

I forced my muscles to remain still as I greeted her with nothing more than a nod, releasing a clipped breath when her eyes turned to Haylee next.

"So you are not the one in trouble this time," Mrs. Walker's clipped tone rang out. "What are the chances your best friend takes the prize?"

Glen cast a worried look Haylee's way before she sat down on the couch, where I should've been positioned. "I didn't steal anything."

"Innocent before proven guilty, isn't it?" Mrs. Walker said. "When, in fact, in my field of work, it's the other way around. Guilty, always guilty unless proven innocent. Let's see the letter then."

The crumpled piece of paper changed hands, and Mrs. Walker's eyes scanned it while standing over us like an executioner. It shouldn't have felt this grave since she was here to help, after all. Besides, there wasn't any available seating for her to lower to our level. Yet the girls cuddling on the couch together, basically chewing their fingernails bloody and my own building nerves made the situation more tense than it should've been. Until Lisa laughed and shook her head.

"Amateurs," she chuckled. "This will be easy."

"Really?" Glen gasped.

"I'll take care of it." Mrs. Walker folded up the letter and tucked it in a jacket pocket, her eyes flicking back to her daughter.

She stiffened. I tensed. It was fun all around.

"Is there anything you want to tell me, Haylee?" she demanded.

"No."

"For crying out loud—"

"Wait, you don't need a statement from me or anything?" Glen interrupted.

Lisa Walker scoffed. "Waste of my time. We'll be calling them to court before they have the chance for any more threats. Once they realize there's no way they'll win, they will back off. Case closed." Her attention turned to me next. "How did you get mixed up in this anyway?"

Haylee's worried eyes begged at me from across the coffee table.

I wanted to rub my hand across my face but dug my fingers into the arms of the chair instead. "We're neighbors."

"Case closed?" Glen echoed blatantly. "What if they are happy to go to court?"

Mrs. Walker narrowed her eyes, and for a moment, she looked gruesome, but then the clint in her eyes and twitch of her lips shattered the illusion. "Then I will hear your statement. I said I will take care of it."

She was really not interested in discussing it further, and I got the impression she hadn't dropped what she was doing to get here this quickly because of the accusation. She was here because of me. And Haylee. And what Haylee had said about her insisting on a background check. I was under inspection. Was-I-good-enough-for-her-daughter type of inspection.

"Neighbors with benefits?" Mrs. Walker's gaze danced around the room, taking in Haylee's jerking and my calculated stiffness.

I caught Haylee's eyes and did my own begging. I refused to lie. "Neighbors with feelings," I amended.

Haylee sagged into the pillow and hid her face behind her curls.

"Haylee?" Mrs. Walker's biting voice rang out, pulling the girl out of her curling position.

Haylee's gaze was all fire when she met her mother's jeer. "What? I told you last time. I'm not having this conversation with you."

"Just tell me one thing, then. Does he treat you well?" A softness I didn't expect to see crossed Lisa's features.

Haylee took no time to reply. "Yes."

Lisa Walker nodded, then turned to me again. "You're leaving at the end of the week, aren't you?"

"Yes." I didn't need the reminder, but coming from her in that sharp tone was the worst.

"That will be resolved then, too," she said, then set to dodge the antiques on her way out, waving a hand dismissively at Glen. "Don't bother standing up, I know where the door is."

The moment Mrs. Walker was out of the room, I was on my feet and between Haylee and Glen on the couch with my arms around my girl. She remained tense until the front door closed with a resounding click, then she melted into my embrace.

"Resolved," Glen huffed. "Since love totally works like that."

It was strange, I must admit, but I had no experience with mothers. Grandmothers, yes, but not mothers. I tried not to think too much of it because, for me, nothing would be resolved when I left, and I hoped Haylee saw it my way, too. I wasn't quite sure if it was me Lisa disliked or the idea of Haylee dating in general. The idea of Haylee dating someone other than me—that got me to squeeze her tighter against my chest.

I breathed in her sweet scent, and whatever clots had begun forming in my gut loosened up. Fuck, I was a sucker for this girl.

"Oh, and she didn't even care about A&R's threat to me," Glen fumed on. "That was just a side-gig. The main issue was that Haylee is seeing someone. That's not normal, is it?"

Haylee's face rubbed against my chest as she shook her head while I mumbled, "I don't know" into her locks.

"It's not," Glen decided. "What kind of mother wants their daughter unhappy? She didn't even ask you if you were happy only if Luke treated you all right."

"Haylee did say she didn't want to talk about it," I offered, not ready to make a judgment of my own, but realizing there must've been a bigger reason for Haylee's jarring reaction. I might've not understood it, but I saw how she'd tensed up. I'd felt her rigid against me before she'd allowed herself to relax. She was still not speaking.

"Whose side are you on?" Glen scoffed.

"Yours. I was just stating the facts."

"The facts are," Glen blabbered on, "that she wholeheartedly didn't care for whatever case is going to be started on my behalf with A&R, and she really doesn't like you, Luke. Coming from her that was mild, too. She can express her dislike in much, much worse ways than simply bidding you good riddance at your departure."

Not exactly the way I would translate Mrs. Walker's actions, but I supposed Glen wasn't far off either. No matter how hard I tried to explain away the frosty exterior of Haylee's mother, I couldn't quite view the situation through her eyes when her daughter hid her face on my chest and weeped.

I remembered Haylee saying her family wasn't like mine, and my heart broke for her again. Family was everything to me. They were my strength, my stronghold to fall back on. If I didn't have that, I'd be lost. I couldn't imagine what it must be like for her not to be able to trust her family with... well anything. The fight in the bar and our relationship possibly being just a few of the things she kept from them.

"I'm sorry," I said quietly. Sorry for the way Haylee was feeling. Sorry for her relationship with her mother being what it was. But I couldn't be sorry for telling the truth.

"At least, she didn't see the black eye," Haylee responded shakily.

That broke me apart.

Just say it.

"What are you most excited about going back home?" I asked Luke on Saturday.

Half of his flat was packed in boxes, while the other half was simply tidied up for the next occupant. One of those boxes had my name on it, and I had a feeling I'd be bringing that one up to my flat that evening, although Luke hadn't yet mentioned anything about it.

"Excited," he echoed slowly, rubbing a hand over his face. "It's hard to be excited feeling *like this*."

"You will see your family, surely that's exciting?" I insisted. The thought of him leaving tomorrow made me feel *like this*, too, but I refused to linger on that. There'd be plenty of time to miss Luke once he was gone.

"Yes, that'll be… exciting. I just wish you'd be there, too."

We were sitting on his sofa, my legs across his lap, his right hand drawing patterns across my back while the left rested on my knee. My arms hung around his neck, but I slid one hand up to cup his cheek. He leaned into the touch.

"Maybe we can plan something?" I thought out loud.

Luke's lips twitched, and some of his spark returned to his eyes. "We can definitely plan something. When will you be free?"

I pursed my lips, thinking about it. "Turtle Bay doesn't matter. I can leave whenever I want to. Just quit, really, if they don't let me take off. The dance studio closes for the summer."

"The farm is beautiful during summer." Luke hummed, his smile growing. "Wait, let me get my tablet."

He moved out from under me and fished around in a bag at the side of the sofa. I watched his fingers tap around the screen, opening a browser and searching for flights to Denver.

"The entire summer?" he asked when the site loaded.

I gasped. "Oh, we're planning right now?"

Luke gave me a peck on my cheek. "Yes, we are planning right now, and I will buy you the tickets."

"I can pay for my own tickets," I argued.

"I'm sure you can, but I will buy them anyway. So, the entire summer?"

I gaped at him for a heartbeat, then forced my mouth to close and nodded awkwardly. "Um... July and August. I can ask about June, but I don't think they'd mind. It's always quieter in June anyway."

Luke smiled as he entered the dates into the website. "Perfect."

I stared at the prices in mild bewilderment as Luke picked the quickest trip across the ocean and added it to the cart.

I swallowed as he didn't even hesitate writing my name in the passenger information. "Wait, we are buying it now? Don't I need to apply for a visa first?"

"You'll get a visa, no problem." Luke grinned at my gobsmacked expression. "Now, your date of birth, Miss Haylee Walker?"

I blushed. "Can I at least confirm with the studio that I can have the entire summer off?"

"Only if you get the answer in the next ten minutes."

An incredulous laugh bubbled up in my throat. "You are joking."

Luke pointed at the timer ticking away on the website, letting you know how long you had to complete the order. Of plane tickets to the USA, no less. Oh my God!

"Okay, okay. I just need a minute."

"While you're at it, I need your ID to fill in the details," he said with a smirk.

My heart pounded away as I handed Luke the card I carried in my phone case while dialing the dance studio.

"This is crazy," I muttered under my breath. "I can't believe you'd do something like this."

"Call it reassurance. A promise."

I liked the sound of that. A much stronger promise than his phone number saved to my contacts. Much, much stronger than that.

Twenty minutes later we had bought the plane tickets and filled in an application for a visa. Now, Luke leaving didn't feel all that sorrowful anymore but more like the start to a new adventure. True, summer was still several months away, but we'd made a promise. A promise that cost Luke one thousand and four hundred pounds!

"I'm excited now," Luke admitted once he'd set the tablet aside. "I can't wait to spend those three months with the woman I love. There's so much I want to show you. *Nonni* will love you. So will my dad. Haylee... I really love you."

I swallowed at the sincerity in Luke's voice. At the intensity in his eyes when he looked at me. My heartbeat picked up, and my mouth felt too dry all of a sudden. We bought a plane ticket for me. We bought a freaking plane ticket for me! Holy gobsmacking shit!

"Luke—Luca." My heart was fighting its imprisonment in my chest, and I was almost certain it would spring free with the next pounding beat and join his. It was already beating for him, anyway. I took a deep breath to calm myself, but it wasn't working. My hands shook. Hell, my voice shook, too, but at least, I got the words out. "I love you, too."

The smile lighting up his face was priceless. It was gorgeous beyond words, and it was all for me. Those same smiling lips kissed me tenderly a moment after, and all my breath whooshed out of my lungs.

"Good, because I've planned my future around you," Luke murmured against my lips. "I'm in way over my head for you."

Then he kissed me more firmly. For a long, breathless moment, we were attached to each other as if air meant nothing; when I was in Luke's arms, oxygen became meaningless. He was all I needed, and *he was in way over his head for me*. He was mine. How did I get this lucky?

Once we did come up for air, my eyes fell on the box with my name on it again. "I've got to ask, what's in the box?"

Luke grinned. "Everything I can't take with me. My heart."

I did my awkward non-eyebrow raise, making his grin even bigger.

"The kitchen aid, pans, some other cooking supplies."

"You're leaving these for me?"

"My heart? Yes, Haylee. I'm most definitely leaving it with you."

I laughed. "I don't think I'll have much use for cooking supplies, Luke. Wouldn't it be better to give those to—"

"To who, Haylee?" he asked. "You're the only one I want to give them to. Besides, you're going to need them for cooking on Sunday."

"What?" I gaped at Luke, not sure I'd heard him right. Or that I understood him correctly. "Sunday's cooking is for the family. It's your family time."

"Red Cheeks," Luke said, his voice sounding gravelly. "As far as my heart is concerned, you are family. I don't want to cook without you."

"I'm horrible at it," I admitted gingerly.

"You'll learn."

I bit my lower lip, staring at the box. It was very sweet of him to leave his *heart* with me. He loved cooking; it was part of him just like dancing was part of me. I'd enjoyed being in the kitchen with him, but we both knew he'd been doing most of the cooking while I watched. I'd been content just watching.

"Red Cheeks," Luke murmured when I'd been quiet for too long. "It was wrong of me to assume you would like to cook with me on Sundays. I'm sorry. We can do something else."

My heart dropped at the controlled expression on his face. He was keeping the disappointment at bay. Or hurt? He'd offered me something he held precious, and I'd just spat on the gesture. It was equivalent to Luke placing his heart at my feet and me stumbling on it and crushing it as I fell. I *had* stumbled.

"No. No, Luke, it's fine. I didn't expect it, but we can try. I will try."

"You don't have to." His arm snaked around my back and pulled me to his chest. His other hand smoothed at my hair as he leaned in close enough that our foreheads touched. "I'll take whatever you can give me, Haylee."

"No, I want to." My throat hurt, and the words came out pathetic, weak. I tried again. "Luca, I want to try it for you. It means a lot to you." I'll just stumble my way through it. It'll be fine.

"We can start with something simple," he suggested, his breath brushing my lips.

"That would help."

Luke closed the distance between us in a barely-there kiss that left my lips tingling. "Thank you," he whispered. "Let me take this upstairs for you."

I laid in bed that night, thrashing and turning while my stomach did somersaults and hollowed out and filled with warmth and cold ice all at once. An intricate dance to be sure, but I couldn't get it to still, and I wasn't able to sleep through the turmoil.

Nothing had gone the way I wanted it to. How come I was so awful at relationships? I couldn't express myself properly, let alone tell Luke what I wanted without getting embarrassed about it. We'd never finished what we'd started on his kitchen counter before Glen's interruption. After the way I'd reacted to his cooking suggestion I hadn't been able to share that I would've liked to stay the night.

He was leaving. We hadn't even—and he was leaving! And the next time I'd see him was eight months away. What if the distance would drift us apart? Why would he wait this long for me, anyway? It's not like I'd given him anything incredible worth waiting for. I'd been a fumbling mess for at least half of our interactions. He might find it endearing now, but the more time passed by the more he'd come to see it wasn't love he'd felt. Then what?

Maybe that's why he hadn't asked me to stay. He didn't want to ruin me in case the distance would tear us apart. Luke would be considerate like that. But he'd bought me a plane ticket. He'd spent so much money on it. Surely, that meant he was serious in wanting to make it work, long distance and all. Surely, we could survive eight months apart.

Eight months! I was already battling with confidence. How was I going to survive eight months like this?

After several more twists and turns, I pushed off the mattress and tiptoed out of my room, clutching only my phone and my keys in my hands. I couldn't stop to think about this or I'd flee back to my room, so I shuffled downstairs to the tenth floor, typing *I can't sleep* to Luke before I reached his door and stood behind it awkwardly. Okay, I should've perhaps thought a little about this. He might be able to sleep just fine. I might be the only one struggling.

Relax. Haylee, just relax. And maybe go back up. Yeah. Just go back to bed.

The phone vibrated between my fingers, and I dropped my gaze on it.

Luke: **Me neither.**

Fuck it. I knocked on his door, holding my breath until he opened it, standing on the other side in grey joggers and nothing else. My eyes trailed up his bare chest to his face as he roamed across my jammies. The very same ones he'd seen me in before. I should've changed into something else. It was too late now.

"Cute," he murmured, lips twitching.

"Hi," I blurted, my cheeks heating up when his eyes met mine, and he wet his lips. I gripped my phone tighter. "I was... ugh... wondering if I could sleep here tonight."

"*La mia casa è la tua.*"

I blinked.

"Come inside, Gorgeous. I'll make tea."

"Tea..." I wasn't there for tea.

"Camomile," Luke replied. "Helps you relax."

There were other things pretty efficient for that, but if he wasn't going to say it he might not want to try those methods. Oh God, how was I supposed to say I wasn't here for tea when he placed that perfect kettle of his on the stove to heat the water. I was heating up along with it. It was so hot I couldn't quite think straight. How could anyone say that it wasn't tea they were standing behind his door for in the middle of the night? Maybe I should just kiss him, that always seemed to work.

Biting down my nerves, I trailed my fingers across the counter top as I rounded the kitchen island to where he stood rather rigidly. His eyes followed my every step until we were facing each other. Silence was like static in my ears. But he waited. My legs shook slightly. He still waited. I reached out and awkwardly placed my sweaty palm on his bare chest. His eyes darkened, yet he waited.

I swallowed, tracing the contours of Luke's pecks with my fingers, and over the bruise on his side. A rapid pulse met my touch when I crossed over his heart. The rising and falling of his chest quickened when I trailed a path down to his stomach.

"Are you going to say it?" he rasped.

The sound—any sound—was so unexpected after the tense silence, and I startled, pulling my hand away and dropping my eyes before I had the chance to realise how silly that was.

"Say what?" I looked back up.

"What you want, Haylee. You know you can say it, right?"

"I was hoping you would read my mind."

"I'm afraid I haven't yet perfected that skill." Luke chuckled. "It's much safer if you tell me so that I don't misinterpret."

"Is there any other reason I'd be here in the middle of the night?"

"I don't know, you tell me."

I worried at my lower lip, trying to form the words in my head before blurting them out.

"God, you're adorable, Haylee," Luke murmured right before he was done waiting and pulled me in for a kiss.

I melted against his chest as his tongue tangled with mine without restraint. When the kettle whistled a long whine, one of Luke's hands reached out to flick the stove off without separating his lips from mine. Then he gripped my bottom, yanking us closer. Close enough that I could feel him through the fabric of his joggers.

He groaned. "Is that what you want, Red Cheeks?"

I nodded, then said a breathless, "Yes," against his lips before he smashed them against mine again.

"See, that wasn't so hard to say," he rasped between kisses. "Now, we know we're thinking about the same thing."

Now, both of his hands gripped my butt before he lifted me up. I held onto his shoulders for dear life when he walked us out of the kitchen, forgetting the bubbling water and camomile altogether.

"You can say no at any point and we'll stop."

I shook my head. "I don't want to stop."

"I'm just saying, Haylee. Any time. You're in charge."

"I don't want to be in charge."

Luke stopped us at his bedroom door, eyes roaming over my face. "Okay, I'm in charge as long as you agree that you can always say no."

"Okay," I said.

"Okay," he rasped. "Good."

Then he carried me across the threshold, closing the door behind us.

From behind the door came a breathless gasp. "The light."

"I want to see you, Red Cheeks."

"Please."

A soft click of the switch flicked the lights off. Then the gasps amplified.

I woke up surrounded by a masculine scent that immediately got me blushing. My body remembered exactly what the owner of that cologne had done to it, and heat pooled up between my legs. Goodness gracious, now I was blushing double.

I pulled the blanket over my head, hiding my face in it. That only served to bring his scent closer to me. I inhaled as the night replayed in my head. Oh my God!

I stayed still in Luke's bed as more awareness returned. He wasn't in the bed with me, though every single part of me knew at one point he had been. Oh, he certainly had been.

I was still tired since we really hadn't done much sleeping. *I should get out of his bed regardless.*

After I found my clothes, I creaked the bedroom door open and peaked out. Luke was in the kitchen, because of course he was. Something sizzled on the pan, and the fresh aroma of coffee wafted through the space. A low humming of a tune I wasn't familiar with accompanied the sound, and I realised it was Luke singing. He smiled to himself—or the bacon—since he hadn't seen me yet. Joy radiated from his every pore, and he was absolutely gorgeous.

I stepped away from the doorway and into the living room. As if drawn by a magnet, his head turned my way, and that smile grew wider.

"Good morning, Red Cheeks."

I grinned. "Good morning, Mr Umbrella."

Epilogue

I rechecked my travel bag for my passport, phone and plane ticket. They were all still exactly where I'd placed them. Glen helped me with check-in, and the much bigger, much heavier bag was now already on its way to the plane. It was time for us to part. Yet, I clung to her like this was goodbye for forever.

"I promise I'll be fine," she said for the hundredth time since her trial started. "I'm in good hands, remember?"

I felt horrible leaving her alone, but there was nothing that would keep me from boarding this plane. We both knew it.

"I still wish I could be there for you," I mumbled as she nudged me toward the security gate.

"You've been here for me. Now, go be over there with Luke. I said I'll be fine, didn't I?"

I checked my documents again, suddenly nervous. In ten hours I would be seeing Luke again. Face to face. Lips on lips. His arms around me, and only the barriers I myself set between us. I missed his voice undistorted by the speakers of my phone. The way he'd chuckle when I said something witty. His eyes would sparkle and he'd either tap his fingers on his thigh or any available hard surface, or he'd give in and touch me. I loved the way he'd search my eyes for permission, take his time making sure I was okay with it first. I missed how my heart would speed up at the smallest of signs that he wanted to kiss me, and the way it had thundered the night we'd been together. I didn't know you could miss someone this much.

I'd been burning food every Sunday since Luke left. Glen had decided to help with the cooking, leaving me more time to stare at the iPad screen, drooling at how good Luke looked, and how comfortable he was moving around his kitchen. Her warnings for when something on the pan started smelling like it was burning weren't always timely either, but so far, nothing tasted bad enough to throw it away. Never as good as Luke's cooking but not outright horrible either.

"You'll still tell me all the big things, right?" I asked Glen.

"Just like you'll tell me everything," she replied with a raised eyebrow.

To this day I hadn't told her any details about the night I'd spent with Luke. She'd tried prying those out of my sealed lips for weeks before giving up on it.

"That's different!" I exclaimed.

"Yes, yes, I get it. I'll let you know if they're taking me to prison."

"They won't be taking you to prison," I argued.

"We'll see." Glen pushed me towards the security gate again. "Go, Haylee, the love of your life is waiting."

My stomach was tap-dancing the entire flight as every minute took me further from the last furthest place I'd ever been from home, and closer to Luke. This entire trip depended on him coming to pick me up. I had no plans further than reaching the Denver airport. After that, I was at Luke's mercy. Entirely dependent.

What if everything was different when I saw him again? Once we were stuck together at his farm, what if we no longer clicked and he'd get bothered with me. What if my imagination had run wild and portrayed him all wrong this entire time?

I didn't sleep a wink, and the movie selection barely managed to keep me distracted. At one point, the stewardesses brought me food, and it tasted fine, but my stomach was all but ready to get rid of it anyway. I almost didn't get to the onboard toilet fast enough; there was a line.

We'd talked almost every day, and still, I was nervous. Three months was a long time to be staying with someone. Oh my God, I'd be staying with Luke for three months. It would be much different than texting or even the regular video calls we were used to. I was overthinking again, and that wasn't even the worst of it. What if he didn't come to pick me up from the airport? What then?

We had talked about all of that, of course, but nine hours locked up in a seat wasn't helping my overactive brain. By the time I landed, I had lived through several pretty horrible scenarios and was ready to face the reality. The reality where my carry-on bag was pulled aside for a drug test, since my jittery movements were suspicious. The reality where I almost didn't get through passport control. The very same where my luggage never showed up on one of the rolling lines.

The baggage claim was emptying out by the time I managed to convince myself my suitcase didn't matter enough to keep on waiting for it. I wobbled my way out without asking for help. My eyes roamed the much busier welcome area for Luke's handsome face. Everything was blurring together, and I couldn't make out any faces, though. When did I start crying?

Just keep walking. I followed the swarm. People hugged and laughed and received flowers, and my head swam from the entire display even as I was unable to make out any details by the time I heard my name called out.

"Haylee!"

I whipped my head toward the sound, searching the crowd until my eyes landed on him rushing toward me with a big smile on his face. Then, his arms crushed me to his chest, and everything within me calmed. I squeezed him back like my life depended on it.

"I missed you so much," I whispered, burying my face in his chest. Sandalwood and something fresh engulfed my nostrils and enforced the sense of safety.

"I missed you, too," Luke murmured against my ear. Then, he pulled back just enough to kiss me deeply, one of his hands cupping my wet cheek.

When he pulled back, his thumb wiped at the tears as his eyes searched my face. "Why are you crying?"

I sniffed, hating the weakness I was unable to hide. "It was a stressful trip, but I'm okay now."

I hugged him again, just to make sure he was really there. Luke dropped his head to the crook of my neck, inhaling sharply. "You smell so good."

"I most certainly don't," I snorted. "I'm in desperate need of a shower."

"Pheromones, remember?" He kept sniffing until I squirmed in his embrace.

"Stop it!" I giggled and pushed him away playfully.

Luke wore a victorious grin, moving only far enough to look me in the eye. "Hello there, Red Cheeks."

I bit my lip and blushed as if on demand. Luke's thumb traced the line of my mouth, freeing my lip.

"Hi, Luca."

"I love it when you say my name." He kissed me again, softer this time.

My lips tingled and my breath hitched, and Luke's tongue flicked in, tasting my mouth. A low hum vibrated through him. Flames ignited within me, and I forgot all the things I'd been so worried about. We melted together, our hearts beating as one, both frantic and needy.

I clung to Luke like he was the very oxygen I needed to survive, and he kissed me like we weren't still standing in the middle of a crowded airport. But we were—we certainly were, and a loud clearing of a throat brought the general noise right back into the forefront of my mind.

Luke pulled away slowly, reluctantly. Next to us, his father raised an eyebrow and his grandmother smiled sweetly, while I choked on my own spit and dropped my head to Luke's chest. Hiding behind my curls didn't help with my heated cheeks.

"You didn't tell me we weren't alone," I muttered under my breath.

Luke chuckled. "There are a lot more people here than just my family, Red Cheeks. Come on, I'll take your bags."

He looked around for my suitcase with a furrowed brow.

"About that," I huffed. "I think I lost my luggage."

"You mean, the airline lost your luggage," Luke specified. "What did they tell you?"

I sucked my lower lip into my mouth and stared at our feet. "I... ah... didn't ask."

The soft brush of Luke's lips on my forehead relaxed my tensing muscles. "I'll take care of it, Haylee. Stay here."

He handed me off to his grandmother, who pulled me into a hug of her own, and I saw him strolling toward an info desk with the confidence I'd been lacking.

"Ciao," I said awkwardly, dragging my eyes from Luke's back to his family. "I'm sorry, I still don't really speak Italian."

"Don't worry, you'll pick it up in no time," Luke's father replied with a grin.

Nonni nudged him. "You scare the girl away, then Luke is heartbroken again. We speak English."

"I am not so easily scared." Not after the kiss Luke welcomed me with. My lips tugged up in a smile. I couldn't wait to kiss him again.

My eyes drifted over to the info desk again, searching for him. His fingers tapped the desk as the woman behind it confirmed something on the phone. As if feeling my eyes on him, Luke turned his head and winked at me. I raised my palm to my heated cheeks as if that would help to cool them.

"*Belle guance rosse*," *Nonni* scolded me, pulling my hand away from my face. "Be proud of your nickname."

"*Guance rosse*," I repeated. "Is that 'red cheeks?'"

"One and the same."

"They can't find it," Luke confirmed what I'd already feared once he got back. He took over carrying my small travel bag and pulled me to his side as he led our small group towards the exit. "It's all right, you can wear my T-shirts and shorts until they figure out what went wrong."

He leaned in closer to my ear, and his breath tickled the delicate skin as he whispered much quieter. "An image I've been thinking of for the past fifteen minutes."

"Okay. As long as you're fine with it."

"More than fine."

Warm air greeted us when we stepped outside, easing some of my headache, and I sighed blissfully.

"I'll take you shopping if there's anything you need," Luke said, dodging the mayhem of people trying to find their way wherever they needed to get.

"Like underwear," I blurted.

"Hmm, you won't need underwear where we're going, but sure."

"Sure." I giggled uncontrollably.

"I'll take good care of you, Haylee. I promise." His arm squeezed me tighter to his side. We'd reached where they'd parked the car, but he was reluctant to let me go. "Your bag will be delivered to the farm once they find it. They have my address."

I pouted. "Everyone but me seems to have your address."

"You don't need my address, Haylee. You have my heart."

"You have my heart, too," I whispered.

Luke kissed me softly, before he threw his keys to his father and dragged me onto the back seat. I melted against his side and rested my head on his shoulder, listening to the car roaring to life.

"Let's take you home, love." Luke murmured, kissing my hairline.

The rocking of the car lulled me further into relaxation, and I closed my eyes, rubbing my cheek against Luke's shirt.

"I am already home," I sighed happily.

The End

Interview with characters of Elevate With Me

Interviewer: Haylee, is trapping Luke between elevator doors your most embarrassing experience?

Haylee: You know it isn't. At the time, I thought it was a close second, but I've reevaluated it since.

Luke: Hmm. I remember you saying you were mortified.

Haylee: Of course you do.

Luke: That you wished the earth would swallow you up.

Haylee: Shut up!

Luke: Meanwhile, all I wanted was for you to look at me. I'm glad we figured all of that out.

Interviewer: Luke, tell us honestly, what were your thoughts on Haylee's pajamas?

Luke: Honestly? Do you think I wasn't honest when I called them cute? I was surprised to see Haylee again but not disappointed in the way we met. She intrigued me.

Haylee: I found it embarrassing, as well. I can't believe we met like that.

Luke: Not embarrassing, Red Cheeks. Memorable. Very much so. I couldn't get you out of my head after that, and that was when I thought you had a boyfriend. I thought he was stupid, too, letting you leave like that. I wouldn't have.

Interviewer: Haylee, how do you think you got a coffee stain on your shirt?

Haylee: No.
Interviewer: No what?
Luke: She's not answering.
Interviewer: It's a simple question.
Luke: Leave it.
Interviewer: But...
Luke: I said leave it. Ask about her favorite song or something.

Interviewer: What is your favorite song?

Luke: The one Haylee danced to in my apartment before our first kiss.
Interviewer: Haylee?
Haylee: I don't have one.
Interviewer: Of course you do.
Haylee: I don't.
Interviewer: ...
Luke: If she says she doesn't, then she doesn't.
Interviewer: What song did she dance to?
Luke: Ask about our favorite meal.

Interviewer: What is your favorite meal?

Luke: Meatballs.

Haylee: You're only saying that because of the way we made them.

Luke: Yes, they taste even better now.

Haylee: Okay. I'll say meatballs, too.

Luke: And chocolate custard.

Haylee: Yes.

Interviewer: Luke, were you going to tell Haylee you were leaving?

Luke: Ask about our favorite movie.

Interviewer: Were you?

Luke: It's The Notebook, if you must know. I never thought I'd like a chick-flick that much, but The Notebook certainly got to me.

Interviewer: …

Interviewer: Haylee?

Haylee: I don't know.

Glen: She likes Dirty Dancing more.

Haylee: Only because it has dancing in it.

Interviewer: Is Dirty Dancing your favorite movie?

Haylee: I don't think I have one.

Interviewer: The night Haylee stayed—

Haylee: No.

Luke: We will not talk about it.

Interviewer: I was going to ask—

Luke: —about our favorite color. Mine's red, but we knew that already.

Haylee: Green.

Luke: Green? Really? Why?

Haylee: Your eyes are green.

Luke: You like my eyes?

Haylee: You know I like your eyes.

Luke: I do? You've never told me.

Haylee: I like your eyes.

Luke: I like everything about you, Red Cheeks.

Interviewer: About your last night in the UK, Luke—

Luke: We said we won't talk about it.

Interviewer: Was it memorable?

Luke: …

Interviewer: It was, wasn't it?

Luke: Ask about our summer plans.

Interviewer: What are your plans for the summer?

Luke: Anything and everything Haylee wants to do.

Haylee: Can we go hiking in the Rocky Mountains?

Luke: Yes.

Haylee: And swimming?

Luke: I'm sure we'll find a place.

Haylee: Will you show me how to farm?

Luke: We'll probably need to help out a little.

Haylee: Do you have horses? Could we go riding?

Luke: I know someone who does. I'll take you.

Glen: I wish I had plans like that for the summer, too.

Interviewer: It sounds like the court case wasn't as easy as Mrs. Walker let on. How is it going, Glen?

Glen: It's fine. I'm fine. Go back to Luke and Haylee's summer plans. That's much more interesting than little ol' me.

Interviewer: You're interesting, and the court case really did not get discussed enough. How are you feeling about your chances of winning?

Glen: I am represented by none other than Mrs Walker herself. If she scares the shit out of me and Haylee, imagine how the opposition feels.

Interviewer: So, you feel good about your chances?

Glen: If I don't mess it up.

Interviewer: What was that?

Glen: Nothing.

Interviewer: About your love life, Glen? Are you seeing anyone?

Interviewer: Hello?

Interviewer: Are you still there?

Interviewer: I suppose that's it for today. Thank you.

If you've got the feeling that Glen has a story to tell, too. You're probably right.

Victoria Liiv's books

YA fantasy

Through Hell & Highwater

Paranormal romance/ Romantasy

Afterworld: Road to Redemption
Fairies of Death
Nature Fairies

Contemporary Romance

Angels Around Us
Elevate With Me

About the Author

Victoria Liiv is a writer, reader, nature lover and traveller at heart. She has been travelling through magical worlds since a very young age and wants more than anything to share that wonder with everyone else eager to escape from all things mundane. Let it be a magical adventure through the slowly darkening Earth or a soul-crushing fight for survival and love while the world burns. Sometimes all it takes is a little bit of romance.

In her everyday life Victoria found the magic in her partner, who gave her courage to move out of Estonia, the country she was born in, to an equally small but more known The Netherlands.

Instagram: @vicwritesbooks

Facebook: @vicwritesbooks

Tiktok: @vicwritesbooks

Printed in Poland
by Amazon Fulfillment
Poland Sp. z o.o., Wrocław

53075606R00138